SPECTRAL EVIDENCE

GEMMA FILES

TREPIDATIO
PUBLISHING

Trepidatio books may be ordered through booksellers or by contacting:
Trepidatio
www.trepidatio.com
or
JournalStone
www.journalstone.com

The views expressed in this work are solely those of the authors and do not necessarily reflect the views of the publisher, and the publisher hereby disclaims any responsibility for them.

ISBN: 978-1-947654-18-1 (sc)
ISBN: 978-1-947654-17-4 (ebook)

Trepidatio rev. date: February 16, 2018

Library of Congress Control Number: 2018933936

Printed in the United States of America

Cover Design: Andrei Bat / 99designs
All images free for commercial use
Interior Layout: Jess Landry

Edited by: Dan Mason
Proofread by: Sean Leonard

SPECTRAL
EVIDENCE

A WISH FROM A BONE

War zone archaeology is the best kind, Hynde liked to say when drunk—and Goss couldn't disagree, at least in terms of ratings. The danger, the constant threat, was a clarifying influence, lending everything they did an extra meaty heft. Better yet, it was the world's best excuse for having to wrap real quick and pull out ahead of the tanks, regardless of whether or not they'd actually found anything.

The site for their latest TV special was miles out from anywhere else, far enough from the border between Eritrea and the Sudan that the first surveys missed it—first, second, third, fifteenth, until updated satellite surveillance finally revealed minute differences between what local experts could only assume was some sort of temple and all the similarly-coloured detritus surrounding it. It didn't help that it was only a few clicks (comparatively) away from the Meroitic pyramid find in Gebel Barkal, which had naturally kept most "real" archaeologists too busy to check out what the fuck that low-lying, hill-like building lurking in the middle distance might or might not be.

Yet on closer examination, of course, it turned out somebody already *had* stumbled over it, a couple of different times; the soldiers who'd set up initial camp inside in order to avoid a dust storm had found two separate batches of bodies, fresh-ish enough that their shreds of clothing and artefacts could be dated back to the 1930s on the one hand, the 1890s on the other. Gentlemen explorers, native guides, mercenaries. Same as today, pretty much, without the "gentlemen" part.

Partially ruined, and rudimentary, to say the least. It was laid out somewhat like El-Marraqua, or the temples of Lake Nasser: a roughly half-circular building with the rectangular section facing outwards like a big, blank wall centred by a single, permanently-open doorway, twelve feet high by five feet wide. No windows, though the roof remained surprisingly intact.

"This whole area was underwater a million years ago," Hynde told Goss. "See these rocks? All sedimentary. Chalk, fossils, bone-bed silica and radiolarite—amazing any of it's still here, given the wind. Must've formed in a channel or a basin...but no, that doesn't make sense either, because the *inside* of the place is stable, no matter how much the outside erodes."

"So they quarried stone from somewhere else, brought it here, shored it up."

"Do you know how long that would've taken? Nearest hard-rock deposits are like—five hundred miles thataway. Besides, that's not even vaguely how it looks. It's more...unformed, like somebody set up channels while a lava-flow was going on and shepherded it into a hexagonal pattern, then waited for it to cool enough that the up-thrust slabs fit together like walls, blending at the seams."

"What's the roof made of?"

"Interlocking bricks of mud, weed, and gravel fix-baked in the sun, then fitted together and fired afterward, from the outside in; must've piled flammable stuff on top of it, set it alight, let it cook. The glue for the gravel was bone-dust and chunks, marinated in vinegar."

"*Seriously,*" Goss said, perking up. "Human? This a necropolis, or what?"

"We don't know, to either."

Outside, that new chick—Camberwell? The one who'd replaced that massive Eurasian guy they'd all just called "Gojira," rumoured to have finally screwed himself to death between projects—was wrangling their trucks into camp formation, angled to provide a combination of look-out, cover and wind-brake. Moving inside, meanwhile, Goss began taking light-meter readings and setting up his initial shots, while Hynde showed him around this particular iteration of the Oh God Can Such Things Be travelling road-show.

"Watch your step," Hynde told him, all but leading him by the sleeve. "The floor slopes down, a series of shallow shelves...it's an old trick, designed to force perspective, move you further in. To develop a sense of awe."

Goss nodded, allowing Hynde to draw him toward what at first looked like one back wall, but quickly proved to be a clever illusion—two slightly overlapping partial walls, slim as theatrical flats, set up to hide a sharply zig-zagging passage beyond. This, in turn, gave access to a tunnel curling downwards into a sort of cavern underneath the temple floor, through which Hynde was all too happy to conduct Goss, filming as they went.

"Take a gander at all the mosaics," Hynde told him. Get in close. See those hieroglyphics?"

"Is that what those are? They look sort of...organic, almost."

"They should; they were, once. Fossils."

Goss focused his lens closer and grinned so wide his cheeks hurt. Because yes yes fucking YES, they were: rows on rows of skeletal little pressed-flat, stonified shrimp, fish, sea-ferns, and other assorted what-the-fuck-evers, painstakingly selected, sorted, and slotted into patterns that started at calf-level and rose almost to the equally creepy baked-bone brick roof, blending into darkness.

"Jesus," he said out loud. "This is *gold*, man, even if it turns out you can't read 'em. This is an Emmy, right here."

Hynde nodded, grinning too now, though maybe not as wide. And told him: "Wait 'til you see the well."

The cistern in question, hand-dug down through rock and paved inside with slimy sandstone, had a roughly twenty-foot diameter and a depth that proved unsound-able even with the party's longest reel of rope, which put it at something over sixty-one metres.

Whatever had once been inside it appeared to have dried up long since, though a certain liquid quality to the echoes it produced gave indications that there might still be the remains of a water-table—poisoned or pure, no way to tell—lingering at its bottom. There was a weird saline quality to the crust inside its lip, a sort of whitish, gypsumesque candle-wax-dripping formation that looked as though it was just on the verge of blooming into stalactites.

Far more interesting, however, was the design scheme its excavators had chosen to decorate the well's exterior with—a mosaic, also assembled from fossils, though in this case the rocks themselves had been pulverized before use, reduced to fragments so that they could be recombined into surrealistic alien patterns: fish-eyed, weed-legged, shell-winged monstrosities, cut here and there with what might be fins or wings or insect torsos halved, quartered, chimerically repurposed and slapped together to form even larger, more complex figures of which these initial grotesques were only the pointillist building-blocks. Step back far enough, and they coalesced into seven figures looking off into almost every possible direction save for where the southeast compass-point should go. That spot was blank.

"I'm thinking the well-chamber was constructed first," Hynde explained, "here, under the ground—possibly around an already-existing cave, hollowed out by water that no longer exists, through limestone that *shouldn't* exist. After which the entire temple would've been built overtop, to hide and protect it...protect *them*."

"The statues."

Hynde nodded.

"Are those angels?" Goss asked, knowing they couldn't be.

"Do they *look* like angels?"

"Hey, there are some pretty fucked-up looking angels, is what I hear. Like—rings of eyes covered in wings, or those four-headed ones from *The X-Files*."

"Or the ones that look like Christopher Walken."

"Gabriel, in *The Prophecy*. Viggo Mortensen played Satan." Goss squinted. "But these sort of look like...Pazuzu."

Hynde nodded, pleased. "Good call: four wings, like a moth—definitely Sumerian. This one has clawed feet; this one's head is turned backwards, or maybe upside-down. *This* one looks like it's got no lower jaw. This one has a tail and no legs at all, like a snake..."

"Dude, do you actually know what they are, or are you just fucking with me?"

"How much do you know about the Terrible Seven?"

"Nothing."

"Excellent. That means our viewers won't, either."

—

They set up in front of the door, before they lost the sun. A tight shot on Hynde, hands thrown out in what Goss had come to call his classic Profsplaining pose; Goss shot from below, framing him in the temple's gaping maw, while 'Lij the sound guy checked his levels and everybody else shut the fuck up. From the corner of one eye, Goss could just glimpse Camberwell leaning back against the point truck's wheel with her distractingly curvy legs crossed, arms braced like she was about to start doing reverse triceps push-ups. Though it was hard to tell from behind those massive sun-goggles, she didn't seem too impressed.

"The Terrible Seven were mankind's first boogeymen," Hynde told whoever would eventually be up at three in the morning, or whenever the History Channel chose to run this. "To call them demons would be too...Christian. To the people who feared them most, the Sumerians, they were simply a group of incredibly powerful creatures responsible for every sort of human misery, invisible and unutterably malign—literally unnameable, since to name them was, inevitably, to invite their attention. According to experts, the only way to fend them off was with the so-called 'Maskim Chant,' a prayer for protection collected by E. Campbell Thompson in his book *The Devils and Evil Spirits Of Babylonia, Vols. 1-2*...and even that was no sure guarantee of safety, depending on just how annoyed one—or all—of the Seven might be feeling, any given day of the week..."

Straightening slightly, he raised one hand in mock supplication, reciting:

"They are Seven! They are Seven!

"Seven in the depths of the ocean, Seven in the Heavens above,

"Those who are neither male nor female, those who stretch themselves out like chains...

"Terrible beyond description.

"Those who are Nameless. Those who must not be named.

"The enemies! The enemies! Bitter poison sent by the Gods.

"Seven are they! Seven!"

Nice, Goss thought, and went to cut Hynde off. But there was more, apparently—a lot of it, and Hynde seemed intent on getting it all out. Good for inserts, Goss guessed, 'specially when cut together with the spooky shit from inside...

"In heaven they are unknown. On earth they are not understood.

"They neither stand nor sit, nor eat nor drink.

"Spirits that minish the earth, that minish the land, of giant strength and giant tread—"

("*Minish*"?)

"Demons like raging bulls, great ghosts,

"Ghosts that break through all the houses, demons that have no shame, seven are they!

"Knowing no care, they grind the land like corn.

"Knowing no mercy, they rage against mankind.

"They are demons full of violence, ceaselessly devouring blood.

"Seven are they! Seven are they! Seven!

"They are Seven! They are Seven! They are twice Seven! They are Seven times seven!"

Camberwell was sitting up now, almost standing, while the rest of the crew made faces at each other. Goss had been sawing a finger across his throat since *knowing no care*, but Hynde just kept on going, hair crested, complexion purpling; he looked unhealthily sweat-shiny, spraying spit. Was that froth on his lower lip?

"The wicked *Uttuku*, who slays man alive on the plain.

"The wicked *Arralu* and *Allatu*, who wander alone in the wilderness, covering man like a garment,

"The wicked *Gallu* and *Alu*, who bind the hands and body.

"The wicked *Lammyatu*, who causes disease in every portion.

"The wicked *Ekimmu*, who draws out the bowels.

"The wicked *Namtaru*, who seizes by the throat..."

By this point even 'Lij was looking up, visibly worried. Hynde began to shake, eyes stutter-lidded, and fell sidelong even as Goss moved to catch him, only to find himself blocked—Camberwell was there already, folding Hynde into a brisk paramedic's hold. "A rag, *something*," she ordered 'Lij, who whipped his shirt off so fast his 'phones went bouncing, rolling it flat enough it'd fit between Hynde's teeth; Goss didn't feel like being in the way, so he drew back, kept rolling. As they laid Hynde back, limbs flailing hard enough to make dust-angels, Goss could just make out more words seeping out half through the cloth stopper and half through Hynde's bleeding nose, quick and dry: rhythmic, nasal, ancient. Another chant he could only assume, this time left entirely untranslated, though words here and there popped as familiar from the preceding bunch of rabid mystic bullshit—

Arralu-Allatu Namtaru Maskim
Assaku Utukku Lammyatu Maskim
Ekimmu Gallu-Alu Maskim
Maskim Maskim Maskim

Voices to his right, his left, while his lens-sight steadily narrowed and dimmed: *Go get Doc Journee, man! The fuck's head office pay her for, exactly?* 'Lij and Camberwell kneeling in the dirt, holding Hynde down, trying their best to make sure he didn't hurt himself 'til the only person on-site with an actual medical license got there. And all the while that same babble rising, louder and ever more throb-buzz deformed, like the guy had a swarm of bees stuck in his clogged and swelling throat...

ArralAllatNamtarAssakUtukkLammyatEkimmGalluAluMaskimMaskimMaskim
(Maskim)

—

The dust-storm kicked up while Journee was still attending to Hynde, getting him safely laid down in a corner of the temple's outer chamber and doing her best to stabilize him even as he resolved down into some shallow-breathing species of coma. "Any one of these fuckers flips, they'll take out a fuckin' wall!" Camberwell yelled, as the other two drivers scrambled to get the trucks as stable as possible, digging out 'round the wheels and anchoring them with rocks, applying locks to axles and steering wheels. Goss, for his own part, was already busy helping hustle the supplies inside, stacking ration-packs around Hynde like sandbags; a crash from the door made his head jerk up, just in time to see that chick Lao and her friend-who-was-a-boy Katz (both from craft services) staring at each other over a mess of broken plastic, floor between them suddenly half-turned to mud.

Katz: "What the *shit*, man!"

Lao: "I don't know. Christ! Those bottles aren't s'posed to *break*—"

The well, something dry and small "said" at the back of Goss's head, barely a voice at all—more a touch, in passing, in the dark. And: "There's a well," he heard himself say, before he could think better of it. "Down through there, behind the walls."

Katz looked at Lao, shrugged. "Better check it out, then," he suggested—started to, anyhow. Until Camberwell somehow turned up between them, half stepping sidelong and half like she'd just materialized, the rotating storm her personal wormhole.

"I'll do that," she said, firmly. "Still two gallon cans in the back of Truck Two, for weight; cut a path, make sure we can get to 'em. I'll tell you if what's down there's viable."

"Deal," Lao agreed, visibly grateful—and Camberwell was gone a second later, down into the passage, a shadow into shadow. While at almost the same time, from Goss's elbow, 'Lij suddenly asked (of no one in particular, given *he* was the resident expert): "Sat-phones aren't supposed to just stop working, right?"

Katz: "Nope."

"Could be we're in a dead zone, I guess...or the storm..."

"Yeah, good luck on that, buddy."

Across the room, the rest of the party were congregating in a clot, huddled 'round a cracked packet of glow-sticks because nobody wanted to break out the lanterns, not in this weather. Journee had opened Hynde's shirt to give him CPR, but left off when he stopped seizing. Now she sat crouched above him, peering down at his chest like she was trying to play connect-the-dots with moles, hair, and nipples.

"Got a weird rash forming here," she told Goss when he squatted down beside her. "Allergy? Or photosensitive, maybe, if he's prone to that, 'cause...it really does seem to turn darker the closer you move the flashlight."

"He uses a lot of sunscreen."

"Don't we all. Seriously, look for yourself."

He did. Thinking: *optical illusion, has to be*...but wondering, all the same. Because—it was just so clear, so defined, rucking

Hynde's skin as though something was raising it up from inside. Like a letter from some completely alien alphabet; a symbol, unrecognizable, unreadable.

A sigil, the same tiny voice corrected. And Goss felt the hairs on his back ruffle, sudden-slick with cold, foul sweat.

It took a few minutes more for 'Lij to give up on the sat-phone, tossing it aside so hard it bounced. "Try the radio mics," Goss heard him tell himself, "see what kind'a bandwidth we can...back to Gebel, might be somebody listening. But not the border, nope, gotta keep off *that* squawk-channel, for sure. Don't want the military gettin' wind, on either side..."

By then, Camberwell had been gone for almost ten minutes, so Goss felt free to leave Hynde in Journee's care and follow, at his own pace—through the passage and into the tunnel, feeling along the wall, trying to be quiet. But two painful stumbles later, halfway down the tunnel's curve, he had to flip open his phone just to see; the stone-bone walls gave off a faint, ill light, vaguely slick, a dead jellyfish luminescence. He drew within just enough range to hear Camberwell's boots rasp on the downward slope, then pause—saw her glance over one shoulder, eyes weirdly bright through a dim fall of hair gust-popped from her severe, sweat-soaked working gal's braid.

Asking, as she did: "Want me to wait while you catch up?"

Boss, other people might've appended, almost automatically, but never her. Then again, Goss had to admit, he wouldn't have really believed that shit coming from Camberwell, even if she had.

He straightened up, sighing, and joined her—standing pretty much exactly where he thought she'd've ended up, right next to the well, though keeping a careful distance between herself and its creepy-coated sides. "Try sending down a cup yet, or what?"

"Why? Oh, right...no, no point; that's why I volunteered, so those dumbasses *wouldn't* try. Don't want to be drinking any of the shit comes out of there, believe you me."

"Oh, I do, and that's—kinda interesting, given. Rings a bit like you obviously know more about this than you're letting on."

She arched a brow, denial reflex-quick, though not particularly convincing. "Hey, who was it sent Lao and what's-his-name down here in the first place? I'm motor pool, man. Cryptoarchaeology is you and coma-boy's gig."

"Says the chick who knows the correct terminology."

"Look who I work for."

Goss sighed. "Okay, I'll bite. What's in the well?"

"What's *on* the well? Should give you some idea. Or, better yet—"

She held out her hand for his phone, the little glowing screen, with its pathetic rectangular light. After a moment, he gave it over and watched her cast it 'round, outlining the chamber's canted, circular floor: seen face on, those ridges he'd felt under his feet when Hynde first brought him in here and dismissed without a first glance, let alone a second, proved to be in-spiralling channels stained black from centuries of use: run-off ditches once used for drainage, aimed at drawing some sort of liquid—layered and faded now into muck and dust, a resinous stew clogged with dead insects—away from (what else?) seven separate niches set into the surrounding walls, inset so sharply they only became apparent when you observed them at an angle.

In front of each niche, one of the mosaicked figures, with a funnelling spout set at ditch-level under the creature in question's feet, or lack thereof. Inside each niche, meanwhile, a quartet of hooked spikes set vertically, maybe five feet apart: two up top, possibly for hands or wrists, depending if you were doing things Roman- or Renaissance-style; two down below, suitable for lashing somebody's ankles to. And now that Goss looked closer, something else as well, in each of those upright stone coffins...

(Ivory scraps, shattered yellow-brown shards, broken down by time and gravity alike, and painted to match their surroundings by lack of light. Bones, piled where they fell.)

"What the fuck *was* this place?" Goss asked, out loud. But mainly because he wanted confirmation, more than anything else.

Camberwell shrugged, yet again—her default setting, he guessed. "A trap," she answered. "And you fell in it, but don't feel bad—you weren't to know, right?"

"We found it, though. Hynde and me..."

"If not you, somebody else. Some places are already empty, already ruined—they just wait, long as it takes. They don't ever go away. 'Cause they *want* to be found."

Goss felt his stomach roil, fresh sweat springing up even colder, so rank he could smell it. "A trap," he repeated, biting down, as

Camberwell nodded. Then: "For us?"

But here she shook her head, pointing back at the well, with its seven watchful guardians. Saying, as she did—

"Naw, man. For *them*."

—

She laid her hand on his, half its size but twice as strong, and walked him through it—puppeted his numb and clumsy finger-pads bodily over the clumps of fossil-chunks in turn, allowing him time to recognize what was hidden inside the mosaic's design more by touch than by sight: a symbol (*sigil*) for every figure, tu-mour-blooming and weirdly organic, each one just ever-so-slight-ly different from the next. He found the thing Hynde's rash most reminded him of on number four, and stopped dead; Camberwell's gaze flicked down to confirm, her mouth moving slightly, shaping words. *Ah*, one looked like—*ah, I see*. Or maybe *I see you*.

"What?" he demanded, for what seemed like the tenth time in quick succession. Thinking: *I sound like a damn parrot.*

Camberwell didn't seem to mind though. "Ashreel," she replied, not looking up. "That's what I said. The Terrible Ashreel, who wears us like clothing."

"Allatu, you mean. The wicked, who covers man like a gar-ment—"

"Whatever, Mister G. If you prefer."

"It's just—I mean, that's nothing like what Hynde said, up there—"

"Yeah sure, 'cause that shit was what the Sumerians and Bab-ylonians called 'em, from that book Hynde was quoting." She knocked knuckles against Hynde's brand, then the ones on either side—three sharp little raps, invisible cross-nails. "*These* are their actual *names*. Like...what they call *themselves*."

"How the fuck would you know that? Camberwell, what the hell."

Straightening, shrugging yet again, like she was throwing off flies. "There's a book, okay? The *Liber Carne*—'Book of Meat.' And all's it has is just a list of names with these symbols carved along-side, so you'll know which one you're looking at, when they're—embodied. In the flesh."

"In the—you mean *bodies*, like possession? Like that's what's happening to Hynde?" At her nod: "Well...makes sense, I guess, in context; he already said they were demons."

"Oh, that's a misnomer, actually. 'Terrible' used to mean 'awe-inspiring,' 'more whatever than any other whatever,' like Tsar Ivan of all the Russias. So the Seven, the *Terrible* Seven, what they really are is angels, just like you thought."

"Fallen angels."

"Nope, those are Goetim, like you call the ones who stayed up top Elohim—*these* are Maskim, same as the Chant. Arralu-Allatu, Namtaru, Assaku, Utukku, Gallu-Alu, Ekimmu, Lammyatu; Ashreel, Yphemaal, Zemyel, Eshphoriel, Immoel, Coiab, Ushephekad. Angel of Confusion, the Mender Angel, Angel of Severance, Angel of Whispers, Angel of Translation, Angel of Ripening, Angel of the Empty..."

All these half-foreign words spilling from her mouth, impossibly glib, ringing in Goss's head like popped blood-vessels. But: "Wait," he threw back, struggling. "A 'trap'...I thought this place was supposed to be a temple. Like the people who built it worshipped these things."

"Okay, then play that out. Given how Hynde described 'em, what sort of people would *worship* the Seven, you think?"

"...Terrible people?"

"You got it. Sad people, weird people, crazy people. People who get off on power, good, bad, or indifferent. People who hate the world they got so damn bad they don't really care what they swap it for, as long as it's *something else*."

"And they expect—the Seven—to do that for them."

"It's what they were made for."

Straight through cryptoarchaeology and out the other side, into a version of the Creation so literally Apocryphal it would've gotten them both burnt at the stake just a few hundred years earlier. Because to hear Camberwell tell it, sometimes, when a Creator got very, verrry lonely, It decided to make Itself some friends—after which, needing someplace to put them, It contracted the making of such a place out to creatures themselves made to order: fragments of its own reflected glory haphazardly hammered into vaguely humanesque form, perfectly suited to this one colossal task, and almost nothing else.

"They made the world, in other words," Goss said. "All seven of them."

"Yeah. 'Cept back then they were still one angel in seven parts—the Voltron angel, I call it. Splitting apart came later on, after the schism."

"Lucifer, war in heaven, cast down into hell and yadda yadda. All that. So this is all, what...some sort of metaphysical labour dispute?"

"They wouldn't think of it that way."

"How *do* they think of it?"

"*Differently*, like every other thing. Look, once the shit hit the cosmic fan, the Seven didn't stay with God, but they didn't go with the devil, either—they just went, forced themselves from outside space and time into the universe they'd made, and never looked back. And that was because they wanted something angels are uniquely unqualified for: free will. They wanted to be us."

Back to the fast-forward, then, the bend and the warp, 'til her ridiculously plausible-seeming exposition-dump seemed to come at him from everywhere at once, a perfect storm. Because: *misery's their meat, see—the honey that draws flies, by-product of every worst moment of all our brief lives, when people will cry out for anything who'll listen. That's when one of the Seven usually shows up, offering help—except the kind of help they come up with's usually nothing very helpful at all, considering how they just don't really get the way things work for us, even now. And it's always just one of them at first, 'cause they each blame the other for having made the decision to run, stranding themselves in the here and now, so they don't want to be anywhere near each other...but if you can get 'em all in one place—someplace like here, say, with seven bleeding, suffering vessels left all ready and waiting for 'em—then they'll be automatically drawn back together, like gravity, a black hole event horizon. They'll form a vector, and at the middle of that cyclone they'll become a single angel once again, ready to tear everything they built up right the fuck on back down.*

Words words words, every one more painful than the last. Goss looked at Camberwell as she spoke, straight on, the way he didn't think he'd ever actually done previously. She was short and stacked, skin tanned and plentiful, eyes darkish brown shot with a sort of creamier shade, like petrified wood. A barely-visible scar quirked through one eyebrow, threading down over the cheekbone beneath to intersect with another at the corner of her mouth, keloid raised in their wake like a negative-image beauty-mark, a reversed dimple.

Examined this way, at close quarters, he found he liked the look of her, suddenly and sharply—and for some reason, that mainly made him angry.

"This is a fairy tale," he heard himself tell her, with what seemed like over-the-top emphasis. "I'm sitting here in the dark, letting you spout some...Catholic campfire story about angel-traps, free will, fuckin' misery vectors..." A quick head-shake, firm enough to hurt. "None of it's true."

"Yeah, okay, you want to play it that way."

"If I *want*—?"

Here she turned on him, abruptly equal-fierce, clearing her throat to hork a contemptuous wad out on the ground between them, like she was making a point. "Look, you think I give a runny jack-shit if you believe me or not? *I know what I know.* It's just that things are gonna start to move fast from now on, so you need to know that; *somebody* in this crap-pit does, aside from me. And I guess—" Stopping and hissing, annoyed with herself, before adding, quieter: "I guess I wanted to just say it, too—out loud, for once. For all the good it'll probably do either of us."

They stood there a second, listening, Goss didn't know for what—nothing but muffled wind, people murmuring scared out beyond the passage, a general scrape and drip. 'Til he asked: "What about Hynde? Can we, like, *do* anything?"

"Not much. Why? You guys friends?"

Yes, damnit, Goss wanted to snap, but he was pretty sure she had lie-dar to go with her Seven-dar. "There's...not really a show, without him," was all he said, finally.

"All right, well—he's pretty good and got, at this point, so. I'd keep him sedated, restrained if I could, and wait, see who else shows up: there's six more to go, after all."

"What happens if they all show up?"

"All Seven? Then we're fucked, basically, as a species. Stuck back together, the Maskim are a load-bearing boss the likes of which this world was not designed to contain, and the vector they form in proximity, well—it's like putting too much weight on a sheet of...something. Do it long enough, it rips wide open."

"*What* rips?"

"The crap you think? Everything."

There was a sort of jump-cut, and Goss found himself tagging along beside her as Camberwell strode back up the passageway, listening to her tell him: "Important point about Hynde, as of right now, is to make sure he doesn't start doin' stuff to himself."

"...Like?"

"Well—"

As she said it, though, there came a scream-led general uproar up in front, making them both break into a run. They tumbled back into the light-sticks' circular glow to find Journee contorted on the ground with her heels drumming, chewing at her own lips—everybody else had already shrunk back, eyes and mouths covered like it was catching, save for big, stupid 'Lij, who was trying his level best to pry her jaws apart and thrust his folding pocket spork in between. Goss darted forward to grab one arm, Camberwell the other, but Journee used the leverage to flip back up onto her feet, throwing them both off against the walls. She looked straight at Camberwell, spit blood and grinned wide, as though she recognized her: *oh, it's you. How do, buddy? Welcome to the main event.*

Then reached back into her own sides, fingers plunging straight down through flesh to grip bone—ripped her red ribs wide, whole back opening up like that meat-book Camberwell'd mentioned and both lungs flopping out, way too large for comfort: two dirty grey-pink balloons breathing and growing, already disgustingly over-swollen yet inflating even further, like mammoth water wings.

The pain of it made her roar and jack-knife, vomiting on her own feet. And when Journee looked up once more, horrid grin trailing yellow sick-strings, Goss saw she now had a sigil of her own embossed on her forehead, fresh as some stomped-in bone-bruise.

"The Terrible Zemyel," Camberwell said, to no one in particular. "Who desecrates the faithful."

And: "God!" Somebody else—Lao?—could be heard to sob, behind them. But: "Fuck Him," Journee rasped back, throwing the tarp pinned 'cross the permanently open doorway wide and taking impossibly off up into the storm with a single flap, blood splattering everywhere, a foul red spindrift.

'Lij slapped both hands up to seal his mouth, retching loudly;

23

Katz fell on his ass, hind-skull colliding with the wall's sharp surface, so hard he knocked himself out. Lao continued to sob-pray on, mindless, while everybody else just stared. And Goss found himself looking over at Camberwell, automatically, only to catch her nodding—just once, like she'd seen it coming.

"—Like *that*, basically," she concluded, without a shred of surprise.

—

Five minutes at most, but it felt like an hour: things narrowed, got treacly, in that accident-in-progress way. Outside, the dust had thickened into its own artificial night; they could hear the thing inside Journee swooping high above it, laughing like a loon, yelling raucous insults at the sky. The other two drivers had never come back, lost in the storm; Katz crawled away and tore at the floor with his hands, badger-style, like he wanted to bury himself alive head-first. Lao wept and wept. 'Lij came feeling towards Camberwell and Goss as the glow-sticks dimmed, almost clambering over Hynde, whose breathing had sunk so low his chest barely seemed to move. "Gotta *do* something, man," he told them, like he was the first one ever to have that particular thought. "*Something.* Y'know? Before it's too late."

"It was too late when we got here," Goss heard himself reply—again, not what he'd thought he was going to say when he'd opened his mouth. His tongue felt suddenly hot, inside of his mouth gone all itchy, swollen tight; strep? Tonsillitis? Jesus, if he could only reach back in there and *scratch...*

And Camberwell was looking at him sidelong now, with interest, though 'Lij just continued on blissfully unaware of anything, aside from his own worries. "Look, fuck *that* shit," he said, before asking her: "Can we get to the trucks?"

She shook her head. "No driving in this weather, even if we did. You ever raise anybody, or did the mics crap out too?"

"Uh, I don't think so; caught somebody talkin' in Arabic one time, close-ish, but it sounded military, so I rung off real quick. Something about containment protocol."

Goss: "*What?*"

"Well, I thought maybe that was 'cause they were doing minefield sweeps, or whatever—"

"When *was* this?"

"...Fifteen minutes ago, when you guys were still down there, 'bout the time the storm went mega. Why?"

Goss opened his mouth again, but Camberwell was already bolting up, grabbing both Katz and Hynde at once by their shirt-collars, ready to heave and drag. The wind's whistle had taken on a weird, sharp edge, an atonal descending keen, so loud Goss could barely hear her—though he sure as hell saw her lips move, *read* them with widening, horrified eyes, at almost the same split-second he found himself turning, already in mid-leap towards the descending passage—

"*—INCOMING, get the shit downstairs, before those sons of bitches bring this whole fuckin' place down around our goddamn—*"

(ears)

—

Three hits, Goss thought, or maybe two and a half; it was hard to tell, when your head wouldn't stop ringing. What he could only assume was at least two of the trucks had gone up right as the walls came down, or perhaps a shade before. Now the top half of the temple was flattened, once more indistinguishable from the mountainside above and around it, a deadfall of shattered lava rock, bone-bricks and fossils. No more missiles fell, which was good, yet—so far as they could tell, pinned beneath slabs and sediment—the storm above still raged on. And now they were all down in the well-room, trapped, with only a flickering congregation of phones to raise against the dark.

"Did you have any kind of *plan* when you came here, exactly?" Goss asked Camberwell, hoarsely. "I mean, aside from 'find Seven congregation site—question mark—profit'?" To which she simply sighed, and replied—

"Yeah, sort of. But you're not gonna like it."

"Try me."

Reluctantly: "The last couple times I did this, there was a physical copy of the *Liber Carne* in play, so getting rid of that helped—but there's no copy here, which makes *us* the *Liber Carne*, the human pages being Inscribed." He could hear the big I on that last word, and it scared him. "And when people are being Inscribed, well...the *best* plan is usually to just start killing those who aren't possessed until you've got less than seven left, because then why bother?"

25

"Uh huh..."

"Getting to know you people well enough to *like* you, that was my mistake, obviously," she continued, partly under her breath, like she was talking to herself. Then added, louder: "Anyhow. What we're dealing with right now is two people definitely Inscribed and possessed, four potential Inscriptions, and one halfway gone..."

"Halfway? Who?"

She shot him that look, yet one more time—softer, almost sympathetic. "Open your mouth, Goss."

"Why? What f—oh, you gotta be kidding."

No change, just a slightly raised eyebrow, as if to say: *do I look it, motherfucker?* Which, he was forced to admit, she very much did not.

Nothing to do but obey, then. Or scream, and keep on screaming.

Goss felt his jaw slacken, pop out and down like an unhinged jewel-box, revealing all its secrets. His tongue's itch was approaching some sort of critical mass. And then, right then, was when he felt it—fully and completely, without even trying. Some kind of raised area on his own soft palate, yearning down as sharply as the rest of his mouth's sensitive insides yearned up, straining to map its impossibly angled curves. His eyes skittered to the well's rim, where he knew he would find its twin, if he only searched long enough.

"Uck ee," he got out, consonants drowned away in a mixture of hot spit and cold sweat. "Oh it, uck *ee.*"

A small, sad nod. "The Terrible Eshphoriel," Camberwell confirmed. "Who whispers in the empty places."

Goss closed his mouth, then spat like he was trying to clear it, for all he knew that wouldn't work. Then asked, hoarsely, stumbling slightly over the words he found increasingly difficult to form: "How mush...time I got?"

"Not much, probably."

"'S what I fought." He looked down, then back up at her, eyes sharpening. "How you geh those scars uh yers, Cammerwell?"

"Knowing's not gonna help you, Goss." But since he didn't look away, she sighed, and replied. "Hunting accident. Okay?"

"Hmh, 'kay. Then...thing we need uh...new plan, mebbe. You 'gree?"

She nodded, twisting her lips; he could see her thinking, literally, cross-referencing what had to be a thousand scribbled notes from the margins of her mental grand grimoire. Time slowed to an excruciating crawl, within which Goss began to hear that still, small voice begin to mount up again, no doubt aware it no longer had to be particularly subtle about things anymore: *Eshphoriel Maskim, sometimes called Uttukku, Angel of Whispers...and yes, I can hear you, little fleshbag, as you hear me; feel you, in all your incipient flowering and decay, your time-anchored freedom. We are all the same in this way, and yes, we mostly hate you for it, which only makes your pain all the sweeter, in context—though not quite so much, at this point, as we imitation-of-passionately strive to hate each other.*

You guys stand outside space and time, though, right? he longed to demand, as he felt the constant background chatter of what he'd always thought of as "him" start to dim. *Laid the foundations of the Earth—you're megaton bombs, and we're like...viruses. So why the hell would you want to be anything like us? To lower yourselves that way?*

A small pause came in this last idea's wake, not quite present, yet too much there to be absent, somehow: a breath, perhaps, or the concept of one, drawn from the non-throat of something infinitely larger. The feather's shadow, floating above the Word of God.

It does make you wonder, does it not? the small voice "said." *I know I do, and have, since before your first cells split.*

But: *Because they want to defile the creation they set in place, yet have no real part in,* Goss's mind—*his* mind, yes, he was *almost* sure—chimed in. *Because they long to insert themselves where they have no cause to be and let it shiver apart all around them, to run counter to everything, a curse on Heaven. To make themselves the worm in the cosmic apple, rotting everything they touch...*

The breath returned, drawn harder this time in a semi-insulted way, a universal "tch!" But at the same time, something else presented itself—just as likely, or invalid as anything else, in a world touched by the Seven.

(*Or because...maybe, this is all there is. Maybe, this is as good as it gets.*)

That's all.

"I have an idea," Camberwell said, at last, from somewhere nearby. And Goss opened his mouth to answer only to hear the angel's still, small voice issue from between his teeth, replying, mildly—

"Do you, huntress? Then please, say on."

—

This, then, was how they all finally came to be arrayed 'round the well's rim, the seven of them who were left, standing—or propped up/lying, in Hynde and Katz's cases—in front of those awful wall-orifices, staring into the multifaceted mosaic-eyes of God's former *Flip My Universe* cast and crew. 'Lij stood at the empty southeastern point, looking nervous, for which neither Goss nor the creature inhabiting his brain-pan could possibly blame him. While Camberwell busied herself moving from person to person, sketching quick and dirty versions of the sigils on them with the point of a flick-knife she'd produced from one of her boots. Lao opened her mouth like she was gonna start crying even harder when she first saw it, but Camberwell just shot her the fearsom-est glare yet—Medusa-grade, for sure—and watched her shut the fuck up, with a hitchy little gasp.

"This will bring us together *sooner* rather than later, you must realize," Eshphoriel told Camberwell, who nodded. Replying: "That's the idea."

"Ah. That seems somewhat...antithetical, knowing our works, as you claim to."

"Maybe so. But you tell me—what's better? Stay down here in the dark waiting for the air to run out only to have you celestial tapeworms soul-rape us all at the last minute anyways, when we're too weak to put up a fight? Or force an end now, while we're all semi-fresh, and see what happens?"

"Fine tactics, yes—very born-again barbarian. Your own pocket Ragnarok, with all that the term implies."

"Yeah, yeah: clam up, Legion, if you don't have anything useful to contribute." To 'Lij: "You ready, sound-boy?"

"Uhhhh..."

"I'll take that as a 'yes.'"

Done with Katz, she swapped places with 'Lij, handing him the knife as she went, and tapping the relevant sigil. "Like that," she said. "Try to do it all in one motion, if you can—it'll hurt less."

'Lij looked dubious. "One can't fail to notice *you* aren't volunteer-ing for impromptu body-modification," Eshphoriel noted, through Goss's lips, while Camberwell met the comment with a tiny, bitter smile. Replying, as she hiked her shirt up to demonstrate—

"That'd be 'cause I've already got one."

Cocking a hip to display the thing in question where it nestled in the hollow at the base of her spine, more a scab than a scar, edges blurred like some infinitely fucked-up tramp stamp. And as she did, Goss saw *something* come fluttering up behind her skin, a parallel-dimension full-body ripple, the barest glowing shadow of a disproportionately huge tentacle-tip still up-thrust through Camberwell's whole being, as though everything she was, had been and would ever come to be was nothing more than some indistinct no-creature's fleshy finger-puppet.

One cream-brown eye flushed with livid colour, green on yellow, while the other stayed exactly the same—human, weary, bitter to its soul's bones. And Camberwell opened her mouth to let her tongue protrude, pink and healthy except for an odd whitish strip that ran ragged down its centre from tip to—not exactly *tail*, Goss assumed, since the tongue was fairly huge, or so he seemed to recall. But definitely almost to the uvula, and: oh God, oh shit, was it actually splitting as he watched, bisecting itself not-so-neatly into two separate semi-points, like a child's snakey scribble?

Camberwell gave it a flourish, swallowed the resultant spit-mouthful, then said, without much affect: "Yeah, that's right—'the Terrible Immoel, who speaks with a dead tongue...'" Camberwell fluttered the organ in question at what had taken control of Goss, showing its central scars long-healed, extending the smile into a wide, entirely unamused grin. "So say hey, assfuck. Remember me now?"

"You were its vessel, then, once before," Goss heard his lips reply. "And...yes, yes, I do recall it. Apologies, huntress; I cannot say, with the best will in all this world, that any of you look so very different to me."

Camberwell snapped her fingers. "Aw, gee." To 'Lij, sharper: "I tell you to stop cutting?"

Goss felt "his" eyes slide to poor 'Lij, caught and wavering (his face a sickly grey-green, chest heaving slightly, like he didn't know whether to run or puke), then watched him shake his head, and bow back down to it. The knife went in shallow, blunter than the job called for—he had to drag it, hooking up underneath his own hide, to make the meat part as cleanly as the job required. While Camberwell kept a sure and steady watch on the other well-riders,

29

all of whom were beginning to look equally disturbed, even those who were supposedly unconscious. Goss felt his own lips curve, far more genuinely amused, even as an alien emotion-tangle wound itself invasively throughout his chest: half proprietorially expectant, half vaguely annoyed. And—

"We are coming," he heard himself say. "All of us. Meaning you may have miscalculated, somewhat...what a sad state of affairs indeed, when the prospective welfare of your entire species depends on you not doing so."

That same interior ripple ran 'round the well's perimeter as 'Lij pulled the knife past "his" sigil's final slashing loop and yanked it free, splattering the frieze in front of him; in response, the very stones seemed to arch hungrily, that composite mouth gaping, eager for blood. Above, even through the heavy-pressing rubble-mound which must be all that was left of the temple proper, Goss could hear Journee-Zemyel swooping and cawing in the updraft, swirled on endless waves of storm; from his eye's corner he saw Hynde-whoever (*Ashreel*, Eshphoriel supplied, helpfully) open one similarly parti-coloured eye and lever himself up, clumsy-clambering to his feet. Katz's head fell back, spine suddenly hooping so heels struck shoulder-blades with a wetly awful crack, and began to lift off, levitating gently, turning in the air like some horrible ornament. Meanwhile, Lao continued to grind her fisted knuckles into both eyes at once, bruising lids but hopefully held back from pulping the balls themselves, at least so long as her sockets held fast...

(*The Terrible Coiab, who seeds without regard. The Terrible Ush-ephekad, who opens the ground beneath us.*)

From the well, dusty mortar popped forth between every suture, and the thing as a whole gave one great shrug, shivering itself apart—began caving in and expanding at the same time, becoming a nothing-column for its parts to revolve around, an incipient reality fabric-tear. And in turn, the urge to rotate likewise—just let go of gravity's pull, throw physical law to the winds, and see where that might lead—cored through Goss ass to cranium, Vlad Tsepesh style, a phantom impalement pole spearing every neural pathway. Simultaneously gone limp *and* stiff , he didn't have to look down to know his crotch must be darkening, or over to 'Lij to confirm how the same invisible angel-driven marionette-hooks were now pulling at *his* muscles, making his knife-hand grip and flex, sharp enough the handle almost broke free of his sweaty palm entirely—

(*The Terrible Yphemaal, who stitches what was rent asunder*)

"And now we *are* Seven, without a doubt," Goss heard that voice in his throat note, its disappointment audible. "For all your bravado, perhaps you are not as well-educated as you believe."

Camberwell shrugged yet one more time, slow but distinct; her possessed eye widened slightly, as though in surprise. And in that instant, it occurred to Goss how much of herself she still retained, even in the Immoel-thing's grip, which seemed far—slipperier, in her case, than with everybody else. Because maybe coming pre-Inscribed built up a certain pad of scar-tissue in the soul, in situations like these; maybe that's what she'd been gambling on, amongst other things. Having just enough slack on her lead to allow her to do stuff like (for example) reach down into her other boot, the way she was even as they "spoke," and—

Holy crap, just how many knives does this chick walk around with, exactly?

—bringing up the second of a matched pair, trigger already thumbed, blade halfway from its socket. Tucking it beneath her jaw, point tapping at her jugular, and saying, as she did—

"Never claimed to be, but I do know *this* much: Sam Raimi got it wrong. You guys don't like wearing nothin' *dead*."

And: *That's your plan?* Goss wanted to yell, right in the face of her martyr-stupid, *fuck all y'all* snarl. Except that that was when the thing inside 'Lij (Yphemaal, its name is Yphemaal) turned him, bodily—two great twitches, a child "walking" a doll. Its purple eyes fell on Camberwell in mid-move, and narrowed; Goss heard something rush up and out in every direction, rustle-ruffling as it went: some massive and indistinct pair of wings, mostly elsewhere, only a few pinions intruding to lash the blade from Camberwell's throat before the cut could complete itself, leaving a shallow red trail in its wake...

(Another "hunting" trophy, Goss guessed, eventually. Not that she'd probably notice.)

"*No*," 'Lij-Yphemaal told the room at large, all its hovering sibling-selves, in a voice colder than orbit-bound satellite-skin. "Enough."

"We are Seven," Eshphoriel Maskim replied, with Goss's flayed mouth. "The huntress has the right of it: remove one vessel, break

31

the quorum, before we reassemble. If she wants to sacrifice herself, who are we to interfere?"

"Who *were* we to, ever, every time we have? But there is another way."

The sigils flowed each to each, Goss recalled having noticed at this freakshow's outset, albeit only subconsciously—one basic design exponentially added upon, a fresh new (literal) twist summoning Two out of One, Three out of Two, Four out of Three, etcetera. Which left Immoel and Yphemaal separated by both a pair of places and a triad of contortionate squiggle-slashes; far more work to imitate than 'Lij could possibly do under pressure with his semi-blunt knife, his wholly inadequate human hands and brain...

But Yphemaal wasn't 'Lij. Hell, this very second, '*Lij* wasn't even 'Lij.

The Mender-angel was at least merciful enough to let him scream as it remade its sigil into Immoel's with three quick cuts, then slipped forth, blowing away up through the well's centre-spoke like a backwards lightning rod. Two niches on, Katz lit back to earth with a cartilaginous creak, while Lao let go just in time to avoid tearing her own corneas; Hynde's head whipped up, face gone trauma-slack but finally recognizable, abruptly vacated. And Immoel Maskim spurted forth from Camberwell in a gross black cloud from mouth, nose, the corner of the eyes, its passage dimming her yellow-green eye back to brown, then buzzed angrily back and forth between two equally useless prospective vessels until seeming to give up in disgust.

Seemed even angels couldn't be in two places at once. Who knew?

Not inside time and space, no. And unfortunately—

That's where we live, Goss realized.

Yes.

Goss saw the bulk of the Immoel-stuff blend into the well room's wall, sucked away like blotted ink. Then fell to his knees, as though prompted, only to see the well collapse in upon its own shaft, ruined forever—its final cosmic strut removed, solved away like some video game's culminative challenge.

Beneath, the ground shook like jelly. Above, a thunderclap whoosh sucked all the dust away, darkness boiling up, peeling itself away like an onion 'til only the sun remained, pale and high and bright. And straight through the hole in the "roof" dropped all that was left of Journee-turned-Zemyel—face-down, from a twenty-plus-foot height, horrible thunk of impact driving her features right back into her skull, leaving nothing behind but a smashed-flat, raw meat mask.

Goss watched those wing-lungs of hers deflate, thinking: *she couldn't've survived.* And felt Eshphoriel, still lingering clawed to his brain's pathways even in the face of utter defeat, interiorly agree that: *it does seem unlikely. But then, my sister loves to leave no toy unbroken, if only to spit in your—and our—Maker's absent eye.*

Uh huh, Goss thought back, suddenly far too tired for fear, or even sorrow. *So maybe it's time to get the fuck out too, huh, while the going's good? "Minish" yourself, like the old chant goes...*

Perhaps, yes. For now.

He looked to Camberwell, who stood there shaking slightly, caught off-guard for once—amazed to be alive, it was fairly obvious, part-cut throat and all. Asking 'Lij, as she dabbed at the blood: "What did you *do,* dude?"

To which 'Lij only shook his head, equally freaked. "I...yeah, dunno, really. I don't—even think that was *me.*"

"No, 'course not: Yphemaal, right? Who sews crooked seams straight..." She shook her head, cracked her neck back and forth. "Only one of 'em still *building* stuff, these days, instead of tearing down or undermining, so maybe it's the only one of 'em who really *doesn't* want to go back, 'cause it knows what'll happen next."

"Maaaaybe," 'Lij said, dubious—then grabbed his wound, like something'd just reminded him it was there. "Oh, *shit,* that hurts!"

"You'll be fine, ya big baby—magic shit heals fast, like you wouldn't believe. Makes for a great conversation piece, too."

"Okay, sure. Hey...I saved your life."

Camberwell snorted. "Yeah, well—I would've saved yours, you hadn't beat me to it. Which makes us even."

'Lij opened his mouth at that, perhaps to object, but was interrupted by Hynde, his voice creaky with disuse. Demanding of Goss directly—

"Hey, Arthur, what...the hell *happened* here? Last thing I remember was doing pick-ups outside, and then—" His eyes fell on Journee, widening. "—*then* I, oh Christ, is that—who *is* that?"

Goss sighed, equally hoarse. "Long story."

By the time he was done, they were all outside—even poor Journee, who 'Lij had badgered Katz and Lao into helping roll up in a tarp, stowing her for transport in the back of the one blessedly still-operative truck Camberwell'd managed to excavate from the missile-strike's wreckage. Better yet, it ensued that 'Lij's backup sat-phone was now once again functional; once contacted, the production office informed them that border skirmishes had definitely spilled over into undeclared war, thus necessitating a quick retreat to the airstrip they'd rented near Karima town. Camberwell reckoned they could make it if they started now, though the last mile or so might be mainly on fumes.

"Better saddle up," she told Goss, briskly, as she brushed past, headed for the truck's cab. Adding, to a visibly gobsmacked Hynde: "Yo, Professor: you gonna be okay? 'Cause the fact is, we kinda can't stop to let you process."

Hynde shook his head, wincing; one hand went to his chest, probably just as raw as Goss's mouth-roof. "No, I'll...be okay. Eventually."

"Mmm. Won't we all."

Lao opened the truck's back door and beckoned, face wan—all cried out, at least for the nonce. Prayed too, probably.

Goss clambered in first, offering his hand. "Did we at least get enough footage to make a show?" Hynde had the insufferable balls to ask him, taking it.

"Just get in the fucking truck, Lyman."

—

Weeks after, Goss came awake with a full-body slam, tangled in his sleeping bag and coated with cold sweat, as though having just been ejected from his dreams like a cannonball. They were in the Falklands by then, investigating a weird earthwork discovered in and amongst the 1982 war's detritus—it wound downward like a harrow, a potential subterranean grinding room for squishy human corn, but thankfully, nothing they'd discovered inside seemed (thus far) to indicate any sort of connection to the Seven, either directly or metaphorically.

In the interim since the Sudan, Katz had quit, for which Goss could hardly blame him—but Camberwell was still with them, which didn't make either Goss or Hynde exactly comfortable, though neither felt like calling her on it. When pressed, she'd admitted to 'Lij that her hunting "methods" involved a fair deal of intuition-surfing, moving hither and yon at the call of her own angel voice-tainted subconscious, letting her post-Immoelization hangover do the psychic driving. Which did all seem to imply they were stuck with her, at least until the tides told her to move elsewhere...

She is a woman of fate, your huntress, the still, small voice of Eshphoriel Maskim told him, in the darkness of his tent. *Thus, where we go, she follows—and vice versa.*

Goss took a breath, tasting his own fear-stink. *Are you here for me?* he made himself wonder, though the possible answer terrified him even more.

Oh, I am not here at all, meat-sack. I suppose I am...bored, you might say, and find you a welcome distraction. For there is so much misery everywhere here, in this world of yours, and so very little I am allowed to do with it.

Having frankly no idea what to say to that, Goss simply hugged his knees and struggled to keep his breathing regular, his pulse calm and steady. His mouth prickled with gooseflesh, as though something were feeling its way around his tongue: the Whisper-angel, exploring his soul's ill-kept boundaries with unsympathetic care, from somewhere entirely Other.

I thought you were—done, is all. With me.

Did you? Yet the universe is far too complicated a place for that. And so it is that you are none of you ever so alone as you fear, nor as you hope. A pause. *Nonetheless, I am...glad to see you well, I find, or as much as I can be. Her too, for all her inconvenience.*

Here, however, Goss felt fear give way to anger, a welcome palate-cleanser. Because it seemed like maybe he'd finally developed an allergy to bullshit, at least when it came to the Maskim—or this Maskim, to be exact—and their fucked-up version of what passed for a celestial-to-human pep-talk.

Would've been perfectly content to let Camberwell cut her own throat, though, wouldn't you? he pointed out, shoulders rucking, hair rising like quills. *If that—brother-sister-whatever of yours hadn't made 'Lij interfere...*

Indubitably, yes. Did you expect anything else?

Yes! What kind of angels are you, goddamnit?

The God-damned kind, Eshphoriel Maskim replied, without a shred of irony.

You damned yourselves, is what I hear, Goss snapped back—then froze, appalled by his own hubris. But no bolt of lightning fell; the ground stayed firm, the night around him quiet, aside from lapping waves. Outside, someone turned in their sleep, moaning. And beyond it all, the earthwork's narrow descending groove stood open to the stars, ready to receive whatever might arrive, as Heaven dictated.

...There is that, too, the still, small voice admitted, so low Goss could feel more than hear it, tolling like a dim bone bell.

(*But then again—what is free will for, in the end, except to let us make our own mistakes?*)

Even quieter still, that last part. So much so that, in the end— no matter how long, or hard, he considered it—Goss eventually realized it was impossible to tell if it had been meant to be the angel's thought, or his own.

Doesn't matter, he thought, closing his eyes. And went back to sleep.

WHEN I'M ARMORING MY BELLY

Much later, he would recall the exact moment when he finally forgot his own name: Face-down on a bumpy mattress smelling of semen and Vicks, with Goran pushing and biting into him at once—dry drag and relentless ache, icy and burning in equal amounts, the full Isobel Gowdie daemon lover treatment. Wasn't like it'd never happened before, and yet, *that* particular time…something broke, never to be repaired. He felt it run out of him like the blood itself, greedily lapped and savoured: Waste not, want not.

When they flipped him over, meanwhile, Cija came settling onto him from above like Fuseli's nightmare or Munch's red-headed whore-dream, her teeth almost meeting around the bed of one nipple—with him in too much nethermost pain even to fuck forward 'til she *made* him, reached back to dip her too-sharp thumbnail right into the seat of his deep, laid-open hurt and *pressed* inward. His hips bucked in a jerky frenzy, and she just laughed to see it; that same laugh they all had, a rippling silver-glass trill, delighted most by the spectacle of damage. Her insides milking him hard enough to bruise all the while, wet and tight and numbing-cold as a close-packed box of snow.

They gave him a bath that night, let the grime and blood soak off in rivulets, exposing all his wounds—healed and unhealed alike—to their careless exploration. Cija ran some sort of hotel shampoo-packet through his hair that smelled of sage and lemon, and exclaimed in surprise at the result: "Ver-y pret-ty," she said, her "outside voice" (as he'd come to call it in his own mind, to distinguish it from either the half-glimpsed roil of thought or that off-putting subvocal communication they used amongst themselves) just a bit too rough, too slow, still tinged with whatever original accent she'd had, even after being run through their million-year proto-tongue Creole as a filter.

Combing her claws carelessly outward from the roots of his overgrown mop, bangs drooping almost to his lower lip now, and scoring away a bit of beard as she did; he damn well knew he'd looked a whole lot pret-ti-er a half-year back, 'round when he'd first started his tour through the circuit—before he'd stopped bathing, or shaving, or talking to anybody he could tell had a pulse. And complaining, as she did: "You *smell* like us, but you *taste* like them. It's very confusing."

Goran shrugged, licking his fingers clean. "Smells like *us*, specific, 'cause we just got done rubbing ourselves all over him. He's not a toy, Cija," he warned.

"But he could be."

And: *Yes*, he wanted to say, *yeah, I could. I can be anything you want. Let me, please. Let me.*

Please.

But it hurt too much, and he didn't know who he was anymore, and then he was gone for a while—extinguished, snuffed out, like a black wax Sabbat candle. He'd been up for what seemed like months, always in transit, passed like a party favour from pride to pride; his fever for assimilation through emulation had spiked at last, and he slept well, dreamlessly. Cradled between corpses.

—

That first bunch of 'em he'd met in an all-night highway strip-mall drugstore, somewhere considerably closer to home. He'd seen them coming from a literal mile away, knowing in his gut how they could him, too: not just background noise, potential prey. That he stood out to them in some way which intrigued, itched at them the way scar tissue did—some frequency they were all tuned to, him and them alike, though he only got the fuzz and the beat, most times. Static and hiss, lost between stations.

"You smell like us," the first one to look directly at him said, words echoing magnified through his skull's orbit, in-mouth/in-mind. And: "I *dreamed* of you," he replied, eagerly. "Knew you was gonna be here."

"Of vampires? Not so special. Many do."

"No, I dreamed *you*: Saoirse, Owain, Chuyia. Y'all met near the Black Sea, on a pilgrimage to Chorazin, right? 'There to salute the Prince of the Air.'"

The first one (Owain) simply kept on looking at him, blinkless eyes almost all-white between slitted white lashes, with a faint black ring 'round each iris and pupils like chips of ice. While the second girl, Chuyia—chai-scented hair in a braid to her waist, one gold strand fringed with small coins linking nostril to earlobe on the left-hand side—cast her red-tinged gaze down at her bare, clawed feet, and murmured:

"…perhaps worth examining at…closer quarters…"

Saoirse tittered and stroked his cheek, her own eyes eight-ball haemorrhage black, each twisted nail frosted a different, inappropriately candy-bright colour. "He's certainly warm enough to seem edible, at least. Whatever *else* he might turn out to be."

Owain shrugged the idea away, like someone ugly-drunk was trying to feel him up. Said: "Just another bug-eater, another would-be tool. There's a new one every mile in this damn country."

"No, I ain't like nothin' you seen before—nothin' like *them*, anyhow. Never have been. But I *am* like you. I mean…" Adding, desperate, as they just kept on staring, fixedly: "Why would I dream you, your names and lives and all, if I wasn't?"

"Why indeed?" Chuyia murmured, as Owain hissed, dismissively. But there was just enough room for one more in the van, as it happened—and after all, they were already hungry.

Their nightside existence turned out to be built far less on glamour and magick than on endless boredom, constant flight. Enabling it was steady yet stultifying work, almost as brain-dead as any other crap job he'd ever had—all but the blood part, coming hand-in-whatever as it did with sex parts of every possible combination. Though even that wasn't exactly the way the books and movies had warned it might be: They needed far less than anyone seemed to think in order to keep going, far more often. Five small meals a cycle, just like that Caveman Diet the girls' magazines kept talking up.

So he settled into the routine, head-first. Drove during the day, when they were asleep; booked the rooms, rented storage spaces, made sure the windows were well-taped over by the time they woke and the evenings well-stocked with a steady stream of treats—hookers fresh enough not to be too diseased, experimenting students, runaway junkie-wannabes who hadn't quite connected with the habit that'd kill 'em yet. And now, never would.

He healed fast, thought on his feet, made a nice chew-toy—and he could at least pass for human still, which none of them could. Once they'd all done him enough in enough different ways, though, that really was it; they were done with him, and made it more than plain, no matter how he pleaded. The most (and least) they could do before leaving was throw him to a new pride, so he could at least try getting what he wanted out of them awhile.

But the next bunch didn't come across either, in the end—nor the next, nor the next after that. And slowly, he came to recognize that whatever mild affection any of 'em might eventually develop for him was entirely predicated on points of difference rather than shared similarities, equally disturbing as they were on both their parts...that what had driven him towards them, in the first place, was exactly what inevitably drove them away in the opposite direction. That they liked him as he was, all (comparatively) weak, confused and buzzing with random pain—strong enough to take their abuse and live, to heal, but not scar-free. And never quite strong enough to stop them doing any damn thing they wanted with him, even if he'd thought to try.

Oh, they could enthrall, all right; he'd seen it done, on more occasions than he could count. But he was not in thrall to them, and never had been. What he did, he did with a clear mind and an even clearer conscience, willingly, in sure and certain hope of due recompense to come. Of the Resurrection, and the Life.

What remained to be seen, however, was how many times a man could be lied to, and still keep on believing; much like any other faith in that way, he guessed, which he had to admit wasn't really enough to keep him from being at least a little resentful.

Backsliding, his Momma used to call it, way back when—*you KNOW how to do right, just don't wanna, do you, boy? 'Cause there's something in you that don't fit with this world, something mean and dead and rotten to the core...and I'm gonna have to beat it from you like a damn rat-killing dog, ain't I, so's you'll get at least a little better. Or so's you won't get no worse, anyhow...*

Ignorant swamp-French bitch.

Momma kept Daddy in the old fall-out shelter under her own Daddy's house, locked down fast, while her and him slept in a trailer in the front yard. At first, growing up, he'd thought it was some game they played between the two of 'em, like other people's parents did—but it went on far too long, never stopped. And one time she'd dragged him down there by the hair, twisting and kicking, with a cat she'd found him playing with hanging slack from her other hand: *Let's make this Daddy's supper!* Threw it in, then, and slammed the door again real quick. Made him watch what happened, after.

Holding him still all the while, his eyes peeled open with a thumb jammed in either corner 'til stars bloomed at the limits of his vision, and whispered: *This is why. Why you are the way you are. Why I gotta do like I do. 'Cause you don't wanna end up like THAT, do you, boy?*

Nobody left alive could tell him exactly what had happened, though some certainly speculated (outside his earshot, as well as in it): Seemed fairly common knowledge how Daddy and Momma had married while still in school, Daddy swapping a low-grade sports career for injury and addiction, while Momma waitressed or hooked just enough to keep them both in generic prescription drugs. How he'd went out to score one night and came crawlin' back at the crack of dawn, burned lobster-red, almost smoking; he knocked Momma down with a slap that unseated her upper-left bicuspid when she answered the door, then opened up a wound in her shoulder, and got busy.

And nine months later, in a sanguinary haze of emergency

transfusions, that's when he was born—with a full set of teeth, already snapping.

When he was old enough to make the highway on his own recognizance, he ran away; authorities brought him back real quick, so he just did it again and so on, 'til she beat on him like he was a rug hung up to dry; daily, habitually, offhandedly. Like hurting him was her hobby. The last time, he made sure to wait 'til she was asleep (roofies stirred in her beer, when she wasn't looking), then set the house on fire. Tried to get Daddy to come with him when he saw him peering out through the shelter grate, but he just spat and yowled, and then it got too hot to stay. So either he survived or he didn't, and then maybe they were back together in some better world, or at least well out of this one; he sometimes mused on how maybe he'd run across him on the circuit, one of these nights, so high he wouldn't even remember how they were related.

Monsters are defined by what they prey on, what they hunt, Chuyia told him once, in a quiet moment. *In the jungle, the most fearsome killers are those who know how to hide, to wait. To pretend. Because the best mask of all for strength is weakness, do you know that? Like Saoirse, with her I'm-lost, I'm-scared, Mister-help-me-please game; you've seen how efficient that is. And you would know that better than most, I think, at any rate: Little trap-door spider, so expert at concealment...do you even remember who you used to be, earlier that same night? Before you found us?*

He hadn't wanted to agree with her, then; just shook his head and looked away, agonized, as she picked his half-healed neck-scars open again, and bent to lick the blood surface-wards. But now, trapped in Cija and Goran's diffident embrace, he knew at last how right she really was...how nice she'd been trying to be, in her own way. The way even he (most times) was to those tricks and treats he brought Chuyia and the others, not because he *had* to, but just because he could. 'Cause it cost him less than nothing.

He couldn't feel anything for "real people," not at all—never before, probably not in future. But at least he felt an attraction, one-sided and screwed as it might be, for things like them; that had to count for something, didn't it?

So: *Thank you*, he'd told Chuyia, as her teeth slid out. And felt her nod against him in reply, ever so slightly, as the pain washed back up over him like a black wave, tinged with red: *Oh no, thank YOU...*

Kissing the whip-handle, the branding iron. Kissing the hand that stroked his hair, stroked him to full attention then slid down even further, all the better to slit his pulsing throat.

—

"Bad teeth," Cija said, examining them closely, running her finger over their ragged grey edges—a dirty old snowbank to her fresh salt-ice, opaque as haematite. "Do they pain you? They must."

"Naw. They come back in like that, after my Momma took a hammer to the first set."

Cija, to Goran: "A joke?"

"Have you known him to?" They both turned to look him at once, this time with slightly more interest. "So. Not a fanatic, after all—a dresser-up, a…poser? Is this the word?"

"It's one. But no, I ain't that, just like I keep on tellin' you. Jah sh'te oupir, kom toy."

"*Oupir? Necht, merkecht.*" Goran paused. "*Dhampir*, perhaps. You know this word?"

"Means—halfbreed? Born, not made. But not like—"

"—us, no, never. Not even if we drain you dry. But if your father was very fresh when he got you, this might explain; dead man's sperm lives for some time after, viably. Why is it you want this so badly, though? You're *not* them, born meat, so find your own way, *your* desire. Hunt accordingly. Why be hyena, if you can be wolf? Don't have to eat our leftovers forever…"

Cija: "You don't have to let us hurt you, either. But maybe you like that."

"Maybe I do."

"Then it's settled. It's what he wants, Goran—you heard him. So very little, really."

"No, I think not. Do you even remember their names, who had you last?"

"Why should I? They didn't want me. Passed me on to you. You even remember *my* name?"

"Benjamin Boucher. Says so, on your driver's license."

He looked down, oddly shamed. Muttered, resentfully: "Y'all say it boo-SHAY. 'Sides…I know *your* names."

"Mmm, no doubt. But, as I say: We leave tomorrow, travelling fast...so fast, you cannot keep up. This is goodbye, little virus. You are...too much work."

"How? *How* am I? I do *everything* for you. Everything! Y'all don't do nothin' for yourselves—"

Cija: "But we don't *have* to, Ben-ja-min, not while we have you. Or someone like you. They are so easy to find, too, always—"

—you know that.

"We can of course pass you on again, if you want. There are more coming always, even now: Mortlake, Hu-shien. Marival, and her get..."

Despair welling up in him, sharp yet removed as the sight of someone else's tears: "But *you* won't, that it? Never? Not under no circumstances?" Goran just shook his head—not unkindly, if not exactly kind. Which only made him snarl, already near weeping: "Well, why the God shit Hell fuck *not?*"

(And Cija, cutting in subvocally, from what seemed very far away: *Oh look, he's* CRYING! Such pure wonder in her voice, such a depthless, awful joy. As though his pain was the sweetest thing she'd ever seen.)

"Because..." Goran said, eventually; a pause, long even for him. And then—

"...I don't know what you would become, after."

Which, he could only think, put pretty much forever paid to *that.*

Goran looked away, pointedly, while Cija kept on grinning, her blank eyes ravenous-covetous. He took a long, sobbing breath, into great silence.

"Then kill me," he said, finally. "Just kill me, right damn now. I *want* you to."

Goran nodded. "All right."

But when Goran's eyes were already rolling back and his own pulse was racing shallow, dying away, he suddenly thought: *I ain't gonna die like this, not after all I done. I deserve more. Who the hell are you to take my life away, anyhow? Even if I did give it? Fuck* YOU, *dead man. Fuck the pair'a you, and not like I usually do...*

So he turned and bit deep into the neck of the monster who had him pinned, instead—battened on like a tick, held fast and didn't let go, not even when a howling Cija ripped his ear off at the root; something inside told him it'd probably grow back, especially if he finished what he was doing. Just kept on drinking 'til Goran groaned into coma, free hand shooting forward to choke Cija silent with abruptly vampire-grade strength before finally turning on her, as well. Strength on top of strength flaring to life inside him, like a double-twisted halogen coil: the wily parasite whose contaminant touch alone had been enough to bring a lion—*two* lions—down.

That was the thing, with vampires: All the ones he'd met, anyhow, before or since. So old, so arrogant. So utterly convinced they'd seen everything there was to see, so sure they knew it all. They never saw it comin'.

It tasted good, too, damn good. And when he caught sight of himself afterwards, shaving dry with Cija's black-handled knife as a haphazard razor, he found he shone so brightly he could hardly bear to look at himself at all—a bleak halo of stolen light all 'round him like some eclipse turned inside-out, Goran and Cija's long, shared midnight ramblings instantly translated to a full-body crown whose crenellations made one point each for every soul they'd ever taken, in turn.

When he finally tracked down Owain and the others, nesting in Montréal, they only had one thrall left between 'em—made him think maybe they'd come down in the world a little, just for a moment, 'til he recalled how they'd always liked travelling light.

Owain opened the door, frowning when he saw who it was. "We told you not to come back," he said, warningly.

He nodded. Told him: "Goran and Cija said 'hi.'"

And again, no immediate warning bells seemed to go off—Owain just turned his back, sighing disgustedly, head cocked at a perfect angle for the upswung axe to connect with; it left his slippery hands with a slight, odd "pop," lodged deep in the pareital lobe. Owain went down, seizing, and he saw Chuyia's blood-dimmed eyes widen from across the room, (pleasantly?) surprised, her mouth moving silently, words booming through both their synapses at once: *Little spider, my born-again jungle creature. Oh, you treasure, you.*

Then she was on him from one direction, Saoirse from the other, tag-teaming him both at once. Not that it ended up doin' either of them all that much good, in the end.

The thrall was just a girl, meanwhile—maybe sixteen and deep-tranced, so much so she beat at him 'til they were all dead, then hugged him tight and cried into his neck: *You're not another one of*

THEM, *are you? Oh God! ARE you?*

And: "Naw, not hardly," he answered, hugging her back. "Me, I'm somethin' else."

Thought about killing her too, little as she and her kind still meant to him. But he forbore instead, for now, knowing full well how she'd be good help and better bait, once he moved on to richer hunting-grounds—first in a long line of leech-traps, soft skin over hidden teeth. Another potential predator's predator, one he could teach the true value of pretending to be born prey.

He caught his own glance in the bedroom mirror, eyes like peridot set in gold, and smiled a jagged black pearl smile. Thought: *My Christ but I'm handsome, all of a sudden. Must be the light, the angle—something I did. Something I am. Something...*

(Someone)

...I ate.

—

They spent the rest of the night dismembering their former masters with all the skill taught by long experience, stopped off at a local hospital to use the biohazard incinerator, slept 'til dawn. Then loaded up the van, him and his new apprentice, and headed for fresher pastures. And every time she glanced at him, all worshipful-drunken, he knew just what it was would keep the vampires flocking to 'em: that endless lust to see your reflectionless self cast back from others' eyes, mirrored a thousand times normal size. Demigod promoted to full God status, if only for the length of time it took to make your victim's gaze fix, dim, cloud over with dust and dreams...go out entirely. After which you moved on, and on.

...You, or someone like you. For they are so easy to find, always...

Well, yeah. But what went around came back the other way 'round, too, that was for damn sure; just as fast, if not faster. And twice as hard.

Because he could still hear them, blaring behind his eyes even as he drove—all those pirate dream-broadcasts spilling out into the night, calling to him. That was how he navigated down this particular lost and endless highway, knowing full well they'd never even think to hide.

And when they finally fucked for the first time, him and the girl, it was in yet another motel, on yet another dirty bed—the old familiar pattern, varying only in how he deliberately forced himself to be gentle with her, pay attention to her pleasure, like he was breaking her cherry for real this time, with all the traditional attendant joys on tap. Physical show of affection, give as well as take, mutual orgasm, "love" (or something like it...'cause what did she know, anyhow? Sixteen. What she understood about love would probably fit on a sleeveless baby tee, with room left over for two whole additional rows of dirty jokes and Internet quotes).

He slit his wrist open with Cija's knife at the height of it, too, and let her drink from him 'til her lips were crimson, 'til she shivered, blinked and near passed out from the desperate jolt of it. Thinking: *Won't make you LIKE me, I reckon, but it's good enough to keep you mine...and that ain't too bad, is it? Considering how I'll for damn sure treat you better than any of those fuckers ever treated ME.*

So. Because he *wasn't* them, he finally knew, not really; never had been and never would be, no matter what. But he wasn't nobody, either—not nothing. Neither wolf nor hyena but something new, something *other*, entirely. A chimera, of sorts.

A victory of half-life over half-death, made unexpected flesh.

CROSSING
THE RIVER

...dreaming evil, I have done my hitch
over the plain houses, light by light:
a lonely thing, twelve-fingered, out of mind.
A woman like that is not a woman, quite.
I have been her kind.
—Anne Sexton

Here's how it probably happens, that first time, if you're anything like me...

Your Momma wakes you in the middle of the night, takes you up on the mountain. Says she has something fine and secret to show you, something that sets you and her apart from all the rest of the common herd. *This here is our'n, baby girl,* she tells you, *gifted by Him who made us to the whole of our blood—and you more than most, darlin'. You more than any.*

And what is it you see once she's got you up there, anyhow? Maybe a dog with horns or a black cat bigger than a bull, a goat with women's breasts and owl's eyes, some sort of beast having ten horns, ten crowns, and on every head the name of blasphemy. Or maybe just a pale man with a black beard and a sad face, like the ghost of Osama bin Laden, who lays one hand on the top of your skull, the other on the sole of your foot and laughs, saying: *Shall I really take you for gift on only your mother's word, all of you, everything which lies between this hand and that? What true mischief could I ever possibly do in this world with such a little one as you, Gley Chatwin's gal?*

If you're anything like me, which most just ain't. Because my Momma was a witch, same as hers, and so on; it's from their side of things that I can't stand the touch of salt, can't cry real tears. But I sure ain't no hill-woman like her, either, out hollering to Old Scratch every full moon—and I never did kiss any man's ass but for money, horns or no. I got my pride.

So: I can throw out a fetch, given time, and dirt enough to build one from. Bring anyone my way and keep 'em long as I want, using nothing but a drop of their blood, a drop of mine and a hank of my own long hair to tie the knot with. Spread out a pack of cards and tell you your future; knock a rag against a stone and raise up a wind, then write nonsense words on myself to whip that same wind into a Force Three twister; make doors slam, tables tap and call up a ghost to talk through me, just like that woman of Endor who got old King Saul in so much trouble with the Almighty.

I've read some books, too; Montague Summers, Scott's *Discoverie*, Stuart's *Daemonologie*. The mighty *Hammer*. I know my history, such as it is. My culture is different than yours, older still than the Travellers with their tricks or the Injuns with their anger—ain't just moonshine and trailers, back where I come from. And I got but two things to blame for everything I've done since, I suspect: Gley Chatwin and the Daddy she chose to get me on her, her cold witch blood and his hot demon seed. Or three, maybe, if you choose—like I do—to also count my own bad self.

But if any of the above meant I could witch myself right in and out of prison anytime I felt like it…well, we wouldn't have too much to talk about, now, would we?

'Course, biology does count for something, at least in terms of execution. If I was a man, they'd probably have to keep me in Ad Seg 24/7, for fear of me trying to stick my dick in anything that moved close enough past me for me to grab at it. Being I'm not, though, my "unrepentant serial sexual offender" sins always tended to err more on the side of *knew I shouldn't've, but I went on ahead and did it anyways*: it, her, him, them. Whatever.

I mean, sure—my not-Daddy messed around with me some, just like everybody else's. But I'll gladly own the rest.

Sometimes I feel like I must've been drunk, high, picking up trade and robbing folks blind for a straight year before the Powers That Be finally got around to slinging me right back in where I so obviously needed to be. Seems like I looked up the once and I was in custody, looked up twice and I was in court, allocuting before sentence. Looked up the third time and I was already dug deep down here in Mennenvale Women's Penitentiary, Block A, max security—sweating hard, getting clean; not such a bad place to do it, either, when all's said and done. Certainly does concentrate the mind wonderfully.

Getting *into* Hell, that's the easy part, always; people do it every damn day, though far more often by accident than by intent. It's getting *out* that's harder, 'specially on demand—though it's not like *that* can't be done either, exactly.

Not so long's you can only make yourself patient enough to wait for just the right sort of…leverage.

One way or the other, what you maybe need to know most about me is this: I don't think of myself as a monster. Never have. Never will.

But then again, I guess most monsters don't.

—

Now, leverage comes in many different forms, by many different methods. I mean, if you're looking to understand just how somebody like me ever came into partnership with two kick-ass do-gooders like Samaire and Dionne Cornish in the first place, much can probably be made of the plain fact that Cornish and Chatwin lie almost right next to each other come roll-call, alphabetically speaking…but then, there's really no earthly reason I wouldn't've noticed them anyhow, eventually—Samaire, in particular. And not for the reasons you might initially assume, given my record.

That same morning, just before the fish truck pulled in, I was lounging at the cell-door with my pretty little Maybelle already all ground up against me, one thigh slung so tight over mine I could fair feel the heat of her through my pants (sweat-moist, or what-have-you), over my hip-pocket. Murmuring in my ear, as she did it:

"They got the Cornish sisters comin' to call in this batch, Alleycat. Pulled life plus nine-nine between 'em both, mainly 'cause of the three strikes rule." Pause. "Well, that, and they had a whole car full'a concealed weapons, when the Feebs finally caught their asses at the Border."

She was mainly putting on a show for rubes like that new CO Brenmer, who threw us a full-gawk double-take as he went by, pulling at his crotch like he'd suddenly noticed someone slipped ants in his shorts.

"Oh, you're so bad, baby girl," I told her, and watched her pout, more in confirmation than denial. "But I guess you aim to be."

"I do."

"Thought so." I pulled her closer, adding, in a murmur: "Hell, ain't like *I* mind."

And oh, didn't she just perk up and glow at that? 'Cause May always *was* easy to please…just as well, what with her being Grade-A born victim meat thrown straight into the lions' den, rare and bloody as any potential bitch-turned-butch might hope for. Her ability to enjoy herself under pressure was probably pretty much all that helped keep her sane, given the circumstances.

Was a time when I could do sweet (if not innocent) fairly well myself, but prison ain't exactly conducive to that. Oh, I guess I could glamour up now and convince you my skinny stringbean bones were sleek and foxy, this hillbilly hatchet-face of mine "interesting" rather than off-putting, my many visible scars fascinating rather than freakish. But one of the few things I like about lock-down is how you can breeze by on half-speed, or even quarter-, you just know how to play it right; talk people in and out of things like a human would, fuck and fight to a stand-still without ever even having to use your own full strength.

That's how I got myself my pocket-money business, running mail and brokering favors; how I snagged May right out from under M-vale's former baddest Daddy-miss of all time, Verena Speller, who—after an extended turn in that extremely locked-down part of Ad Seg known as the Finishing School—eventually decided that having only three super-stacked blonde groupies with Nazi nicknames in her Aryan harem was probably impressive enough.

No magic involved in either case, nor (in fact) did it need to be... just like with fishing in Head CO Guard Erroll Curzon, King Prick in a whole jailhouse full of corrupt hacks, and so in love with his own piggy self that I sure didn't have to raise any Hell but the usual in order to convince him he was the one raping *me* every so often, not the other way 'round.

"I ain't afraid of you, Chatwin, you goddamn witch," he'd say, not even knowing how right he'd got it. And I'd just nod along, smiling. Thinking: *'Course not, boss. Not like I scare MOST folks, after all.*

Hell, sometimes? Sometimes, I even scare myself.

So he'd lumber on and off, huffing hard. And every time he did, I'd inject just a hint more of my poison in him, to keep him firmly on the hook; never did have to worry about falling pregnant, which was a mercy. Going by past record alone, I don't really think I can conceive—not with a human man, anyhow. Not with the legacy of what my Momma conjured up coursing through my bloodstream.

Holler magic—blood, tears, sweat and spit. Bodily fluids of all descriptions. The good part is, it's very direct. Bad part...well, *one* bad part...is, it sure won't get you out of jail, not once you're already in. Not when any given escape scenario means you gotta beguile each and every one of the hundred-some people between you and the front door individually, one by one by one. Daily penal system grind aside, ain't no one has *that* sort of time to waste.

And: "Here we go," Maybelle said, jumping off of me, while the PA simultaneously crackled and Guard Curzon's voice rang out: "COUNT, LADIES! ALL ASSES TO THE RAIL!" A general stomp and shuffle, a screech of contact locks; the gates slid open, admitting our newest members. And here was where I finally saw the Cornish sisters for myself, as they stepped onto Mennenvale Block A, with my very own eyes: caul-touched, always slightly narrowed against the light.

And just like that, not even a minute gone, I knew Samaire Cornish—the younger, taller, even blonder of the two—was my sister. Not just a sister, a fellow practitioner of the Art—like Gioia Azzopardi, Dom the Cop's *stregha* widow, or that gal they call Needle, over in Psych—but a true something-sibling, with Hell's own mark spread all over her too-calm face like an invisible stain. I think I know my own bad blood well enough to recognize the taint of it in others, even when it's hid inside their veins.

I also noticed that while both of 'em were cute in their own particular ways, all their (many, inventive, enticing) tattoos were strictly magical in intent. Tough little Dionne had the Gran Tetragrammaton on the back of her neck, Solomon's Seal overtop her heart and the holy name of Saint Michael Archangel girding both arms, just like the warrior she was; Samaire's whole rangy body, on the other hand, seemed inked up with spell-script specifically designed to not only keep things out but keep things in, as well.

Those images looped above and beneath her skin, buzzing against each other like rot.

Not that anyone but me could have told, by either witch-sight or plain-sight. But then again, that is precisely why they call such things "occult." From the Latin, *occultus*, "to conceal." Because their true meaning, their real story is...

...a secret.

—

What I knew about the Cornishes before I met 'em boiled down to what everyone else did, albeit with one very important difference. In a nutshell, the sisters' act had kept 'em criss-crossing backroads America for upwards of seven years now, laying a trail of odd mayhem that'd grown into sketchy legend. They robbed gun-shops and places of worship, desecrated graves and left arcane graffiti behind; kicked ass, too—an unholy lot of it. And told the FBI that the people they'd killed along the way weren't people at all but demons in human form, preying on the innocent. That they'd *had* to kill 'em, along with anybody those demons'd touched, to keep Armageddon far off and little children safe at night. Which was why, in the main, they were in here now.

Digging back, what seemed to've kicked it all off was the State-assisted death of the man whose name they both wore, Jeptha Cornish. Their paper trail started where his finally went to ground: Raised off the grid by like-minded outlaw parents, a demon-slaying cult of two, up 'til Jeptha was popped by the law for killing his common-law woman Moriam, somehow managing to reduce her body to a flesh slurry so fluid its provenance had to be back-traced through her daughters' DNA. Local constabulary thought he might'a used a woodchipper, though they later had to admit they couldn't find that, either—along with much of a motive, beyond the usual hit parade of *well, he's weird and well, so was she and since when's a damn domestic get this complicated, for shit's sweet sake?*

Money, sex and/or parentage, the Jerry Springer trifecta. Maybe she'd been cheating, or maybe he'd just thought she was; maybe he'd figured out Samaire might not be his after all, not to mention the basic difficulty inherent in some self-taught backwoods exorcist's wife popping out hellspawn on the down-low, no matter how that circumstance might've originally come about.

The girls went into foster care either way, separated for most of high school; Dionne did a tour in Iraq, then rabbitted after she got tapped for stop-loss turnaround, taking a load of Army weaponry with her when she did. Samaire, armed with a sprinter's scholarship and a panel of genius-level IQ scores, managed to make it into law school by twenty, but dropped out just before finals of her second year. Her neighbours-in-residence said she got a visit from some woman looked almost exactly like her, except for being half a head shorter, about a week before she packed up and hit the highway. And the rest, as they say, is history.

Like most history, though, the really intriguing bits are always those ones which rarely get written down. Like the difference between the official version, say, and mine: Where most probably considered Samaire and Dionne Cornish either crazy or faking, I knew they were right. Didn't necessarily mean I approved of their methods, let alone their *raison d'être*—they did kill monsters, after all. Awkward.

Yet that, more'n anything, was what made Samaire's potential heritage issues so very…interesting, might be the word. Especially within context.

—

Back in the now, meanwhile, the new fish got 'emselves all lined up, "yes sir"-ing quick-smart in turn, as Guard Curzon checked their names off his print-out. "Ahmad, Zaidee. Burch, Lisanne. Cornish, Dionne. Cornish, Sahmeyer…"

"SahMEERah," the Cornish in question corrected, quietly.

Curzon frowned. "What'd you say there, convict?"

"That it's pronounced SahMEERah. Boss."

"Oh, really. And what is it makes you think I give a good god-damn about cross-checking the correctness of all your little bio-graphical details? I look like Oprah friggin' Winfrey to you, cup-cake?"

Others might've met this sort of dickery with a similarly harsh word, or even a punch, and ended up in Ad Seg for a month as of Day One for it; Dionne sure as Hell looked like she wanted to kick him where it counted, from the way her fists balled up. Samaire, though, just shrugged, and made herself look somehow small—small as a gal who loomed over Curzon by a good two inches while slumping ever could, at any rate. Projecting, if not saying right out loud: *Nope.*

"Thought not," Curzon shot back, and flounced off to finish count, Guard Brenmer hot on his heels. Which left us all alone together, free to get acquainted however we felt most inclined.

—

But I didn't approach 'em right then, no. I watched 'em a while instead, from long-range—across the yard, passing in the halls, two tables over in mess. Sent Maybelle to do fly-bys; she told me how they'd been split up for work (Samaire got library, Dionne got work-shop), but stuck together as cellmates (no surprises there). Kept my eyes peeled for whatever scuffles might arise, so's I could confirm for myself both what quarters said scuffles might come from, and how the Cornishes might deal with 'em, if and when they did.

Now some fools will speak from hubris and say that we women are too frail to fight, and some'll speak from rosy innocence and say we're too compassionate. Neither of these is true. What is true is that unlike men, women—*most* women—don't fight for *fun*. A woman throws down with you, she wants you either dead, or beaten bad enough you'll never look her in the eyes again. Two women throw down, it don't stop until it stops for good, or *gets* stopped. Which is why women mostly don't start a fight unless we're either damn sure we'll win or we got no other choice, and why we learn right quick to tell the fights we can win from the ones we can only hope to survive.

Even the dumbest of M-vale's denizens, it seemed, could see with a single look neither Cornish was a winnable fight. Around them the subtle vicious swirls of violence roiled on, while they floated through it like pumice in a Yellowstone caldera, untouched, untouchable. Model prisoners, 'cause they could afford to be. And because…they needed to be.

No, it was the *guards* they had to fool, not us; it was the men with the keys they wanted to be overlooked by, the watchdogs they had to bore to sleepiness. That extra edge of alertness Maybelle reported, that I saw for my own self, whenever a bluebird came within hearing of their constant low mutters to each other: the tension, the flickering eyes, the expert balance of submissiveness, dullness and sullenness, thrown over that spark of sharp defiance like an oil-rag wrapping carbon steel. That it took me so long to realize what it all meant is some embarrassing, in full honesty.

Once I *did* realize, though…well. I never have been one for wasting time, once the course of action is clear.

—

"You two're thinkin' on escape, ain't you?" I said, sliding in between both Cornishes without any fair warning, as they leant up against their usual staked-out corner of the prison yard. Dionne reacted pretty much just like I'd expected she might to this display of unmitigated gall: shifted back into fight-stance and fisted one hand, while the other went on the sly for that shank she kept shoved down the back of her pants. But Samaire just drew herself up to full height and shot me the downwards cut-eye, before asking, calmly—

"And…you would be?"

"Oh, just another poor victim of stunted parental creativity." I stuck out my own hand, so fast she almost couldn't help but take it, if only for a second. "Allfair Chatwin—Alleycat, they call me; looks like 'all-fair,' sounds like Ah-la-fAHr. Kinda like bein' named Cinderella, back where I come from."

Dionne glowered at me, and snapped: "Don't say word one to this bitch, Sami. I've been askin' around; she's nobody we need to know."

"Oh, I'd say that probably depends, pretty gal."

"On what?"

"On whether or not it's true your li'l sister's Daddy wears the same set of horns mine does." She flushed a bit at that, but didn't

argue; though it might still be a sore spot, the concept obviously wasn't really up for debate. So I simply smiled, and continued.
"'Cause if he does…"

"*If*," Samaire put in, raising a brow.

"…Well. Then I think we might be fit to do some business together."

Dionne and Samaire traded looks; Dee's seemed to read like she
thought she could probably stab me quick and walk on 'fore the
guards noticed, but Samaire's half-shrug, half-headshake seemed
less for than against. So Dionne let out a breath, and stepped back
just far enough to let me get between her and her sister—metaphorically, at least. Especially considering exactly how little wiggle
room she'd left me to work with…

(For now.)

"I mean, you *do* need to get outta here too, am I right? Go back to
savin' the world, and all." Now it was my turn to get looked at. "So…
how's that goin' for you, anyways?"

Dionne: "Like it's any of your damn—"

But: "Not as well as I'd hoped for, considering," Samaire replied,
cooler than cool, at almost the same moment. "But I take it you have
suggestions."

'Cause she could see it on me too, 'course; no way she couldn't.
We *all* know each other by sight, if nothing else.

I nodded. "Now, don't get me wrong," I began, "I hear you're
an educated woman, so I know whatever sort of craft you practice
probably got to have mine beat all to Hell and back, just on the
reference material. But I been in here long enough to learn this
much: Craft in itself ain't gonna get you through gate one, let alone
out those front doors without anyone puttin' a bullet through ya…
or better still, through *her*."

Dionne snorted loudly at the very idea, naturally—but Samaire's
eyes flicked over nonetheless, automatic as a skipped heartbeat, like
she was already checking for damage. And: *Well-a-day*, I thought to
myself, wonderingly, as I so often had before. *Ain't family something
SPECIAL?*

Best earthly way to get an otherwise smart person to do somethin' stupid under pressure that I ever have tripped across, inside jail
or out of it, hands damn down.

"I'm listening," was all she said in return, though. Which was more'n good enough.

I walked her through what I knew about M-vale's various pitfalls, as gleaned from tales of other past break-out schemes (sadly truncated in their execution, most often), then sat there while Samaire walked *me* in return through what she'd decided on when she first heard the verdict read out on her and Dionne, and why it wasn't quite coming together the way she'd thought it would.

"I usually practice hierarchical magic," she said. "But that's pretty tool-heavy for in here—not least since they took all my supplies away, before we even went to trial…"

"Uh huh. Good luck gettin' hold of 'a hazel-wood wand new-peeled' on the black market, not to mention the steel caps, lodestone and virgin cock's blood you'd need to consecrate it." Adding, as she stared: "What? You think just 'cause I ain't been to university, I don't know my basics?"

She kept on staring a second, then shook it off. "Okay," she said, finally, pointing to a sinuous double line of text snaking up around her right-side humerus. "If you're really up on your *rituale magiciae componentum*, then—what's *that*?"

I just grinned: Man, *far* too easy.

"Why, that there'd be protection against demons if you read it one way and a binding on your own demon blood if you read it the other, written in the language known as Crossing the River—*Transitus Fluvii*, as the dead Roman tongue would have it. Y'all don't know everything just 'cause you read a book or two got written before Gutenberg made up his first Bible, Princess."

Dionne, impatiently: "Look, so you know some shit, and she obviously knows some of the exact same shit…was there gonna be a plan in here somewhere, or what?"

"Like you say, wizardly workings tend to take the sort of accoutrements our current position renders pretty much inaccessible," I told Samaire, ignoring the unsolicited commentary from the peanut gallery. "So why not go the opposite route?"

"Such as?"

"Holler magic. Y'all might have heard of it."

"Sure. That's the tradition where every spell involves wearing your materiel in your crotch for a day or so."

I nodded, unoffended: "Ain't fancy, I'll grant you, but it's simple, cheap—"

"If you don't count the boiled-down human body parts you usually build it from," Dionne muttered.

"—and it *does* work...'specially so when you got *two* qualified people doin' it, 'stead of just the one. And that's my main point, Princess: You ain't ever gonna get where you want to by exactly *when* you want to, not without help from another worker. But if you was to lay your high-class hexation next to my gutter witchery and let 'em cross-pollinate—feel on each other awhile, or such—might be they'd both end up movin' a tad faster, to our mutual improvement."

"Like a sort of a...really *skanky*...feedback loop."

"Well, I never did go too far through school...but metaphorically, sure. Why not?"

The Cornishes exchanged another glance. "Look, Sami, you already know what *I* think," Dionne said, at last. "Witches are witches. Plus, word on the yard is, banking A-Cat here'll do anything more'n lie right to your face, then kick you down and fuck you ain't gonna get you anything but kicked down and fucked even harder. But we both already know you're gonna do what you want, just like always."

Samaire nodded. To me: "So, assuming everything she's said is true—how could I ever trust you to hold up your end of the bargain? What do you want to get out of here for, anyhow?"

Never you mind, kin-killer, I almost snapped back. But said instead, out loud—

"You kiddin' me? I want to be out of here to be out of here, Princess, same's anyone else. 'Cause it's cramped, your options for fun are substantially limited, and I been here more'n long enough already. 'Sides which, you sure don't have to trust a person to work with 'em. That's half the fun, ain't it?"

She looked at me then, long and level, eyes hard.

"Tell you what," she said, at last. "If it turns out I do find I need you for—anything—I'll go ahead and have Dionne let you know."

I nodded, thinking: *That's all I ask.*

—

That night, in the slice of space between count and lights-out, Maybelle'd already laid there pouting for quite a bit before I finally wised up enough to look over and notice. She'd seen me getting what looked like up close and personal with Dee and Samaire, and that made her nervous; guess she was a bit too well-used, at this stage of the game, to think goin' back on the market was a good idea, particularly if she wanted to trade up (rather than down) from where she was right now. So she wanted some token show of reassurance she really wasn't in immediate danger of bein' thrown over for a newer model, which I—truth be told—was more'n happy to provide.

"Them Cornishes got each other, darlin'; they ain't plannin' to be in here long enough to need anybody else, even if they either of 'em swung that way. Not like I need you, anyhow."

"You need me, A-Cat?"

"Let me demonstrate."

After, while she dozed—all awash with dreamy dreams of how the two of us were both gonna squeeze, hand in hand, through whatever magickal escape hatch Samaire and I ended up cobbling together dancing in her empty blonde head—I studied the darkened ceiling and thought yet once more about that no-contact buzz I'd gotten just from standing next to (not-so-) little miss Princess; how she couldn't helped but've felt it too, rippling up and down those carefully tattooed limbs of hers, the shiver before the quake. And how it'd probably only get stronger yet, the longer we stayed in proximity—ratcheting up unstoppably as we drew ever closer, like the static charge hum just before a flashbulb's flare, or the filament whine as a lightbulb bloomed to full incandescence...

Dee might not be able to *feel* it, bein' what she was, but she'd sure made certain I knew she didn't like what she almost *thought* she saw going on: protective, like some five-foot nothing Mama Bear with her claws out, ready to fight to the bitter end. Which I guessed I could understand, though only in principle. 'Cause me, I never did know what it was to have a sister, not even half of one...but then again, the pull I felt towards Samaire wasn't entirely familial, as Dionne could no doubt tell; things always were a whole lot slipperier down in Hell than they were here up top, 'specially in the bonds-of-kinship department.

I did need to know what-all they were planning to do next, though—about me, as much as anything else—and the surest way to find out was to send something to listen at their keyhole. Which I could certainly do, for all I hadn't in quite some time—and like any other muscle, a witch's craft does tend to get a mite...tight, if she doesn't let it out for exercise on the regular.

So I shut my eyes, said a few choice words under my breath, bit my own lip 'til it bled and took a deep old swallow. And a few moments later, I coughed out a little red glob of sickness onto the cell floor…dirt from my insides, stuck together with Hell-juice and ill-will. A fetch, just like my Momma taught me to make way back, long before I ever saw any Dark Man on top of any hill.

A beat more, and it opened two tiny black jewels to look my way, stretched out its spun-glass wings (still tinged pink with spray) and rubbed its delicate stinger-legs together in greeting. Its voice rose up drily, echoing off the concrete walls—a thin, companionable, whispering vibration.

Let me do thy will, Lady? the fetch asked, eager, inside my skull.

Gladly, I replied.

—

Over in their own cell, meanwhile, Samaire sat cross-legged on one bed with her eyes all rolled back like she was meditating, while Dionne paced the floor, one hand on her shank. Announcing, as she did—

"Look, this is just a *bad* idea, Sami, twenty years or not—that bitch is everything we ever fought, all wrapped up in a hag-ridin', Devil-worshippin' bow. Even layin' aside what we already hear about how she conducts herself on the strictly human tip, she's the sort of witch who probably takes names and steals babies—and we're gonna let her back *out*, where she can get at the next given normal comes along, just to serve our interests? That ain't buddies."

I never stole a baby in all my life, I thought to myself, huffily, as the fetch hovered inside a vent above them, watching their debate through dim, colourblind eyes. Then added: *'Course, I never really had to, just 'cause I needed the parts. There's abortion parlors all over the great state of Alabama, after all…and they dump out their trash like clockwork, twice a day.*

(Ah, the conveniences of modern living.)

Samaire, unmoving: "*Not* helpful, Dee."

"Right. 'Kay." A beat. "Seriously, though, Chatwin's Hell-bait; we've killed enough like her to fertilize a car-park. A witch is a witch is a—"

"—witch, yeah, I got it." A pause. "So what's that make me?"

Dionne stopped, mid-stride. "Not *her*. You get that, *right*?"

"Except...I am."

"But you *use* this shit, Sami. You don't let it use you. That's the difference."

Samaire opened her eyes at that, and raised a doubtful brow; she looked down at her hand, studying that wrap-around ribbon of *Transitus Fluvii* circling the arm it attached to, like she could see things movin' underneath it.

"Six of one," she said, half to herself. Then: "You hear that?"

"What?"

"That...buzzing."

Okay, time to go.

They both turned toward "me," then, and I knew the fetch had almost reached its expiry date. So I peeled my consciousness back from it in long, sticky strings, letting its sight grow ever fuzzier, bleeding away pixel by pixel. 'Til the bond between us finally grew so tenuous I barely even felt a thing when Guard Curzon swatted it from the air as it flew from vent to vent, and crushed it messily beneath one boot. I could hear Brenmer through the wall, muffled, as he blurted out—

"Damn. How those things get in here, anyways?"

Curzon, stomping on: "Fuck if I know. Maybe they can smell all the pussy."

Which was crude, as ever. Yet not entirely inaccurate.

I turned over, wondering if Samaire would bother sending a fetch of her own to watch me sleep—or if she even knew how to make a fetch, considering who'd raised her. One way or the other, I wasn't about to lose a good night's shut-eye over it.

Things learned so far: Cornishes don't want to work with me, but too bad, 'cause they ain't exactly got another choice to switch to, I thought. *So let 'em sweat on that a while; hell, I got time.*

Nothin' but.

—

That was Friday. And a day or so later, I come 'round a corner in the library—mail-cart in hand—to find Dionne waiting on me between the stacks, arms crossed and scowling, with Samaire looming right behind.

"...We might need your help, after all," was all Samaire had to say, after a moment.

And: "Oh, Princess," I said, "tell it to me again, will ya? *Slower*."

—

"What do you know about Abramelin the Mage?" Samaire asked, as she pumped a thirty-pound barbell in the southmost corner of the weight-pile, with Dionne spotting. I sat down nearby, took up a pair of ten-pounders and started doing curls, to cover my reply:

"Abramelin? He thought all worldly phenomena were produced by demons working under the direction of angels; we all come with a guardian angel and a demon attached, the one liftin' us up, the other suckin' us back down, like gravity. Thought initiates could make 'emselves *into* angels, for as long as it took to control the demons..."

"...by using spell-squares. Five-line palindromes that read the same up and down, forward and back. The most famous of which being..."

"...the SATOR box? 'SATOR, AREPO, TENET, OPERA, ROTAS: Hold this in thy right hand, ask what thou wilt, and it shall be delivered.' No tools necessary, 'sides from pen, ink and willpower. But the thing also repels witches somethin' fierce, so too damn bad we can't either of us use *that*..."

"That's right, we can't." She pumped up one more time, shelved it, and lay there a moment, sweating. Before adding—

"But Dionne can."

We both shot Dionne a glance, like we'd been choreographed that way; Dionne—who'd been watching this little back 'n forth of magickal esoterica like it was a Satanic tennis game—flushed deep, looking uneasy for maybe the very first time since I'd made her acquaintance.

"Hey, man," she said, "I don't...*do* magic. Ain't my style. I just don't got it in me."

Samaire nodded. "You're not trained, no—but seriously, Dee, once it's made, this item's pretty much idiot-proof." A beat. "No offense."

"None taken. If it repels witches, though, then how are you guys supposed to make it?"

"Take turns. A-Cat does a character, I do a character, out of order. You hold the paper, so we don't even have to pass it back and forth. Easy."

Dubious: "Oh yeah, sounds it."

For once, I had to agree. "Yeah, it's a neat little concept—'cept we'd have to shield ourselves, somehow, just to stay in the same damn room while Lady Di here worked her will on the thing. You got any bright ideas about *that*?"

"...Not yet. I thought, though, with both of us going full-bore—"

"Princess, I can't shield *myself* from the SATOR box, let alone you too."

And there it sat, for a minute; I could see her thinking on the problem—hard, straight white teeth just denting her lower lip—which was a sort of pleasure in itself, for all it went on just a shade too long for comfort.

"We'd need a jolt, then," she said, at last. "Some sudden extra burst of power, like jump-starting a...car battery, or whatever—"

"Sacrifice, sure. So kill somebody."

Dionne, without even thinking twice, like she'd just remembered she was the *big* sister here: "We're not gonna do that."

I looked right on past her, straight to Samaire, the more innately practical of the two. "Let me, then; you know I'd do it. Do it in a damn minute, I thought it'd get us outta here..."

"Well, demonstrably, Alleycat!" she snapped back. "But we won't."

"Okay, then: Fuck someone, that'd work almost as well. Or are you too damn good to do that, either?"

Now it was her turn to blush. "Not with you," she said, shortly. Adding, as I looked back at Dionne, cocking one eyebrow: "And not with her, either—I mean, Jesus! Just what the Hell is wrong with you, anyways?"

Quantifying that one'd've probably took us all night, so I just shrugged. "Does sort of limit our options then, don't it?" I pointed out, instead.

"I can still figure something, given time," Samaire muttered.

Time. Which we had, again, and didn't have, in just about equal measures—but I knew enough not to push.

"Well, okay; you just go on ahead and do that, then. I need a couple of days to myself, anyhow."

"Why?" Dionne asked, suspiciously.

I shot her a smile. "Oh, nothin' too strenuous. Just gotta wrap up some…unfinished business."

—

Obviously, it had already occurred to me that trying to tote Maybelle on top of everything else would be a tad—difficult, at best. So while the Princess dicked around trying to figure out some slightly less morally suspect way to render her otherwise brilliant escape plan's kicker fully functional, I went ahead and got my pretty May to help lay the seeds of its other components—conceal Abramelin's SINAH box (SINAH, IRATA, NANIR, AXIRO, HAROQ) somewhere in her regular haunt, the laundry, so it could buy us the sort of violent yet short-term distraction we needed to slip the rest of our business past the COs, while they were a bit too conveniently caught up in something else to notice.

According to Abramelin, SINAH meant "hatred." The SINAH box was thus most often used "to create a general war"—a riot, say— which, because the square wasn't perfect, wouldn't go on forever. It'd start slow, working on whatever threads of conflict were already there, 'til the conflagration finally bloomed into full effect…and really, M-vale was (by definition) just chock full'a people who couldn't keep it in their pants for long, literally or figuratively, on *both* sides of the uniformed divide.

"Like yourself," Dionne supplied, when I suggested this tack. To which I simply smiled, freely admitting—

"My impulse control *can* be somewhat inconsistent, dependin' on circumstances."

"Yeah, I hear that happens a lot, with people who end up in jail."

"It does. Welcome to the curve, ladies."

Naturally, though, there was a second element to trusting Maybelle with the SINAH square—mainly, that it got her out of my hair long enough for me to go through her stuff, and get some of her hair. Then get naked and take a steamy trip through the showerroom, where I rifled the discarded brush of the next long-haired woman I saw: In this case, a hot little Latina Queens baller named Felicia Suarez who saw me hovering near her stuff and scowled like she would've happily thrown down with me right there and then, if only the floor hadn't've been so damn wet.

"Stay on your own side, *mami*," she told me. "I ain't lookin' to switch teams."

I shrugged, thinking: *Hmmm. Too bad for you, then, darlin'—'cause you may be in for somewhat of a surprise.*

By chow-time, when Maybelle drifted back my way, I'd already had more'n enough opportunity to tie the two of 'em together by those two locks of hair in a classic holler lust-knot. And sure, she was just as attentive as ever, 'til she glanced up to see Felicia comin'. A stammered excuse later, Maybelle went off to get "another chocolate milk," and didn't come back 'til count; the two of 'em disappeared under the stairs for maybe half an hour, re-emerging with disordered hair and their shirts tucked back in wrong only to head in opposite directions, fast, and blushing; sort of cute, when you thought about it. Though probably a bit off-putting for *them*.

"That was...really crude," said Samaire—who'd seen me snickering to myself, and obviously wondered what the joke was—after she'd finally figured out what just happened.

"Could'a just made 'em kill each other, and solved both our problems," I pointed out. But she kept on shaking her head, like a damn looming metronome.

"You don't *have* to do things like that," she said, finally. "To *be* like that. You just...don't."

"Probably not; I just *am*. You too, gal. And one of these days, you really gonna have to start to relax, lay back and enjoy it." I paused. "'Sides, you *do* kill your own. Don't you?"

Dionne, quickly: "They're not our *own*."

"'Course not, Lady Di. But then again...I wasn't talkin' to you."

Another head-shake, but slower this time. I saw something nasty bloom in back of Samaire Cornish's too-calm eyes, and felt my heart leap in recognition—a shark ill-hid under blue water, sniffing 'round for blood.

"We kill monsters, not people."

"Not even people who *are* monsters?" When she didn't answer: "And what about the half-monsters, Princess—the low-down dirty 'breeds, like you 'n me? But I don't suppose you wanna look too close at *that* one, now, do ya?" I laughed out loud. "Gal, you got issues."

And now Samaire was watching me *really* close, like she was studying hard on how good my head would look, severed and stickset. Took her a beat yet just to collect herself far enough to say—

"My dad killed my mom for getting raped by demons, Ms. Chatwin. So yes, my feelings about heritage are… complicated."

"Uh huh? Well, *my* Momma killed my not-Daddy for bein' human, pretty much. That, and he owed her money."

Dionne stepped in between us, then, clowning hat on firm. "See?" she said, lightly. "It's like I always told you, Sami—*never* lend to family."

Good save; even Samaire had to smirk a bit at that, boiling off the tension. But it didn't surprise me much, even so, when—later that same afternoon—I stepped into the mailroom supply closet pushing the cart before me with one hip, only to find Dionne's shank suddenly pressing up against my carotid.

"Listen up, bitch," Dionne began, a bare voice in the dark, low and grim and even. "I know how you think I'm some kind of dead weight 'cause my blood's a hundred percent human, but here's the deal—we get out, we give you a head start, and that's all. You're a monster, we're monster-killers. End of story. Nod if you understand me."

I did, quick-smart. "Won't happen again," I managed, voice thin with effort.

"Good." The blade drew back—but she leaned forward nevertheless, whispering right in my ear: "Oh yeah, and by the way…try to fuck with my little sister again, and I'll cut your damn tits off."

"Message received, loud and clear."

"Better be," she told me. And was gone, into that same darkness, long before I could get up the nerve to look 'round.

—

On some level, I truly do think I believed I was doing Maybelle a favor—but I also know *she* didn't see it as such, because for the next couple of days she followed me around, alternating frantic make-out sessions with Felicia with equally frantic apologies to me. On the surface, she seemed genuinely horrified both to have "cheated" on me in the first place and by her utter inability to not keep on doing so, any and every chance she got; at base, she was scared shitless I might kick her to the curb, so's she'd be back out on the market again, with no one to protect her at all.

"Think you might be doin' Felicia somewhat of a disservice there, darlin'," I pointed out. "She seems a loyal sort, from everything I've heard; I'm sure she'll stand by you."

"Don't make fun of me, A-Cat! I just...why did I *do* that? I just don't *understand...*"

"Well, c'mon, gal: Seriously, it's okay. You two seem very happy together."

"But I'm not! A-Cat, please don't cut me loose, please. *Please.*"

And there I was, still trying to be nice, but really; this was all getting somewhat ridiculous.

"Maybelle," I said, "you just need to *step off*, right now. Stand on your own two. It's pitiful."

I just walked away and left her standing there, lips trembling, with nary a backwards glance. And the very next time I saw her was when Guard Curzon came by our cell, as per the Warden's request, to take me to the morgue.

It's harder to kill yourself in M-vale than you might think, 'specially if you're dumb. But she'd managed it, nonetheless: Drank a bleach cocktail, industrial-strength, and crawled in between two heavy machines to wait it out, making sure nobody'd find her 'til the worst was long over. She didn't look too kissable afterwards, what with her mouth all gone blue and vomit in her long, blonde hair. Still, I bent down so we were nose-to-nose, shooting Curzon a glance that penetrated even his rhino skin; made him step back, shut the door halfway behind him, and give us some time alone.

To this day, I'm not all too sure what I really felt for her, if anything—though I certainly did appreciate the effort she put into things of an intimate nature, 'specially where I was concerned. But at the time, all I could think was—

Guess she really did LOVE *me—how 'bout that. I mean...fancy.*

Turns out, Maybelle didn't just stay with me 'cause I made it impossible for her to be elsewhere; she was mine 'cause she *wanted* to be, all along. Unlikely. Surprising.

...Depressing.

Yet potentially useful, all the same.

I rummaged 'round in my bra for an empty aspirin bottle I'd found on the infirmary floor one day and managed to keep hid, a secret bit of inexplicable contraband saved for just such an occasion, through all the subsequent strip-searches in between. Slid my thumb to line both triangular childproof seals up, and popped the lid. After which I leant down to the china-pale curl of Maybelle's ear, closed and dumb now as any empty snail-shell, and murmured into it:

"*O lenti, lenti curite noctus equii*...come back to me but a spell, honey, 'fore you go gentle into that good-night. Shed that cocoon on your way to wings. Break off just some tiny unnecessary bit of yourself and leave it here, for me, to remember you by."

Took but a second or two for my words to reach her, trailing down the snarled and fading synapses of her dead brain. And then I saw it right at the back of her throat, a dim light flickering between her stained teeth, on the necrotized black skin of her tongue—some merest fragment of sweet Maybelle Eileen Pine's soul, like a fluttering luminous moth, snared in her very last wisp of earthly breath; dull as a sub-molecular Los Alamos half-spark, powerful beyond Oppenheimer's fondest dreams yet struggling still against death's inertial pull, its foul gravity. Trying blindly to force its way up to me who loved it, against all hope, or logic...

I sucked what was left of Maybelle's pathetic little soul in hard, lip to lip, so close I felt the bleach yet left there start to crisp my skin. Then spat it right back out into the aspirin bottle, along with a smear of my own black blood, to keep it trapped there 'til I needed it.

And: "Thank you muchly, baby girl," I sang out, briskly, straightening again. "Never think, wherever you do end up, that I'm not grateful for your sacrifice—because I really, *really* am."

Like I said—hadn't seen that one comin', though maybe I should've. But I surely did appreciate the gesture, all the same.

"Your jolt, Princess," I told Samaire, much later, as I placed the bottle in her hands.

—

The riot broke out on a Tuesday, over in the mess hall—something about somebody either encroaching on somebody else's territory or looking a bit too hard at someone else's woman, which soon enough swelled to embrace the shank-wielding triple-header of all good prison conflicts: race, face, personal space. Not that I was there to witness it first-hand, of course...since I knew enough to avoid getting myself inconveniently locked down before all the fun began, I'd already made sure to turn Guard Curzon's piggy eyes firmly back on me, long before that particular storm ever started to break.

So here we were instead, in that same supply closet, deep in congress—his version thereof, anyhow—when the alarms went off; he jumped for his gun and stick, only to find 'em suddenly both in my hands instead. Then went backing away from me at an awkward half-shuffle, with his pants down 'round his knees and his dick flapping free, 'til he ended up just where I wanted him—right overtop the most sinister of Abramelin's squares, which S.L. MacGregor Mathers says "should never be made use of," and must be buried in a place where the intended victim will walk over it in order to work to fullest capacity:

CASED—overflowing of unrestrained lust;

AZOTE—enduring;

BOROS—devouring, gluttonous;

ETOSA—idle, useless;

DESAC—to overtake and stick close.

The CASED square can render its wielder invisible, under the right circumstances (along with gaining them access to all nearby hidden treasures, works of art and statuary), so at first I'd thought of that... 'til the Princess herself had pointed out a peculiar secondary characteristic of the square which might be just as useful to our cause, given the restrictions we were laboring under. Or even more so.

As Curzon's foot made contact, he froze stock-still, unable to shift a quarter-inch further either way. "Uh," he said at the feel of it, intelligently. Then: "Oh, my God. What the good goddamn shit Hell?"

I just smiled, feeling my own skin ripple as his form flowed up and over mine, from face to naughty parts and everything in between. "'Lo, Erroll," I said. "How's it hangin'?"

He gaped at me a while, not even resisting when I unbuttoned his shirt, shucked the rest of his pants down and gently encouraged him to kick his boots off, too, like some five-foot-ten toddler. Finally, he observed—with the stunned yet slightly self-pleased air of somebody who's just figured out what the word hidden in that big Saturday morning paper jumble must be—

"—You really *are* a witch."

"Yup. Now, how 'bout takin' one last ride on the ol' skin snake, just for luck?"

"...What?"

71

"Aw, don't fret, cupcake—you ain't actually my type, anyhow. Sleep."

Thus, all tricked out in Guard Curzon drag, I hiked up "my" key-belt and headed for the workshop. Passed Guard Brenmer on the way—ensnared by a howling knot of women, caught in the very manhood-destroying act of getting beat down and having his shit took by unarmed vagina-bearers. "Erroll, help!" he yelled at me, as I went by; I shot him the double finger, and kept right on going.

The Cornishes I found backed into a corner, shoulder to shoulder, kicking and punching at all comers like some well-trained Ultimate Fighter tag-team. And: "You two, warden's office!" I yelled, discharging "my" weapon into the air, only to barely avoid being flattened in the resultant rush for the door.

Which is how we finally came, at long last, to the point of the whole damn exercise: trading letters forth and back, each to each, like some calligraphy lesson from Hell, while Maybelle's captive soul-fragment flickered and spat and flared in sympathy like a late-night TV-blue bug-light. While that same static charge buzz tuned up and down our bodies, meshing us together in a true witches' cradle of probability strings, drawing sparks. I could see Dionne's back-muscles twitch with tension, as the free ends of her hair started to lift; saw Samaire's blue eyes darken yet once more as her bad blood rose to meet mine, studying me like I was some book she had to strain just in order to read, and wasn't even sure she really wanted to, when all was said and done. But it wasn't exactly like she could *stop*, either...

And me looking right on back, thinking: *Oh, you wanna think you're like* HER, *that you're not* like me...*but truth is, Princess, it's the whole other way 'round, 'cause the only thing you and Miss Dee really got in common's the pussy you both slid out of. You just want to be normal, so bad it keeps you up nights, taste of it like a mouthful of blood; Hell, I can't blame you for that. But one day, all those restraining tattoos, all that save-your-soul script you got all over you? They're gonna just flare up and crisp off, like paper in fire...*

(Like a tower falling, struck by lightning, now and forever more. Like Babylon. Like Charn.)

...*yeah.* JUST *like that.*

And then, then—that's when we're *really* gonna get to see some fun.

Charging each other up, winding that phantom winch of combined power ever higher, higher, higher. 'Til our fingertips met across the paper and our heels began to lift, describing a slow, concentric circle in the air like we was two antimatter planets drawn into orbit, an incipient black hole twisting reality's fabric 'til it bent and broke. A paradox waiting to happen.

A howl of wind from nowhere, brisk and bleak and bone-stripping, as the lights pulsed and the sirens wailed on; it was completed, as that poor Daddy-betrayed fool Jesus Christ would say. The SATOR box was done.

I laughed out loud, hair cracking like a whip. And heard Samaire yelling to Dionne even from the very depths of her frenzy, over it all: "*NOW, DEE, NOW—NOW NOW NOW NOW, DO IT DO IT DO IT—DO IT, DO IT GODDAMN NOW!*"

Dionne raised the square, snug in the whirling widdershins circle of our arms, and spoke the words, her merely human voice near to cracking with strain. And we were off, gone, spiraling fast through time and space, hovering through the fog and the filthy air—out of M-vale at last, chased and dragged by Abramelin's devils and angels alike, while Maybelle's soul blew/boiled off in the other direction with a thin, despairing cry...

Samaire had her eyes closed, but Dionne had hers open; I made sure of that. So when I hove in to kiss Samaire, before either of them knew enough to protest—sudden as rape, my tongue hook-probing deep, scratching on hers like oh-so-voluptuous Velcro—there was no way Dionne could stop herself from doing just what she would have under any other circumstances: lunge to thrust herself between, SATOR box forgotten in her haste, still trailing from the same fist she was aiming for my jaw.

It touched us both at once—repelling factor back on full, with no Maybelle for protection—and hurled us to the four winds' tornado-churned quarters, faster than thought; Dionne one way, Samaire and I the absolute opposite. We came down hard, falling fast into black. Then awoke later—*much* later—all on the cold hill's side...

...with no one left near to hold onto, in this dim twilight world, but each other.

—

Samaire looked over at me, head hung down, her eyes like bruises. "Where's…Dionne?" she managed, at last.

"Dunno," I said, fighting my own fair share of post-spell-travel nausea. "Could be…anywhere, really."

She shook her head. "The SATOR box…must've touched us. Thrown us…ugh, *Jesus*." Rolling onto her knees, she heaved upwards, gained her feet and stood there, weaving. "Where…?"

I shrugged—then spat, and wished I hadn't. "Damn if I know. Sorta looks like…Alabama, I had to take a guess." Clawed my own way to standing, using a handy tree, and tried a weak version of my normal charming grin out on her: "Aw, but don't you worry none, pretty gal—given all that excitement we left behind us, I'll bet you five bucks she already must've dropped it."

"You don't get it, Alleycat. I need my damn sister!"

And: *For WHAT, exactly?* I could've said. *'Cause you feel guilty you can do things she can't, and never will? 'Cause you're so all-fired hot to get back to killin' things that're more like you than she'll ever be, just 'cause your old man taught you to? Same old man ended up turning your Momma into hash, as I recall, 'cause he couldn't stand having another creature's fingerprints left on her…and that was just too bad, by Dionne's standards, wasn't it? Too bad for your Momma. Too damn bad for YOU…*

If this actually *was* Alabama, I knew a hill somewhere 'round within walking distance where I could surely introduce her to the Daddy we both shared, for what I knew would be the first time. Put his one hand on the crown of her head, the other on her ankle, and know he'd answer each and every question she might have for him in between. We could be true sisters yet, dance at the Sabbat in our naked skins and sup on broiled corpse-flesh; ride the night astraddle like those carrion storm-birds of old Greece, seeking always for prey, and scour this land of any fool who dared think fire, or salt, or a whimpered prayer to some unhearing God would ever keep him and his safe for long from such as she and me.

But: Looking at her now, I knew it was far too late for that. Her hands were clenched against me, closed and hard like her heart; them ropes of Crossing the River were dug in too deep between the layers of her skin for anything short of a roadside conversion to ever disarm 'em—though it'd have to be one gained on the way to Dis, Hell's own lead-walled capital city, 'course, rather than on the way to Damascus.

Ah well, I thought. And said, out loud—

"Suppose you probably oughta go back for her, then. While you still can."

She knew what I'd done, then, without a doubt; got it all in one, like the brilliant bitch she was. And kept on looking at me nonetheless, appraisingly—less with hate than a vague sort of sorrow, albeit one which came liberally admixed with a caldera's worth of barely-veiled, magma-hot rage.

"...I'm gonna find *you*, too, Allfair Chatwin," she told me, without much affect, as the air between her long fingers began to spark and whine again. "Eventually."

To which I nodded my head, briefly, in what probably looked—from her angle—like acceptance. And replied:

"Oh, but not too soon, I hope. Princess."

—

Took half a second for the rift to pop open again, behind her, and the other half to close once she'd stepped back through. Then I was all by my lonesome in the dark, dark woods once more, a state of affairs which sure did seem to call for immediate relocation—so I started out walking, whistling softly; an old holler tune my Momma always used to sing me, back in the day, on empty nights like these...

> *Don't the moon look pretty, shining down through the trees...*/
> *Said don't the shining moon look pretty, Lord, shining down*
> *through the trees...*/
> *Oh, I can see my baby, Lord Lord Lord...but he can't see me...*

I went looking around for a highway, found one. Started walking. And after a while—

—well, that's when you picked me up. Didn't ya?

Turn in here, darlin'.

SPECTRAL
EVIDENCE[1]

"The dust still rains and reigns."
—Stephen Jay Gould, *Illuminations: A Bestiary*

Preliminary Notes

The following set of photographs was found during a routine reorganization of the Freihoeven Institute's ParaPsych Department files, a little over half a year after the official coroner's inquest which ruled medium Emma Yee Slaughter's death either an outright accident or unprovable misadventure. Taken with what appears to have been a disposable drugstore camera, the photographs had been stuffed into a sealed, blank envelope and then tucked inside the supplemental material file attached to Case #FI4400879, Experiment #58B (attempts at partial ectoplasmic facial reconstruction, conducted under laboratory conditions).

---

[1] Metaphorical license, naturally: Nothing here constitutes proper legal 'evidence' of anything, by any stretch of the imagination.

Scribbles on the back of each separate photo, transcribed here, appear to be jotted notes done in black ink—type of pen not readily identifiable—crossbred with samples of automatic writing done by a blue felt-tipped pen with a fine nib; graphological analysis reveals two distinct sets of handwriting. The original messages run diagonally across the underside of the paper from left to right, while the additional commentary sometimes doubles back across itself so that sentences overlap. Where indicated, supplementary lines have often been written backwards. Footnotes provide additional exegesis[2].

Photograph #1[3]:
Indistinct interior[4] of a dimly lit suburban house (foliage inconsistent with downtown Toronto is observable through one smallish window to left-hand side); the location seems to be a living room, decorated in classic polyester print plastic-wrapped couch 1970s style. A stuffed, moulting sloth (*Bradypus pallidus*), mounted on a small wooden stand, sits off-centre on the glass-toppped coffee-table.

Notes: "House A, April. Apported object was later traced back to Lurhninger Naturalichmuseum in Bonn, Germany. Occupants denied all knowledge of how it got there, paid us $800 to burn it where they could observe. Daughter of family said it followed her from room to room. She woke up in bed with it lying next to her."[5]

Commentary (Forwards): "Edentata or toothless ones: Sloths, anteaters, armadillos. Living fossils. A natural incidence of time travel; time travel on a personal scale, living in two places at once, bilocation. Phenomena as observed. I love you baby you said, I can't do it without

---

[2] All footnotes were compiled throughout March of 2006 by Sylvester Horse-Kicker, Freihoeven Placement Programme intern, at the request of Dr. Guilden Abbott.
[3] Photographs, as indicated, are not themselves numbered; numbers assigned are solely the result of random shuffling. The fact that, when viewed in the order they achieved through this process, the eventual array appears to "tell a story" (Dr. Abbott's notes, March 3/06) must be viewed entirely as coincidence.
[4] Most photos in the sequence are best described as "indistinct."
[5] Research prompted by details in commentary has since indicated that "House A" may be 1276 Brightening Lane, Mimico, owned by William McVain and family. On April 15, 2004, at the request of McVain himself, Slaughter and her Freihoeven control partner, Imre Madach, were sent to investigate on-site poltergeist activity. Activity had apparently ceased by April 20, when they filed their report; the report contains no mention of monetary reimbursement for services, which the Freihoeven's internal code of conduct (of course) strongly discourages.
N.B.: "There remains the question of exactly how McVain knew who to contact initially, not to mention the further question of who inside the Programme might have authorized Madach and Slaughter's travelling expenses—though grantedly, travel to Mimico [a suburb of the Greater Toronto Area, easily reached by following the Queen Street streetcar line to its conclusion] wouldn't have cost them much, unless they did it by taxi. Inquiries into why any letters, e-mails, or phone calls exchanged between McVain and Madach/Slaughter seem not to have been properly logged are also currently ongoing." (Dr. Abbott, ibid.)

you, I cut the key, you turn it. But who opens the door, and to what? Who knows for sure what comes through?"[6]

Commentary (Backwards): "Apports are often difficult without help, so try using lucifuges for guidance. Circle is paramount; Tetragrammaton must be invoked. They have no names."[7]

Photograph #2:
Equally dim, angled upwards to trace what may be marks of fire damage—scorching of wallpaper, slight bubbling of plaster—moving from ceiling of kitchen down *towards* sink. The highest concentration of soot seems to be at the uppermost point. Wallpaper has a juniper-berry and leaf motif.[8]

Notes: "House D, May. We were becoming popular in certain circles. Family had two children, both sons, both under three years old; nanny reported the younger one was playing in his high-chair during breakfast when his 'Teddy-thing' suddenly caught fire.[9] Subsequent damage was estimated at $4,000; we received an additional $2,000 for making sure it wouldn't happen again."

Commentary (Forwards): "We need something more spectacular baby, a display, like Hollywood. Fire eats without being eaten, consumes unconsumed, as energy attracts. Come at once from whatever part of the world and answer my questions. Come at once, visibly and pleasantly, to do whatever I desire. Come, fulfill my desires and persist unto the end in accordance to my will. I conjure thee by Him to whom all creatures are obedient, and by the name of Him who rules over

---

[6] Samples sent to Graphology for comparison suggest the initial notes on each photo were made by Madach, while the backwards commentary comes closest to a hurried, clumsy imitation of Slaughter's normal penmanship. Forward commentary, on the other hand, can probably be attributed to former Freihoeven intern Eden Marozzi, who was found dead in her apartment on Christmas, 2005; going by records left behind, Marozzi had apparently been assisting Madach with his work on Slaughter's unfinished channelling experiments. As we all know, it was Madach's proven presence in her apartment at the time of Marozzi's death—as revealed by evidence gathered during the Metro Toronto Police Department's initial crime scene investigation—which, along with a lack of plausible alibi, would eventually lead to his subsequent arrest on charges of murder in the second degree.

[7] "Mention of 'lucifuges' would seem to indicate Slaughter—and Madach?—were using hierarchical magic to accelerate or control—generate?—poltergeist activity at McVain house. Worth further inquiry, after cataloguing rest of photos." (Dr. Abbott, ibid).

[8] Attempts to identify this location have, thus far, proved inconclusive. Dr. Abbott is undecided, but tentatively calls it as either 542 McCaul or 71B Spinster, both of which were visited by Slaughter and Madach in connection with repeated pyrokinetic poltergeist incidents. One family has moved out leaving no forwarding address, however, while the other proved spectacularly uncooperative, no more detailed analysis seems forthcoming.

[9] If we assume the photo was taken at 71B Spinster, it may be relevant to record that the child in question sustained burns severe enough to require partial amputation of three fingers from his left hand.

thee[10]. So this one goes out to the one I love, the one who left me behind, a simple prop to occupy his time. And why Teddy-'thing,' anyway? God knows I couldn't tell what it was before, afterwards."

Commentary (Backwards): "By this time, I can only think they were already watching me closely."[11]

Photograph #3:
Murky yet identifiable three-quarter study of Slaughter, who appears to be in light mediumistic control-trance. Orbs[12] hover over her right eye, pineal gland and heart chakra, roughly the same areas in which she would later develop simultaneous (and fatal) aneurysms. She sits in a rust-red La-Z-Boy recliner, feet elevated, with a dust-covered television screen barely visible to her extreme right, in the background of the frame.

Notes: "House H, July. Inclement weather with continual smog warning. Séance performed at the request of surviving family members, with express aim of contacting their deceased father; a control spirit was used to produce and animate an ectoplasmic husk patterned after his totem photograph, freely donated for use as a guided meditational aid. Mother cashed out RRSPs and eldest daughter's college fund in order to assemble the $15,000 required to remove 'curse'[13] afflicting their bloodline."

Commentary (Forwards): "But he died of natural causes so it's not so bad, right, not like we did anything really, and if you keep having those migraines then maybe you should take something, maybe you should just relax baby, let me help you, let me. Don't be like that, let me, why you gotta be that way? Palpitations, you say that like it's a bad thing, that's what I love about you baby, you have such a big heart: a big fat heart full of love and warmth and plaque and knots

---

[10] This "anthology incantation" seems to have been compiled from several different ones, all of which appear in the legendary grimoire *Lemegeteon*. Dr. Abbott confirms that the Freihoeven's library copy of this text was misplaced for several days in November of 2004, half a year prior to when the first photo was taken; this theft coincides with Madach's brief tenure as volunteer assistant librarian, before forming an experimental field-team with Slaughter.
[11] By "they," this commentator may mean the aforementioned lucifuges or fly-the-lights—elemental spirits identified with fire—who Eliphas Levi calls notoriously difficult to control and naturally "hateful towards mortals."
[12] Sphere-shaped visual deformities of the emulsion or pixels, often observed at sites where teams are trying to record various psychic phenomena.
[13] "This just gets better and better." (Dr. Abbott, ibid).

and pain. So just breathe, just breathe, just breathe, go do some yoga, take a pill, calm the hell down. You know we can't stop yet."

Commentary (Backwards): "Them either."

Photograph #4:
Close-angled shot of greasy black writing sprawled across what looks like the tiled wall of a bathroom shower-stall; letters vary radically in size, are imperfectly formed, seem (according to Graphology) inconsistent with "tool-bearing hands."[14] Letters read: "aLWaYs TheRe."[15]

Notes: "Automatic writing observed at Apartment C, renewed five separate times over a period of eight days. When advised that a cleansing exorcism was the best option, owner refused to cooperate." [16]

Commentary (Forward): "We have to stop we can't. We have to stop we can't. We have to stop stop stop we can't can't can't, oh Christ I want to STOP this, what are you, stupid? There's too much at stake, we're in too deep, no going back. WE CAN'T STOP NOW."

Commentary (Backwards): "Behold, I shall show you a great mystery, for we shall not all sleep, but we shall all be changed. And you can consider this my formal letter of resignation."

Photographs #5 to #9:
After close examination by various Freihoeven staff members, photographs #5 through #8 have been conclusively proven to show one of the Institute's own experimental labs. The blurry image in the extreme foreground of each seems most consistent with

---

[14] "'Tool-bearing'? Most messages of this type are produced telekinetically." (Dr. Abbott, ibid)

[15] Naturally enough, opinions vary as to who (or what) might be responsible for these markings.

[16] The single shortest annotation. This photo has since been tentatively identified—within a fairly narrow margin of error—as having been taken inside Slaughter's former condo, the site of her death. Even more significant, in hindsight, may be Dr. Abbott's recollection (confirmed through studying her coroner's inquest file) that Slaughter's body was found in her bathtub on August 23/05, partially immersed in shallow water.

an adjustable Remote Viewing diorama[17] which was set up in Lab Four from approximately September 15 to December 15, 2005. Much of the background area of each photo, on the other hand, has apparently been obscured by new visuals somehow imposed over an original image, by unidentifiable means; portions of the emulsion have been either destroyed or significantly altered, creating a visual illusion not unlike the "chiaroscuro" effect observed in certain Renaissance paintings which, while being restored, turn out to have been painted over a primary image that the artist may have wanted to either alter or conceal.[18]

As usual, even these partially subliminal secondary images are best described as indistinct and difficult to identify and/or categorize. Nevertheless, extensive analysis has revealed certain constants, i.e.:

- That background areas correspond with rough approximations of Photos #1 through #4, with the exception/addition of:
- A figure, face always angled away from "the camera," whose physical proportions seem to match those observed in photos taken of Slaughter, pre-mortem.[19]

Photo #9 was taken elsewhere; the diorama shown in Photos #5 through #8 is notably absent. A grey-painted stretch of wall, the hinge of a partially open door and the angle of lens during exposure all suggest that the camera may have been mounted on a tripod inside one of the Freihoeven's many industrial-sized storage closets, but not enough distinguishing marks are visible to establish exactly which one (there are six on Floor Three alone, for example, near the location of Lab Four).

---

[17] Invented by Dr. Abbott as part of his 1978 dissertational work at the University of Toronto, these are often used as a meditational aid during guided remote viewing sessions: The "navigator" or non-psychic team member will set the diorama up to roughly approximate the area he/she wants to access, then talk them through it on a detail-by-detail level until their trance becomes deep enough that they can guide themselves on the rest of their mental journey.

[18] "This is a prime example of what is commonly called 'spirit photography'—in this case, a Directed Imagery experiment involving Marozzi that may have been infiltrated by outside influences, producing the photo. These influences may have been, as Slaughter's commentary suggests, lucifuges originally suborned into helping her and Madach perpetrate their various psychic frauds; since Slaughter, the person with genuine paranatural power in their equation, was probably the one who did the actual invocation, the lucifuges would have seen her as their primary oppressor, and directed their revenge against her in specific. Even were we to take all of the above as being empirically 'true,' however, once the lucifuges' malefic influence had already brought about Slaughter's death (if that is, indeed, what actually happened), one would tend to assume that they would have no further interest in the case…or that, if they did, their campaign would shift focus onto Madach, the sole surviving author of the original invocation. And in that case, why harass Marozzi at all?" (Dr. Abbott, ibid.)

[19] Note to self: Why am I here? Wasn't there some other, slightly less insane place I could have gotten a summer job at? I *knew* Eden; a sweet girl, if easily influenced, overly-fascinated by/with psychic phenomena and those Freihoeven members who claimed to work with/produce them. Emma Slaughter looked at me in the halls once as I passed by, and I dreamed about it for a week—still felt her watching me, wherever I went. Is this relevant? Is recording stuff like this *science*? (S. Horse-Kicker, March 2/06)*

*"A valid question, Sylvester. Thanks for your input." (Dr. Abbott, ibid.)

Notes [collated into list-form for easy reading]:
(#5) "Subject was asked to visualize inside of House X. One hour fifty-three minutes allowed for session; results varyingly successful."

(#6) "Subject was asked to visualize interior of Facility H, no specific target. Agreed to deepen trance through application of Batch 33. Three hours ten minutes allowed for session; results varyingly successful."

(#7) "Subject was asked to visualize office area within Facility H, with specific reference to files stored on Public Servant G's computer. Five hours seventeen minutes allowed for session; results inconclusive overall."

(#8) "Subject was asked to visualize home office area inside House Z, with specific reference to correspondence stored in file-cabinet with plaster gargoyle on top of it.[20] Given sample of handwriting to meditate on, with double dose of Batch 33. Session interrupted at eight hours two minutes, after subject began to spasm; results inconclusive."

(#9) "Subject entered trance on own time, without instruction, after having self-injected a triple dose of Batch 33; session interrupted after approximately one hour, when subject was accidentally discovered by navigator. Limited amnesia observed after recuperation. Having no idea what image is meant to represent, impossible to say if session was successful or not."

Commentary (Forwards) [as above]:
(#5) Unintelligible scrawls.

(#6) Same.

(#7) Same, interrupted only by a shaky but repetitive attempt to form the letters E, Y, S.

(#8) In very different handwriting, far more like that usually used

---

[20] "That sounds like *my* office. Investigate? I have vague recollection of anonymous notes sent to me last year, shortly before Emma's death..." (Dr Abbott, ibid.)

for backwards commentary: "See here, see there, trying so hard, how could I help but answer? Because he likes girls who see things, yes he does; little pig, little pig, let me come in. This world's a big wide open place, up and down and all in between. Not so fun to see around corners when you know what's waiting, is it?"

(#9) Back to unintelligible scrawls.

Commentary (Backwards) [as above]:
(#5) "can"

(#6) "you"

(#7) "hear"

(#8) "me"

(#9) "now"

Photo #10:
At first misidentified as one of the actual MTPD crime-scene photos taken at the Marozzi apartment on Christmas Day, 2005, this image also demonstrates "spirit photography" alterations of a subtly different (yet far more disturbing) sort. Analysis has revealed that the apparent main image, that of Eden Marozzi's bedroom and corpse, is actually incongruent with other elements in the photo—specifically, the time visible on Marozzi's bedside clock, which places this as having been taken a good three hours prior to what forensic experts established as her physical T.O.D.

Further examinations, including x-rays administered at the Institute's expense, have since concluded that this first image has been recorded not on the photograph's own emulsion but on a thin, rock-hard layer of biological substance[21] overlaid carefully on the original photo. Beneath this substance is a simple holiday-style snap, probably taken with the camera on a timer, that shows Marozzi and Madach embracing at Marozzi's kitchen table, both wearing party hats

---

[21] Possibly ectoplasm, a substance occasionally exuded during séances, made up of various dead material from the medium's body.

and smiling. The remains of a Christmas dinner surrounds them; if one looks closely at the bottom centre of the photo, an opened jewel-box explains the ring visible on Marozzi's finger.

In the mirror behind them, however, a third figure—familiar from the previous array of "guided" photos—can be glimpsed sitting next to them, its hand half-raised, as though just about to touch Marozzi on the shoulder.

Notes: "Merry Christmas, Eve, from your Adam. A new Paradise begins."

Commentary (Forwards): "Fruit of knowledge, fruit of sin, snake's gift. This is what you want? This is what you get: the bitter pill. Fly the lights, lights out; out, out, brief candle! Goodbye, my lover. Goodbye, my friend. Goodbye, little girl who didn't know enough not to get in between. You can tell her I picked the wallpaper out myself. Ask her: How you like me now? Pretty good oh God God God God God."

Commentary (Backwards): "And on that note—did it really never occur to you that allowing someone used to working outside her body to be disembodied might not be the world's best idea, after all?"[22]

Conclusion:

With Imre Madach in jail, Emma Yee Slaughter and Eden Marozzi dead, and the official files closed on all three, the discovery of the preceding photographic array would seem—though, naturally, interesting in its own right—fairly extraneous to any new interpretation of the extant facts of the case.

---

[22] To this last bit of commentary, Dr. Abbott asks that a partial transcript of his most recent interview with Freihoeven psychic control group member Carraclough Devize—held March 4/06, during which he showed her what are now tentatively called the Slaughter/Madach/Marozzi photos—be appended to this report:
Devize: (After 120-second pause) Oh, no. Christ, that's sad.
Abbott: What is, Carra?
Devize: That. Don't you…no, of course you don't. There, in that corner, warping the uppermost stains. See? You'll have to strain a bit.
Abbott: Is that…an orb?
Devize: That's *Emma*, Doc. Face-on, finally. God, so *sad*.
Abbott: (After 72-second pause) I'm afraid I'm still not—
Devize: (Cuts him off) I know. But there she is, right there. Just about to take shape.
Abbott: Not fly-the-lights?
Devize: *Emma* had fly-the-lights, like mice or roaches, except mice and roaches don't usually…anyway. But Madach, and that poor little spoon-bender wannabe Barbie of his? By the end, what *they* had…was Emma.

Recommendations
- From now on, access to/possession of library books on the Freihoeven collection's "hazardous" list must obviously be tracked far more effectively.
- In the initial screening process for evaluating prospective Freihoeven employees, whether contracted freelancers or in-house, far more emphasis needs to be placed on psychological mapping. Issues thus revealed need to be recorded and re-checked, rigorously, on a regular monthly basis.
- Similarly, fieldwork teams should be routinely broken up after three complete assignments together, and the partners rotated into other departments. This will hopefully prevent either side of the equation developing an unhealthy dependence on the other.
- Finally, the Institute itself needs to undergo a thorough psychic cleansing, as soon as possible; lingering influences must be dispelled through expulsion or exorcism, and the wards must be redrawn over the entire building. Outside experts, rather than Freihoeven employees/experts, should be used for this task (Dr. Abbott suggests consulting Maccabee Roke, Nan van Hool, Father Akinwale Oja S.J. or—as a last resort—Jude Hark Chiu-wai as to promising/economical local prospects).
- Photographs #1 through #10 will be properly re-filed under #FI5556701 (cross-referentials: Madach, Marozzi, Slaughter).

Filed and signed: Sylvester Horse-Kicker, March 5/06
Witnessed: Dr. Guilden Abbott, March 5/06

GUISING

When I was a kid, out in the woods on the Dourvale Shore, I saw faces in the bushes, sometimes: wizened like nuts, smooth like peeled birch, smiling, snarling, but always with holes—small or large, dark or empty—where you'd expect their eyes to be. Sometimes, at night, I saw wavey little versions of those faces looking out of my bedroom walls, from the spaces in the pattern of the wallpaper.

You probably think I'm speaking metaphorically. Everyone else did, for years—said it was just hypnagogic imagery, a kind of waking dream, a manifestation of the trauma going on around me. And after getting tired of attempting to persuade them otherwise, I eventually managed to kind of convince myself they were right.

But I really wasn't speaking metaphorically then, and I'm sure not doing it now.

I remember trying to draw the face I saw most, then having

that drawing taken away from me by my grandmother, who burnt it in her iron-bellied kitchen stove. I remember she and my Dad arguing about it, later on, when they thought I couldn't hear.

This was just after my parents broke up, when Dad took us home to Overdeere, to stay with his mother until he got a job that'd support us. He'd been a late baby, and as a result, my grandmother was the single oldest person I'd ever seen. Her heavy braid of hair was the dull brownish-yellow of nicotine stains, matching the DuMaurier cigarettes she was always chain-smoking, her hands wrinkly-soft and peppered with age spots. She kept her teeth in a jar and her own "eyes" in a case—they were contact lenses, really, but that didn't stop my Dad from telling me, when I asked once where Grandma was: "Oh, she's upstairs, sweetie, taking her eyes out."

"I'll be out of here by Christmas," Dad told her, to which she simply sniffed.

"You'd better be," she replied.

Dad and Mom just didn't get along anymore, was how he'd eventually explained it, and I'd nodded as though I agreed—though, looking back, I found I couldn't really remember when they *had*. They were different people, to say the least; she came "from town," which in this case was Barrie, and had hoity ideas about what constituted decent living standards. Dad, on the other hand, was a Lake of the North boy, born and bred—managed to bull his way through a Forestry degree, but not quite to find a place in his preferred area. She'd stood there with a disapproving look on her face, watching him slip down into a Rona Gardening job ("You'd be a glorified florist, Kieran!") which eventually became unbearable, after which he got his trucker's license and began to do long-haul, gone three weeks out of every four. Her own stuff she could do from home, at night—she'd majored in Computer Tech, with a Design minor, which kept her busy building other people's websites. But it wasn't enough.

I don't blame her, I guess—not now, anyways. But I did then.

Most days, in fact, I can barely remember her face, aside from that one photo the papers found, reduced to newsprint or LCD pixels. All I have left of her is her scent, a celebrity perfume they don't make anymore, and the memory that the day she finally took off, she was wearing her favourite set of green ribbons trimmed with silver foil in her long, dark hair. Just gone, out the door and down the road in a cab to meet the boyfriend we'd never known she had. And the next day, Dad's car pulled out of our former driveway in the exact opposite direction, with me riding shotgun and everything we had in the back.

A week later, we were setting up in my grandmother's spare room, where the air stung with dust and the furniture hadn't been updated since 1973. Its single window looked straight out into the top sections of a British-style boundary-setting hedgerow whose roots her own grandfather supposedly laid, but which had been left to grow wild since the Korean War. Before that, however, the old man had done his work well—the fruit of his labours grew ten feet high and three feet deep, forming a close-knit lattice of stick-bone bars in winter, a mulch-fed mini-forest every other time of year. What light seeped through was green, and when you stood right next to it, your hands and face turned pallid, bruisy, veins gone suddenly delicate under leaf-thin skin. The shadows it cast made you look as though your blood had turned to chlorophyll.

"Best to stay out of the woods, kiddo," Dad told me, that first day. "It's an obstacle course back there—deadfalls everywhere. A kid I knew growing up fell down a crevasse once, broke his leg, didn't get found for almost a week. Never was right in the head, after that."

"Don't forget the Hell Holes," my grandmother called, from the kitchen.

"Yeah, that's right." To me: "There's Hell Holes, too—sudden falls, straight down, nobody even knows how deep. The limestone forms bubbles, just gives way underfoot."

"It's because of the swamps. That's where the sulphur gas comes from, too."

"Hydrogen sulfide, Mom. It just smells like sulphur."

"Same difference! That stuff'll knock you out, and it catches on fire, you aren't careful. So no mucking 'round with matches!"

"She's not gonna do that, Mom. You're not gonna do that, honey, are you?"

"No, Dad," I lied.

———

It was hard to find a way under the hedge, but I finally managed it. I had to dig around at the bottom, where the stakes holding the ethers in place had started to break down, 'til I found a place so damaged by underground digging, frost and blight that a pathway large enough to crawl through had opened up. It was narrower than me, but I wriggled through, like a worm—emerged on the other side covered in juice-stains and dirt, with cobwebs in my hair and bugs down the neck of my sweater. When I slid it off to scrub my face, a grasshopper fell out, still kicking.

Beyond, the woods began in progress, with no clear line of demarcation. You just looked up, and there they were; there *you* were, more to the point. Where the trees came in so close they shut out the sky, ferns grew so deep you couldn't see where to step, and every weed you brushed past left part of itself behind—clinging, scratching, stinging. The only way out was up, through the underbrush, the terrain getting steeper until weeds gave way to moss and the hill beneath emerged: a massive, pinky-grey blister of granite scored with hand-deep gouges where fresh acorns collected, cushioned on a rotten mush of old ones.

When I got up high enough, the rock flattened out, forming a little shelf, maybe three feet by six. And on that shelf I found an equally tiny camp-table centre-set, haphazardly nailed together from wood, stripped grey by weather. The hill went up behind it, so slant it formed a sort of seat, so I plumped myself down and looked at the table-top, where a word had been carved, in strangely beautiful script: SARACEN.

"That's my cousin's name," a voice said from behind me.

Another little girl had come up, so silently I'd never heard her. She was literally leaning out of the brush above, hanging in over my shoulder, so close I couldn't even jump; denied room to react, my heart just gave a little knock, and I looked at her, swallowing.

"Oh?" I managed, finally. "Uh...that's cool. I never heard of a guy named Sara..."

She corrected me: "Sara*cen*, his name is. They're folk from away, unbelievers in Turkish climes, on the other side of the world. My mother says his mother liked the sound of it, when she was carrying." She peered down at the carving with interest. "Must be he played here too, once, though I can barely credit it."

"They live nearby, your family?"

"All around. We're many, hereabouts."

"We just moved here. Well, Dad and me."

"Aye, I ken. You're Jess Nuttall's boy's girl."

"My name's Nuala. What's yours?"

"They call me Leaf."

She had a high, hoarse voice, not much wind to it, and rough, though that might have been the rhythm of her speech. I was too young to know her accent—it all just seemed strange to me, foreign somehow, with no clear idea beyond that. Years later, it occurred to me that she sounded as though she'd learned English from someone with a thick Scots burr, but spoke it with most of a North Ontarian honk, aside from certain differences of pronunciation.

"How old are you?" I asked. "I'm nine."

She struck a theatrical pose and told me, deadpan: "Oh, I am old, old. I have seen five forests come and go, but never before have I seen beer brewed in an eggshell."

I goggled at her. "You're kidding, right?" And she laughed, high and sweet, a child's laugh like any other, save how I immediately wanted to hear it again.

"Cert," she said. "I'm...kidding, only. I have nine years as well, myself."

Looking back, I can see that she said the word "kidding" as though she'd never heard it before, but liked it. It made her grin, wide, which in turn showed how charmingly gappy her teeth all were, not to mention larger than you'd expect given her size. So much so that when she put her jaws back together, I swear I saw her bottom canines slightly dent her upper lip.

"Do you guise?" she asked me, a moment later. Then explained, spurred by my obvious bafflement: "Put on a face, I mean—make masks, pretend."

"Like...play dress-up, is that it? Or like for Hallowe'en?"

"Aye, that: all Hallows. Samhain Night."

"Well, sure, I guess. Don't you?"

"Aye, ever. We call it the glamour."

"*The* glamour?"

"So I said."

Leaf and I played for what didn't seem like hours, but when I realized the sun was going down, I started back. "You could come for dinner," I offered, not actually knowing if that would be okay with my grandmother or not. But she just shook her shaggy head, solemnly.

"I'm wanted home," she said. "And besides...no, better not."

"You can come anytime," I said. "Tomorrow, maybe."

"Or you, up here."

"I'm starting school soon. Will I see you there?"

"Not too likely."

"...Tomorrow, then. Here."

She laughed again. "Aye," she said. "If I don't see you, first."

—

You're wondering why I'm telling you all this, no doubt. Like, *what's the damn point, Nuala?* And then you maybe remember what I let slip about my mother, back there—what I grazed over, more like, without explanation—and think, annoyed: *More about that, that's what I'd like to know. Not all this backwoods* Stand By Me *crap—"it was the best of summers, it was the worst of summers..."* I mean, Jesus.

Well, at the time, for me, my mother had *already* disappeared. None of us would know anything more until six months later, when two nice officers from the Ontario Provincial Police came asking whether or not we'd had contact with her since a month previously. We were as surprised as anybody else to discover she'd apparently left that boyfriend of hers the same way she'd left us, except far more precipitately: without warning, in the middle of the night, leaving all of her stuff behind. None of which kept the OPP from making him their primary suspect; he had a record, after all, though most of it was for minor drug charges and public intoxication.

A year after that, some hikers exploring the fens around Chaste found her purse nestled high in a tree. Inside was her wallet, most of her hair and a few of her teeth, fresh enough to get DNA from the pulp and roots. My mother's boyfriend was arrested, protesting vociferously. The Crown argued that he probably threw her down a Hell Hole, of which there are several in Chaste's vicinity, though why he didn't do the same with her purse was never explored. That they found a thriving grow-op inside his garage probably didn't help.

He's been in jail for over ten years now, up at the Kingston Pen. I was asked to make a victim's statement at his first parole hearing, but I told them it would upset me too much, which they accepted. I was later informed that he did not, in fact, make parole, because he'd been caught multiple times holding drugs for other inmates.

These are the facts. The truth, so far as I've since been able to figure it, is rather more slippery, and difficult to prove—as it often is. But here, in particular...

Much like beer brewed in eggshells, what came next is definitely odd enough to merit comment, no matter *how* old you might be.

—

At school I soon fell in with a little group of kids my age. Still, I always found a reason to sneak off and meet up with Leaf, at least a couple days a week. She showed me paths I could never find again on my own, taking us all around the area: to the Lake, the dumps out back of the Sidderstane cannery, even that overgrown ghost village by the Dourvale Shore my new friends talked about in whispers. One afternoon in October, we sat together inside a saltbox house whose interior had fallen to ruin, leaving only the outermost portions: four windowless walls, crooked and rickety, held together mainly with vines. Two trees grew up through the middle, where the floor used to be, and their branches made a sort of roof.

"And where's she now?" Leaf asked.

"Don't know," I replied. Then added, quickly, as though to convince myself: "Don't much care, either. She never bothered to call since we got here, never even bothered to write...I mean, not like she doesn't know where we *are*. She just doesn't give a heck, so screw her."

Leaf nodded. "Mothers shouldn't leave," she said. "It's not right."

I laughed, bitter. "I'm okay without one, I guess," I said. "So, what about *your* Mom? She nice?"

"Oh, I love her dearly. Her, my brothers and sisters, our cousins..."

"No Dad?"

"Somewhere," she said. "We don't make ourselves, aye? But he's no part of us, really." Since I didn't know what to say to that, we sat a few more minutes in silence, watching the trees move overhead—comfortable, somehow, even in our discomfort. I could hear her breathing, a faint, sighing song, same as the wind which scattered dead leaves at our feet.

"I'd help with your sorrows, Nuala, if I could," Leaf told me, eventually, putting her cold little hand on mine, with an odd gentleness; I remember how overlong her nails were, black at the broken tips, and that they scratched just a bit, for all her restraint. Looking up at me under the shaggy fringe of her hair, her eyes ever-so-slightly a-gleam, and asking: "You know so, don't you? For you're my friend, my only."

"I know, Leaf."

"Though you have friends elsewhere, now, I hear."

"What, Grace and Milton, Heather? They're just kids in my class, like—somebody to eat lunch with, or hang at recess. *You're* my *best* friend."

"And you, for me, always." She nodded at the sky, like she saw something floating up there, coming closer. "Will be All Hallows soon. Do you think to guise that night, and walk out begging?"

"Um, not so much. I mean, there's that thing at school, the costume party. But we're all a little old for trick or treat, right?"

Her face fell. "I'd hoped you would," she said, at last. "For my family celebrates that night, and I'd have you meet them, if I may. 'Tis a great rout, always."

"Well..." And now I felt bad. "Where do they have it, usually?"

"Oh, hereabouts. The Shore's ours, to do with as we please." She gave me a shy glance. "I could come meet you, the night of, at your school. Bring you here."

I hesitated. "You do that, the guys'll want to come along too."

"Then let them. All will have safe passage, so long as I'm near."

In the trees, a bird sang; the sun was sinking, colours changing. The wind blew a little colder, and I shivered, even in my jacket.

"Sure," I said, finally. "That'd be good."

—

Dad was out on a run Hallowe'en week; he'd gotten his passport updated the month before, so it probably involved crossing the border. Which left my grandmother and me rattling around together, me working on my costume, her doing the stuff she usually did.

"What do you know about fairies, Nuala?" she asked me, the night before: Devil's Night, Mischief Night, when all the older kids were supposedly out egging house and TPing trees. Then continued, not waiting for an answer: "In the old days, my folks used to say Hallowe'en was when they let the ghosts of the damned out of Hell, and that's why we dressed up—so they wouldn't know who we were, if they met us out after dark. You go back further still, though, it wasn't ghosts they meant at all, but the *Daoine Sidhe*, the good folk. Them under the hill."

"What hill, Grandma?"

"Any hill, I guess. But 'round here, they mostly meant Druir Hill, on the Dourvale Shore; don't suppose you go anyplace near there, do you, when you crawl out under the hedge?" At that I looked up, shocked, which made her give a grim little smile. "Oh yes, my girl, I know all about that—think you were the first ever got that same notion? Think again."

"*You* did?"

"Many a time. Up the hill, past that table...there was a boy I'd meet there, sometimes, came right out of the woods. Mrs. Sidderstane's son, from up at the big house, who wrote his name on the table top with his knife."

Saracen, I thought. *Unbeliever, from away.*

"Oh, and he was handsome, too, with his blue eyes, though there was something about the way he looked at you..." She shook her head. "Any rate, the Shore's not a good place, 'specially at night, though I know you kids think it's some sort of amusement park. All the things your Dad and me warned you about, they go double up there. And Hallowe'en's the worst time to go, bar none."

"Because of fairies?"

"Because I say so, miss. Now promise: you go out in *that*"—she nodded at my princess dress, my tinsel crown, the little mask of tissue-paper veiling I was pinning to it—"you stay away from there, far as you can get. Or you don't go at all."

"I promise," I said.

"I wish I believed you."

"I *promise*, Grandma."

"Well, it's on you, now. I've said what I could."

And she shrugged, turning back to the stove where she had biscuits baking. But I could see her eyes were wet.

Why wouldn't you want them to know it was you, though? The fairies? That was what I should have asked—so she could tell me about changelings, or girls caught in rings, boys caught under hills. How time bends in the tunnels, so you might come in one end a child and leave the other an old, old man. How no matter what they serve you, you shouldn't eat, because then it gives them power over you...and besides, it's all nothing but dead leaves, really: leaves, and mulch, and bones. Nothing but glamour.

God knows I *would* have asked, had I only known to; just like I wouldn't have done what I did the next night, I'd only known it was a bad idea. But I guess you can say the same about a lot of things.

—

Heather was a princess for Hallowe'en too, it turned out—a *space* princess, like from *Star Wars*. Grace was a kitty-cat. And Milton was doubling his fun by wearing a werewolf mask on top of his hockey sweater, so he wouldn't have to choose between the two things he liked best, monsters and sports. "I can play goal for Frankenstein against Dracula, now," he told us, muffled. "Beat *that*, Barbies!"

He danced with all of us in turn, though, once the music started—and later we all danced with each other, bopping around in tandem to Men Without Hats while the big kids passed tissue paper in front of the disco lights to make them strobe. Then grabbed a few Cokes and went outside to cool down, chatting our way past the smokers, the neckers and the scrappers, right to the forest's edge. Which is where Leaf met us.

Not much of a costume, per se—just her usual clothes, threadbare and dusty, so out of fashion they almost looked cool. But she was wearing the best mask I've ever seen bar none, before or since: close-fitted enough you couldn't see any seams, moving with her breath. It had lumpy skin, pale like a potato, a pig's nose and dim little red eyes, and the mouth stretched so far in either direction that if the corners hadn't hit its ears—those lobeless curlicue holes, with their flared and pointed upper ridges of cartilage—it almost looked like they might have just kept on going 'til they met, and the whole top of her head popped off.

"Nuala," she greeted me, her voice hardly even muffled. "And these your friends, of course: Heather...Grace. Milton."

Milton didn't quite recoil. "Uh...yeah, hi. Nuala, who's this?"

"Leaf," I said. "*You* remember. She's taking us to a party, at her place."

"Leaf who, though?"

I shook my head, only then realizing I'd never actually asked. But: "Redcappie," Leaf replied, without hesitation. "Leaf Redcappie, they call me."

Grace made a little noise. "I have to go home," she said. "Heather—you should come too."

Heather snorted. "What for?"

"*Redcappie*," Grace hissed back, and Heather swallowed, starting as though she'd suddenly remembered something, while Milton and I just watched, confounded.

"Oh yeah," Heather said, at last. "Yeah, we—have fun, you guys."

"Heather?"

She and Grace had already grabbed hands, however, eyes darting, poised to turn. "Have fun," Grace threw back, over her shoulder. "And, um, nice to meet you, Leaf. Tell your folks...uh, anyhow."

"*Grace*, what the *spit*, man!"

But they were out of range now, almost out of sight. They didn't look back. Milton and I swapped glances, then looked to Leaf, who didn't seem surprised.

"Wish them good even," she said, "and you two as well, if you'd rather not come with, also. For 'twas good enough to see you the once this night, Nuala, in your guise."

I looked back at Milton, who shrugged. "Let 'em go," he said. "I'm always up for a party, 'specially someplace new. This one's been pretty lame, so far."

Then he smiled at me, so I smiled too—and from the very corner of my eye, I almost thought I saw Leaf smile, even through the skin of her amazing mask. She reached out one hand, and I took it.

Into the woods we went, all three—but when November finally dawned, on the cold hill's side, only one of us came back.

—

I remember waking up, on my back, covered with dew. I was cold, and my eyes hurt. I think I'd been crying.

I remember stumbling home, through the woods. Crawling back through the hedge, so clumsy I tore myself on its twigs.

I remember what Dad's face looked like, when he opened the

door and found me wavering there. My grandmother sitting at the kitchen table, face in her hands, her shoulders shaking.

Heather and Grace came to visit me in the hospital, two days later, and stood looking at me for a long minute, still hand in hand, like they'd never broken apart in the last seventy-two hours.

"We thought you'd be okay, is all," Heather said, finally. "You guys. Because you knew her."

"Uh huh," I replied, voice slow and grating, through my swollen throat. "I...*thought* I did, yeah."

"So what happened?" Grace asked. "To Milton?"

"...Don't know."

And after we'd all taken a few minutes to digest that: "Well," she couldn't quite stop herself from saying. "You know that's your *fault*, right?"

(Right.)

Once I was well enough to travel, my Dad finally left Overdeere again, taking me with him. We moved first to God's Lips, then Barrie (ironically enough), then Mississauga, then Toronto proper. I graduated high school there, made Ontario Scholar, got into U of T. My grandmother was dead by that time, of course; she left everything to Dad, who left it in turn to me, as I only discovered after he had a fatal heart attack earlier this year.

I majored in History, with a minor in Library Sciences that I parlayed into my own personal line of research. Eventually, I stumbled upon the Connaught Trust, where the records that had eluded me thus far are kept. Which is how, years on, I learned the truth behind the Dourvale Shore's legendary reputation—about those three bloodlines of Overdeere which supposedly trace themselves back to Scotland, to the fairies, each family's lineage weaving back and forth and in and out of the others' like worms through a dead dog's heart: the Druirs of Stane Hill, lofty and secret, plus their descendants the Sidderstanes, who lend their name to the Cannery, and own most of Overdeere proper. Not to mention the poorest of all their many poor relations, the Redcappies.

Though few of this latter clan have ever been seen in town, they did once own a set of houses in Dourvale in 1935, before the development collapsed, leaving the village untenanted and derelict. And this also happens to be when the youngest Redcappie family member was a nine-year-old girl named Duille, which—in Scots

Gaelic—means "Leaf."

Old, old, her voice sighs through my head sometimes, at night, when I'm alone. *Old, I am, and so strange. Like beer brewed in an eggshell.*

But that's not the whole of it, not yet.

Roughly a year after that Hallowe'en, two hunters tracking a downed duck found the hairy tip of a werewolf mask's ear poking up out of the sod on Stane Hill. Their dog began to whine and dig at it, and as they struggled to pull him away, one hunter felt rather than heard a faint, erratic knocking from beneath their feet. Ten minutes of frenzied excavation later, they broke through a blister in the earth and uncovered a thin, dirty boy in a hockey sweater, his mask's orifices clogged with dirt. When he finally stopped crying and screaming, he told them his name was Milton Recamier, and that he thought he'd been trapped down there for a few days. Maybe a week.

The authorities said he must have fallen into a Hell Hole and been trapped underground, but Milton claimed he'd been stuck inside the Hill itself, breathing its rock like air. Unsurprisingly, he quickly ended up in a mental institution, where he stayed until he changed his tune.

When we were both sixteen, I was visiting friends in God's Lips when he suddenly walked up to me on the street. He looked ragged, literally and figuratively, with a weird sort of eczema at his temples that I later realized might have been the result of electroshock therapy.

"She told me to give this to you, if I saw you again," he said, handing me a package.

"Who?"

"Leaf."

It was an old paper bag, opening folded and scotch-taped to create a seal, and by the time I'd unwrapped it, he was already too far away to call after him, even if I'd been capable. Instead, I just looked down, frozen, my chest hot and hollow. Because what it held was—

a knot of ribbon.

Green.

Trimmed in silver foil.

The kind my mother was wearing, the day she left.

—

I'd help you if I could, Nuala. For that you're my friend. My one. My only.

—

So little of that night I recall, still, at all. Shreds and patches.

Inside Leaf's relatives' house—the Hill?—it was bright (dark), and hot (cold), full of figures (yes) in costume (no), adults and children (maybe), men and women (likewise); I remember shouldering my way through a crowd of whirling, laughing, dancing creatures, humming along and toe-tapping to music I thought I recognized somehow, even though I was equally sure I'd never heard it before. Milton was spun off, whirling away through the darkness, borne on the riotous tide; Leaf clutched me close and let him go, pulling me past reams of food spread out on tables, glistening and delicious-smelling, a feast for the ages. (But: *Don't eat any, Nuala, not one bite,* I felt her say, right into my ear's hiddenmost whorls, so they vibrated secretly. *It will do you no good, if you ever wish to leave here.*)

Milton, in the distance, was cramming his face with both hands. He looked like he enjoyed it, at the time, and whenever I think about it now, I really hope he did.

"Have to sit down," I told her, indistinctly, to which she shook her head: "Nay, but keep on, I pray—slack not, 'tis only a little way further. We're almost through."

Pulling me on, on, ever on, past men with horns and girls with tails, faces with two mouths, faces with none. Eyes and teeth and glittering scales, leaves and vines and fruit blooming straight from skin, crowns of candles lit like marsh-flame, guttering in the darkness. Past the flap of wings and the brachiating leap of things high above, hurling themselves back and forth as though from branch to branch in some massive, invisible copse of trees.

And then, suddenly, in the very midst of it all—a dark young man, blue-eyed and handsome, emerged full-blown, coming towards us through the crowd. Leaf tried her best to avoid him, but he eddied forward, blooming up between us with his arms crossed, frowning down. And I saw (*thought* I saw) that when he blinked, his lids—long-lashed, luxuriant, shadow-touched at their rims, as though lined with kohl—shut the wrong way 'round entirely: not from the top, down, but from the bottom, up.

"Cousin Saracen," Leaf murmured, masked head suddenly hunched, as if she feared to be hit. And: "Leaf," he said, his voice strongly Scots-burred, original template to her merest imitation, "what is't ye've done, my poor, small fool? Tae bring *this* one here, tonight..."

"I thought to show her, only. Only that."

"Ye should not have, as well ye know."

"Yet she's blood, kin—Jess Nuttall's boy's girl. You remember, aye? And...my friend, also."

"That's no account of mine, girl. Ye know my mother's views."

"But—"

He waved her protest away. "Show her the whole truth, Leaf, then loose her tae go, while she still can. Bid her see straight what she half-glimpses already, and let that be an end on't."

"And what of her company?"

"Him? Oh, he's e'en now caught, mazed fast—our families must have their will of him, to work away his debt. No concern of either of ours, therefore—not like her."

Leaf sighed. "I know it," she said, softer still, almost into her neck.

And...first we were standing there, then we weren't, swerved sidelong into some smaller chamber all filled with moss and apples, sticky-sweet and vaguely rot-stinking. By my foot, the pale flower of some woman's hand reached up from further down, submerged below the wrist in the rocky floor, splayed fingers discoloured by decay.

"Don't look there," Leaf told me, raising my head by the chin, as my vision swam. "Here, Nuala, best of all friends. Look to me, only. Look to me."

And her mouth opened, the mask's mouth, wide and wider, wider still. 'Til it seemed the entire top of her potato-pale skull might tip back, drop free and roll away, leaving her nothing but teeth and tongue, gaped open wetly to the world. Except...

...it wasn't a mask, of course. At all. Just her, the real her, finally visible, without the lies. Without—

—"The glamour."

I don't know what I said. What noises I might have been making. Which is odd, because I know for sure that I could hear her—

Leaf, bending in above me herself as her cousin watched, lowering herself so we were eye to eye once more, where I crouched gibbering on that half-rotten, hand-flowered floor. And saying, sadly, as she did:

"Tonight we guise no more, for 'tis the time of it—this one night of all the year, when we may walk abroad unremarked-on, wearing our own faces in jest as we cannot, any other time, or risk a broken covenant. And I did so want you to see me true, if only for the once."

I gaped, and she sighed, and her cousin reached out a six-fingered hand to my shoulder, pushing me out through the Hill's wall. I saw the roots and stones rush by me, *through* me, sifting my very atoms, resistlessly as rain. And then it was dawn, the cold light of day, and I was lying staring up into the sky, my spine hurting, every bone in my body lit up with what seemed like one single, awful ache.

They still ache like that, sometimes, even now. That's when I know I'm seeing something I should probably pay attention to.

—

Here are some things I believe, now, though I have little or no proof for them:

My mother is probably the tree they found her purse in, hands upflung into pleading branches like Daphne, with bark growing over every part of her. Or maybe she's a stone instead, standing frozen somewhere on Dourvale's streets, with only the sun crawling across her skin to tell her time is passing. Maybe she's buried in Stane Hill, same as Milton once was, except further down. One way or the other, I don't expect to find her alive. I don't expect to *find* her, not even if I was to finally start looking.

At Stane Hill, the Druirs' seat, Leaf touched me to get me in, not that she probably needed to, and I touched Milton to get him in, not knowing he wouldn't be able to leave without me 'til he'd worked off the food he took. Blood opens the door, you see—both ways, probably.

The older I get, the more I watch Leaf's cousin surface in me— handsome Saracen with his poison-blue eyes, eternally young and unspeakably old, who once carved his name on a table to impress

102

my grandmother, back when she was still sweet young Jess Nuttall. I sit in my apartment with my part-fairy bones aching, off and on, longing for my great-grandfather's hedgerow, the hole beneath and the woods beyond. It's my inheritance, after all.

We have the stink of human on us, we quarterlings, too much so for the eldest of our blood to ever find us sweet, Leaf's voice whispers to me sometimes, late at night, whether I'm dreaming or awake. *The hills will not open for us; the rings are closed forever. Who can we turn to, therefore, except each other? Which is why no one will ever be coming for you but me, Nuala, just as no one will ever be coming for me, in the end, but...probably, possibly, if I only wait long enough...*

(Oh, how I hope, my dearest, my only friend. Oh, how I pray.)

...you.

I know myself, you see, at last. I'm no monster; not that Leaf was one either, not entirely. But in one particular, I agree with her completely: this Iron World hurts me, and I'm tired of guising. I want to take off my false face and see the one beneath, maybe the same one I used to draw, over and over: wrinkled like a nut, peeled like birch. And one day soon...

...*very* soon, most likely, given it's October again, and Hallowe'en draws near...

...I will.

BLACK
BUSH

Oh, everyone will see, yes, and everyone will know
That boy, you reap what you sow.
—16 Horsepower

After a spell, I found myself on the road once more, tracing that wandering track up over the mountains towards Black Bush way. But the ruts were far too muddy and churned-up for thin-soled prison shoes to weather, so I stuck my thumb out and cocked my hip, waiting on a ride. One stopped soon enough, confirming I still had it.

"They call me Tad," the driver told me, as I slid myself in. He was all done up in a flannel shirt and a cap that said *Free Can of Whoop-Ass with Billy-Bob Teeth*—maybe my age or older but hard-traveled, with a recreational user's roster of barely suppressed tics and the same long build most everyone from the Bush tended to share, all hard muscle and sharp, mismatched teeth. Lot like looking in a mirror, come to think, give or take the dangly bits, which was a draw in itself.

I smiled sidelong, and cast him an upwards look through the long brown shadow of my hair. "Allfair Chatwin's my name," I said. "Alleycat, too, sometimes—or A-Cat, if you prefer."

"Not Gley Chatwin's gal, that was?"

"The same. Why—you happen to know my Momma? Plenty did."

Careful: "Know how she was a...wise woman, sure 'nough."

"Why, ain't you nice: What she was was a *witch*, mister—pure holler, born and bred."

"Like yourself?"

"Wouldn't be too likely to say outright, if I was—'less there was something in it for me to do so."

He nodded once, sage as a judge, which didn't surprise me as much as it might've. For they're practical folk, thereabouts—and better yet, they do know how to keep their mouths shut.

"Heard you was locked up, is all," he said, once another long moment had passed; I saw his eyes go wandering off, fingers twitching just a bit on the wheel, like he was trying not to think too long on a series of bad thoughts passing through his skull.

To which I simply shrugged, and replied: "Well, darlin'...I'm out now."

—

Back in Mennenvale Women's Penitentiary—M-vale, they call it—the other cons was always shoving all manner of contraband up inside 'em, from condoms full of smack or pre-paid phone cards to all heinous manner of tools, keys and other potential sharps; a difficult proposition at the best of times, no matter how carefully you might wrap 'em beforehand. Not me, though: get-back just wasn't worth the put-out, in my never-anything-like humble opinion. 'Sides which, and far more to the purpose, it never did seem to fool anyone for long; after all, once people know you come with a ready-made drop-bag stuck 'tween your nethers, it really is always gonna be the first place anyone ever thinks to look.

Then again, I knew one gal, harder than most, who cut herself a flap and slid the razor-blade that'd made it underneath, like stuffing an envelope; let it heal up good and tight, then tattooed something extra-dark overtop. (Where? In one of those complicated feminine places the Inquisition used to search for witch-marks, and always find 'em.) Give her but a minute to scratch, and it came sliding back out, quick as you please. I guess that was one situation where it really did help not to care 'bout pain, or scarring—or much've anything else, for that matter, 'cept making sure she always had a last-ditch exit plan socked away for the proverbial rainy day.

Couldn't ever quite go there myself, in spite of M-vale's fine capacity to spread suffering virulent as any clap-dose; guess I'm an optimist at heart, underneath it all. But if I was to make that same call, the only weapons I'd need were the ones I was born with: two kinds of bad mixed up and shook to make a new, all the more toxic for its alchemy. Full of poisons, my very blood, rheum and juices natural spell-ingredients, napalm-components kept separate for transport, yet all-too-easily mixed.

How I got into Mennenvale most know, 'least 'round these parts. How I got out's a tale in itself, but never you mind—we'll cover that later. Back to me and Tad.

—

The road ran out soon after, so we pulled over and parked awhile in under the lowest-slung trees, as a sudden rain begun to fall. His lap seemed a good place to wait the storm out, so I wound both my hands in his hair and gave myself over, sucking breath from him the way cats do from sleeping babies 'til at last he gave out a choked cry and went silent, slumped sideways 'gainst the driver's side door.

We renew ourselves in our own special ways, I thought, *according to our natures.* And I shivered all over at the feel of his brief candle passing me by, night-bound—familiar but not, considering how long it'd been since I indulged myself in this particular way. It left me sated yet slightly sad, for he hadn't seemed a bad sort, in his way. But then again, I'd seen a dark spot hovering over his face in the rearview, and a flat white one in either eye like the inverse shadow of two silver pennies waiting to touch down and seal his lids across: Bad tidings already on their way, and soonish. Perhaps I'd simply slid my way between this moment and that, bringing fate's promise to full flower only a skootch or two before its due time.

Had him some fair-to-middling product still left in his glove compartment, though. So I took that, along with what little cash money his wallet held, and a gun so old it might've fought for Patton, and walked on up the trail that I knew lay hid behind that massy curtain of waterlogged leaves.

—

Now, here's the thing. Holler witchery starts deep in the body, same's everything else—life and death, fruit and filth, a constant push-pull of meat and bone versus energy and entropy; it's fueled by spit and blood and juice, always swallowing something here to shit it forth somewhere else. Everything gained through this tradition is paid for, and the price is always the same—flesh, and plenty of it.

Which is why, my Momma used to claim, we are the true root and branch of all subsequent witchery, even the hoity Latinate hierarchical yammer my half-sister Samaire Cornish practiced—that tall, blonde rake of a gal, covered all over in arcane tattoos meant to guard 'gainst the pull of her own demon heritage. Samaire, taught to hate everything she was and borne along in her other half-sister's wake, playing the hunter's game, spending out her life's coin on fatal-hot pursuit of the same wicked things she ought to embrace as her truest kin. That's if she knew what was best for her, which she all-too-obviously didn't...

(Ah, but I aimed to change all that, eventually. If I possibly could.)

One kiss alone I'd ever had from my Princess, got under duress, during the escape she and I—and Dionne Cornish, who'd once threatened to cut my tits off if I didn't stay away—had supernaturally connived, by matchmaking our two traditions together, to win all three of us out through M-vale's iron walls. Yet here she was still, run through me like some pleasant disease; finding her would be hard, I had no doubt, yet more than worth the effort. And I had my ways and means.

I well remember the day the Warden called me in to tell me my Momma was dead at last. How they'd found her laid up in that hovel of a house, all swole up and black and covered in flies, with 'coons gnawing away at the bare meat of her feet. Someone had cut the tall crown of hair that used to fall straight to her thighs when unbound and carried it away, to use in witch-balls, or other such tokens. Someone else had cut away her nose and mouth-skin like Tobit did for Ashmodai, to show his devil-rid love the lips she'd hung on last night, and break the spell she lay under for good. And in between her eyes some third had cut a cross to bleed her of all her power. I could only hope it hadn't helped him much—that she'd given at least as good as she'd got in those last moments, leapt up high with her claws out like any nighthawk, before they finally pulled her down.

Since then, through the vine, I'd heard how neighbours had broken our homestead down for parts and crushed each brick of it with a rock, burnt what was left, then plowed the ash over with salt. But my Momma they'd paid a sin-eater to carry away on his back, hoping she'd ride him 'til she found herself a proper place to rest, and leave them all the hell alone. Him they'd found face-down at the edge of a swamp the next spring, a mask of half-froze mud cutting off his air, and the assumption had been that what was left of Gley Chatwin's body now lay somewhere underneath that same mucky water. Which at least made it as good a place as any other to start looking.

I wanted words with her, you see—one word, in particular: the name she'd used to call my Daddy up, so's he could get me on her. For being that he was the same creature'd once got Samaire Cornish on her own mother Moriam, I felt for sure I'd be able to use that connection to trace like a reel whose either end was a hook sunk deep into both our flesh, and pull us together once more. And after that?

After that, Dionne or no Dionne, I reckoned that blood would tell. *True* family, spawned in the same Pit, 'stead of raised up apart in separate Social Services petri dishes. Blood would out, come up hard like a flash flood, and Lady Di would find her tough little self swept away in its wake, witch-killing knives and all.

The swamp was up the hill, just over a ridge and through some trees, where the moss dipped low and cracks brought up a welcome whiff of sulphur. If I could just get there, I felt, things would fall right into place.

Except that, when I did...what-all I'd been after was just plain gone. Whole place *and* my Momma's body, together.

—

I'd been caught in Alabama, that last time, but one step from the Trail's end...recalled that much clearly, though not a lot else. Back then, crank and liquor'd been my poison, with the occasional side of junk to bring me down; truckers were my source of transportation, recreation, prey. Kept myself high enough to forget I could do magic, or want to, beyond the usual: glamouring, bewitchment, knowing at a glance where best to put my fingers—whether a man (or a woman) was worth my efforts, and for how long. A couple times I sent the Law 'round me on the highway, or made fools think my thumb and forefinger could shoot bullets, but eventually, that just wasn't enough; kicks got hard to find, and the price of keepin' myself entertained went up, accordingly.

Back at M-vale, the prison shrink asked me once if I was sorry for what I'd done, all the trouble and harm I'd caused, the people I'd hurt, while expressing myself the best way I knew how. I knew what he wanted to hear, 'course, but I figured hard truth was probably the best policy for both of us, in the long run.

"That'd be not at all, doctor," was my reply. "Not one little bit. Ain't thought of them since, even for an instant, and don't expect to do so."

'Cause yeah, I've been beat down and fucked a good few times, just like I've done the same elsewhere, to others; sowed my unfair share of pain, some of which I do regret, so far's I'm able. Still, I ain't been too hard done by, in the main, and most've what I got, I frankly asked for. I know what I am—something wicked from a long line of such and proud of it, like Jezebel, or Lilith. Like that great whore of Babylon who consorts with the Beast at End Times, whose house shall be overthrown and never more inhabited, except by owls and satyrs and dragons.

Only person folks 'round me ever fool's themselves, assuming I don't.

I can't remember now, exactly, what it was that first set me off. Maybe just Momma's own bad example, for watching her conduct herself was always as much pain as joy to me. Like most witches, she lived a half-life at best, lazy and dirt-poor and subject to fate and the State's whims as any other during the daytime, only to gain and revel in terrible power at night. But even then, her craft waxed and

waned all month long, moon-wise. She never did learn to read or ci-
pher, nor owned more'n two dresses at a time, nor shed her essential
liking for hard booze and handsome, stupid men whose passions
ran cruel as her own. Wasn't much of a housekeeper, neither. Hell,
I didn't know what it was to sleep up off the floor 'til I run off and
begged refuge in my friend Orpah Cleves's not-Daddy's trailer, and
look how *that* turned out.

"There's something right bad in you, you Devil's whore-piece!"
her Momma yelled at me as she drove me off, throwing rocks—
little thirteen-year-old gal with eyes blacked and split scalp oozing
blood, and her a full-grown woman makin' horns, like she thought
I'd curse her where I stood. "Worse'n Gley by far, and that's sayin'
something!"

I spat, and grinned to see her cringe from it. "What's in me, Gley
Chatwin ain't seen but the once since it laid down atop her!" I threw
back. "My Daddy's a prince of the power of the air, bitch; I got
more jolt in the littlest part of me than most in this holler'll see 'fore
they're bones in the ground. And it was that no-'count man of yours
first laid his hands on me, not the other way 'round—shouldn't've
tried to take the trip, he couldn't pay the fare."

"Don't you never come back 'round here, you know what's good
for you!"

"Don't look to. But if you know what's best, you better damn well
hope I don't!"

And I never did, 'til now.

—

Standing on the flats where that swamp used to be, my prison
shoes crammed down inside poor Tad the driver's boots like insoles
and their tight-laced tops rubbing a blister on either ankle, I narrowed my eyes and swore outright: "Well, I'll be God-damned for
sure if I ain't already, which I damn well know I *am*."

"That's what I'd heard, all right, if you're who I think," a voice
replied. "So...are you?"

I turned, and there was a girl standing under a lightning-struck
locust tree with her puffy jacket's hood up and hands dug deep in
both pockets. From what-all I could glimpse of her she struck me
as blonde, or maybe just mouse with possibilities; her eyes were the

same sort of blue as her thousand-times-washed men's jeans, worn high and belted tight. Except that they were hard instead of soft, as imperturbable as cross-cut stone.

I nodded. "And who'd you be?" I asked.

"Doll Tearsheet."

"A good old name. Would that be of the Step-Stair Tearsheets?"

"The same, though we ain't been out that way since six-six or six-eight, to hear my Grandmomma tell it. I was looking to find my brother in there—Harlan Tearsheet."

"When'd he pass?"

"Now, that I don't know. But I dreamed of water three nights runnin', dark and mucky and still, with poison oak roots all through it. So I figured this might be where he was laid, probably staked down with ash." She looked down. "He was a cunning man, or tried to be."

"You don't say." I shook my head. "No man born who likes it when there's something they don't get to touch, is there? But those of Adam just ain't fit for what we do."

"I know it. He didn't."

"You got the Mark on you yet, Doll?"

"No ma'am, and I don't look to have one, either. I don't need that sort of trouble."

"Sound right knowledgeable, though, for someone ain't interested."

"I got some grammarye from an aunt of mine had Hoppard blood. 'Nough to know not to mess with it, anyhow."

"For fear of the Fire?"

"Naw, not as such. Just seems to take a toll, is all."

"It does that," I agreed. "Still, this here's a hard world for them got given a gift, and don't use it."

"True, but this here's a hard world regardless, ain't it?" She gave me a sly look, from under pale lashes. "Does seem like we're bound in the same direction, though."

"Does, at that. Care to travel in company awhile, Miss Doll?"

"If you do, sure."

"Well, then."

We walked a while in silence; I thought hard on what to do next, and she let me.

"To move a whole tract of land like that..." I said, trying the idea of it out aloud. "Take a full coven, to start with, and one of the Fallen to help. But that leaves traces, and I don't see none." I frowned, reminding myself how not everyone was quick as my Momma'd been to lie down wide-legged for anything had horns; some young witches, in particular, found the thought of it demeaning. "So—witchery *without* goety, and plenty of it; these gals were pilin' what they had together and usin' it like a toolbox. But thirteen alone wouldn't be enough. A coven of covens, then, like twenty-six strong, or thirty-nine...damn. That's a lot of airborne pussy."

Doll nodded. "That's what Harlan said that bitch Orpah Cleves was schemin' on, last time we spoke. Said she wanted to unionize."

"Oh yeah?" I snorted. "And what then—collect dues? Do up a newsletter?"

"If he was privy to her full plans, he ain't passed that part on to me. Just how he was goin' t'court day after tomorrow, send her t'jail if he could; that'd cut the head off the snake. Other ones'd go back to skin-changin' and callin' up storms after, or sendin' scarce animals after folk interfere with their crops. Weed, mostly—that was what he was plannin' on gettin' her put away with."

"Folk 'round here don't like it much when you truck with the Law, as I recall."

"That's still true. But sometimes...sometimes you gotta take help where you can."

I laughed. "And he thought to get away with it, given the numbers? *Gal.* I'd guess you already full-well know just how bad one witch can be, let alone a whole army of 'em."

Her shoulders rose, making her hood bulge like a ruff, mouth all one white line. "Told you already how he only *thought* he was cunning."

I almost shrugged myself, but thought better. From what-all she'd described, this Harlan Tearsheet sounded like someone worthy of respect, to me: Irrefutably wrong-headed, yet ambitious, too—for magic took *effort*, no matter what those barren of it might think. Took sacrifice, most often literal.

But then again, even if she no longer had it in her to respect that shiftless brother of hers, Miss Doll surely loved him still. Or she wouldn't even be here.

The woods got darker, true night. A moon rose up, then guttered, and a mighty rushing sound was heard from all corners, as something flapped 'cross it—a mess of somethings. Above, the stars went out, scratched at by a horde of besom-tails dropping downwards, out of the sky. And high overhead this foul and foggy rising wind I heard all manner of feminine voices screeching to each other, like owls after bats.

"That you and yours, Orpah Cleves?" I called up, shading my eyes.

"You know it is, Alleycat."

I almost thought I could see her hovering there, cocooned in ointment-reek and darkness, hair flapping like a flag. She'd always been the prettier of us, full-fleshed and long-legged with a high nose and flat cheekbones, those bold eyes set at a near-Indian slant. First gal I ever played 'round with; I remembered us lying in the moss next to a trickle of cold spring-water, finding faces in the tree-bark, the wind-shook green leaves, each passing cloud. Remembered her following me down the mountain, too, begging me not to let her Momma drive me off—yelling how she'd been wrong-done as well by that not-Daddy of hers, and needed my help to flush the leavings out. *'Cause I can't have his baby, I just can't, and who-all else can I cry to? God damn you, Allfair Chatwin, there's nobody I know can do the things you do!*

To which I called back: *'Cept my Momma, you catch her sober, or any ten other witches. Or you yourself, you want it so damn bad, so long's you're willin' to pay for it...*

Which she always would've had to, one way or t'other. And looking at her now, I could only guess she did.

"Hey, gal!" I said. "Been a Methuselan spell since last I heard your voice. Still and all, close like we been, you of anybody oughta know better than to put yourself in my path."

"I wouldn't, save how you already put yourself in mine."

"Uh huh. Well, c'mon, then—let's parley."

I beckoned her further down, and she came, dipping 'til her boot-heels brushed the tree-tops. A wild light flickered crown-like through her unbound tresses, or maybe just lit up those white streaks running through it, milkstone seams on a black rock-bed. Time hadn't treated her too badly—better'n myself, I'm sure, with my own hair in rat-tails, Tad's army surplus coat swimming on me and my M-vale A Wing jumpsuit-top peeled down to make the rest of it look like a pair of muddy orange slacks.

"Saw what you done with the swamp," I told her. "That's some fine work."

"Testament to the unknown strength of women in combination," she replied. "And without a single scrap of devil-might, either."

"Noticed that, too. Quite the break in tradition."

"Well, you was the one first pointed out t'me how once witches get their Mark, they turn lazy—lie 'round, act like junkies, let their familiars do all the work. And them that's lazier still go on and devil-deal directly, then settle in on gettin' petted if they do 'nough ill to satisfy and beat on if they don't, like the King o' Flies is their pimp..."

"Hold on, now. That's my Momma you're talkin' 'bout. And my *Daddy*, too."

"I've heard you say worse."

"And that's my right, like it's yours to reject all Hellish influences, if doin' so makes you feel better 'bout the damage you wreak. I ain't about to tell nobody how to practice, let alone how to preach. But I want them bones you took."

"What, Tearsheet's?" She cast Doll a contemptuous look. "That's between me, him and whoever else aims to fulfill his threats 'gainst my domain—*this* bitch, I guess, if she ain't too fear-froze to do more'n gasp over it."

I shook my head. "Hell no, I don't have one earthly care over what you do with *those*. It's Gley Chatwin's bones I'm speakin' of, and those belong to me, if they do anybody."

"Hmmm." A beat went by, her riding the forest's hat and me not breaking gaze, hands curled in my pockets, 'til: "Naw, can't let you have them neither, Alleycat. Not when I know what you want 'em for."

"You go cold turkey, so everyone else has to? That ain't any sort of democracy I ever heard of."

"More like an enlightened monarchy, I 'spose. Every coven needs its devil, if only 'cause they're used to the idea; I'm it, for now, 'til they learn better. And when I die, my bones go back in the pot, community property, to be held in trust."

"Fine for you, very enlightened. But it ain't a policy you get to start with somebody's already damn well dead, not when there's someone else has a prior claim. So bring out them bones—her brother's, too, just 'cause you got me offended. I ain't about to say it twice."

"Look where you are, where you been. You got no power over me."

"What I am is Gley Chatwin's only child, a sick ball a' witchery cut up with Hellfire, and everything you know, you learned from *me*. Not to mention how where I *been* is ten years outta *this* shit-hole, with time enough to think and read on things you ain't ever even heard of—time to practice 'em, too. You really want to throw down?"

"Goddamnit, Allfair...this ain't none of your business! You run off, remember? Left all the mess for me. Well, I cleaned it up, and now I get to keep what I caught. So pack up little miss Won't-Do-Her-Duty here, and get the hell out of my woods."

"Uh uh, woman. *You* get outta *my* sky."

Orpah widened her eyes at that, just long enough for me to jerk Tad's Patton gun from my waistband, hork a wad of spit and blood down the barrel, and shoot. It hit her in the shoulder, sending her spinning; she gave out a cry, cast a handful of witch-balls down, narrowly missing me and Miss Doll both. "Run, gal! While you still can!" I yelled her way, but she stood there, seemingly spot-rooted with fear, 'til I had no leisure time left to pay her any further notice.

For that wind was back, all at once and all around, lowering in like a storm, clouds abruptly black with the shadows of other witches rising up to Orpah's defence.

I kept on horking and firing, enspelled bullets popping apart into stinging fetch-gnat swarms, but eventually, those ran out. A half-second after she heard my hammer click twice, Orpah came swooping down so she and me were almost within kissing range. "Might be jail ain't left you quite as smart as you made out, if that's all you got," she told me.

I laughed again. "Or might be this here's where I all the time aimed to end up, so thanks for playin'."

Orpah snapped her teeth at me like a dog, then opened her mouth a bit further, like she was fixing to retch out a fresh curse-hex all over my mocking face. But before she could, young Doll slid some sort of stoppered-up hooch-bottle she'd been keeping up her sleeve out into her palm, and whipped far enough forward she could bust it quick-smart 'cross Orpah's high-set nose. Announcing, as she did: "That's her, so go to it!"

While Orpah yowled, something like a squished-down ferret jumped clear as the glass broke, unwinding itself mid-air into a flapping skin-cloak, wide and flat as a furry, airborne ray. It engulfed most've Orpah, and set in to squeeze. Her face, already bloody, straightaway begun turning purple; I could hear a couple bones crack, or maybe just grind. The broom veered off one way, her body another, plunging to the dirt-and-weed-entangled forest floor. Above, meanwhile, the coven of covens all shrieked out together at the feel of it and dipped off in varying directions, too stunned to keep up their bombardment.

Best friend I ever had, I thought, and shrugged. Then grabbed Doll by that same sleeve and whisked her aside, into a pocket between two trees, a trail no one but me could see, or step on. "Hey!" she yelled, or started to, but shut up admirably fast, once my finger sealed her lips.

"Hush," I told her. "That was the whole of your plan right there, yeah? Pretty much?"

A sullen teenaged nod.

"Then hurry up and keep quiet, you ever want to see that wayward brother of yours again, 'cause I got somethin' else entirely in mind—somethin' you'd never think of, not in a million years."

"You don't know me so well, ma'am."

"Oh no?"

———

Certain principles run 'cross all cultures, as Samaire Cornish could probably tell you. Hell, she probably did a dissertation on it. Our Lady of the Upside-Down is one of these, queen of the primal Ds: Death, Despair, Darkness, Decay. In old Sumer, they called her Ereshkigal, who hung Her trespassing sister Inanna's naked body at Her gates like a rag on a stick; 'round Mexico way she's *La Flaca*, the Skinny One—Santa Muerte, Beautiful Death, patroness of assassins and thieves. And here on the mountain?

Here, we call her the Rot-Pearl Queen, the Chigger's Bride, who does away with every secret thing left to lie untended in the deepest of the hillside thickets. She who carries the will-o'-the-wisp and leads poor travelers astray, her stiff hair full of tiny clattering bones and dead leaves. She whose footsteps leave little black holes of mould, whose hand is white as peeled birch-bark, whose lightest touch means madness.

Most run to avoid her, and never speak her name aloud; most barely dare to think it, lest she catch its echo, and attend.

But like we've discussed already, on several different occasions—I ain't most.

—

"That thing you threw," I tossed back at Doll, as she pulled herself headlong through a brake of dead blackberry thorns, barely pausing to hiss where they tore what little skin her jacket left unwrapped. "Old Harlan's demon familiar, right?"

She nodded. "Found it buzzin' 'round his place like a two-pound mosquito, all pissed; must've been feedin' it bits of himself, I reckon, since he didn't have nothin' else on offer. So I drew blood into that bottle, waited 'til it climbed inside, and...like you saw."

"Hard for a man to get hold of one of those without bearing a true Mark, willingness to bleed or no. Though it can be done, so long's you're willing to bed down in strange places—as old Bishop Gorlois found out when he raised up that many-mouthed starfish of a thing and bound it to the Olek Psaltery, charging it to make sure his grimoire'd survive the Burning Times, even if he didn't. For once they've had a taste of human meat given, not taken, they never do like it when somebody else cuts off their supply."

She nodded, mouth twisting, a weird shred of pride overtaking her close-kept game face. "So might be he *was* cunning, after all."

Might be. For all this was proof how Harlan Tearsheet'd likely done at least enough research to point him towards something half-forgot, hungry after worship the way a junkie hungers after his or her jolt of choice. The Queen, in other words.

Those who did Her service got service in return: They weren't any harder to kill, but harder by far to keep dead. A useful quality in general, but particularly so right now, given both our specific goals.

"Where are we?" Doll asked, glancing 'round, distrustingly. Smart as she'd proven to be, I was sure she'd probably already cottoned on to the fact that the trees were growing widdershins and wrong-way-'round, that the very ground beneath our feet had an unfamiliar lack of give to it, that the stars above were knit in patterns unseen for millennia: We were elsewhere, having shimmied ourselves straight through the mirror-surface gate of the Queen's domain without her initial notice, albeit with my full connivance.

"Oh, never you mind," I replied, smiling. "Real question should be—who is it lives here, exactly? And what are we gonna offer Her for safe passage, when She realizes we're already at her door?"

Such pretty eyes Miss Doll had, 'specially when they flew all the way open like that. And when I caught them starting to narrow again as she glimpsed something over my shoulder, coming through the trees—while I heard for myself the creak and sigh and moan of its passage, those same trees contorting away to let it through, like they feared to let its skirts brush their roots. I knew we really were in the right place, after all.

"Your Majesty," I said, turning, my head hung down respectfully. "I come to give You sad news of one dear to Your heart, and beg a boon meant to help repair his circumstances, likewise."

Her voice was soft, like a corpse well time-seasoned for dismemberment 'fore digging commenced; it spiraled up from inside like a tapeworm you hadn't known you harboured, unspooling segment by segment, fit to make you retch. But I stayed right where I was, and let it wash over me, wash through me, a maggoty wave of awful. I knew I could take it.

Witch-woman, devil-child, you enter my realm uninvited, without parole. You bring your apprentice here under false pretenses, and walk without respect, disturbing everything. You constitute a living insult. Why should I forgive you?

"Because, my Queen...I do it for love."

From my first kiss on, I've been able to fool with just about anyone, I put my mind to it—always could. Some people might call that a curse (the white coats have a specialized name for it: Polymorphous perversity), but I choose to take it as a gift; the gift of turning trash into treasure, no matter the circumstances. In other words, I can find a thrill on any given dungheap, even with the heap itself, and while I'm in the thick of it, it will be real. Or seem so.

Six of one, I say.

Do not think to play with my affections, Allfair Chatwin. Perverse as you are, you hold no true desire for me.

"Maybe not, but Harlan Tearsheet did, sure enough; does still, wherever he might be. And this gal loves *him*, in turn—enough to come here. Don't that count for anything?"

Should it?

"I think so. Oh, fear is easier to call up than love, by far—but the best sort of worship comes from both, don't you find?"

Apparently, she did.

—

This next part is somewhat hard to talk about, and harder to think on. Yet it had to be done.

Never thought of myself as much of a teacher. That's too like mothering, by far. But right here is where I gave Doll Tearsheet a lesson in true *magie noire*, with its pleasures and pains admixed—showed her how there's always a price, just like I told you, and you can't hire nobody else to pay it for you. And it can't be too small, what you give up; can't be too easy, or they don't like that. You gotta feel like you're actually payin'.

I asked and was given, which meant I owed, so I paid. I gave myself over, stuck my hand in the tiger's mouth—my left, both dominant and sinister—and trusted I'd get at least enough of it back to go on with. Felt the Rot-Pearl Queen's tongue lick away flesh and skin and sinew together from my ring-finger, debriding it 'til there wasn't nothing left but naked bone gone cold and stiff as marble, a corpsefinder-candle alit with dim blue flame; bit my lip 'til it bled, but I never gave out even a squeak, 'cause I knew that'd pile insult on insult. And this was justabout the last place on earth I wanted to try and leave while yet unforgiven.

You have grit, witch-woman. Backbone. The Queen's words traced each of my vertebrae in turn, told them in turn, an ossuary rosary. *Let us say you find my acolyte and release him—for this, I will consider our business concluded. But as to your apprentice...*

"Don't think she considers herself such, Majesty," I managed, through a torn, sour-salt mouthful.

This distinction means nothing to me. She will have to make her own peace, in her own way.

"Might be you tell her that yourself, then."

I felt Her dreadful gaze shift off me, to where Doll stood once more statue-rigid, studying the turf under our feet. And: *Oh, I know she hears me,* she said, with just a hint of amusement, a spreading black-on-black stain. *Do you not, little girl? Perhaps you will take on your brother's burden, like any sin-eater, once he has done his purpose—if you wish to bury him again after, that is, and leave him to his rest. If you wish him to lie still, when you do.*

Doll shivered a bit herself at that, like she was shaking off the ague. And then we were alone again once more, together—back in the world, with only my single-digit Hand of Glory to light our way through a forest so dark, so deep, it was like we were walking the ocean's floor at its very lowest point, where nothing lives that's ever seen a hint of sun at all.

We walked a long way, mainly in silence, but we did find that swamp, eventually. I knew it for what it was the moment my foot touched water, not least 'cause my finger went out—knelt down in the cold and sucking mud right there to plunge both hands in like Pontius Pilate, mouthing my heartfelt thanks, and let something all-too-familiar 'neath the surface wrench the damn thing free like a frozen-off wart, juncture already itchy-healed.

No wedding ring for me, I thought, without a shred of regret. Then got back up, all a-creak with effort, and brushed my knees off, best I could. "Now," I told Doll, "given what-all I've expended thus far, there's a couple of somethin's I need from *you* in return, missy."

Dubious: "Like what?"

"First off, a bit of witch-work, which I know you're familiar with, for all you say you ain't interested: Shed a drop or two of blood and let it tug on you, then study, 'til you find where that boy of yours lies sunk. And conjuration skill aside, I'll just bet you know how to cook a meal using whatever you find, too, don't you? Most mountain-folk do."

"...Uh huh."

"All right, then. Get cracking."

—

What Doll put together was a mess of handy, hardy fare, such as my Momma and I'd sometimes subsisted on, whenever she blew her Welfare check on cheap liquor and bad men: sorrel tubers sliced sidelong and stick-roasted, with watercress and chicken-of-the-woods mushrooms for seasoning, and a dark, flat bread baked from cattail flower and acorn-meat in our fire's ashes to serve it on, like them edible platters in Ethiopian restaurants. I helped here and there in the preparation, but felt the spell'd work better if the meal was made mainly by a loved one's hands.

"Now lay it out," I told her. "Like you're servin' Sunday dinner. Go on, gal."

"Where?"

"On *him*, of course."

I flipped my hand a tad dramatically at the part of the swamp she'd scoped, and up rose Harlan Tearsheet's body in response, or what was left of it. Outer bits'd mostly been gnawed away, with the rest of it froze underwater for some good time, gone thin and sere and slippy; his teeth grinned like keys on a busted-up piano, eyes sunk so far back in his head you could hardly reckon their colour anymore, canted so they stared two entirely different ways.

Doll drew her breath and didn't let it back out, like she was fortifying herself, or at least trying her best not to heave. But at this point, I think she'd seen enough of my works to trust I knew best what I was doing.

A string of hors d'oeuvres, still lightly smoking, trailing from throat to sternum to belly. She took one, bit the tiniest piece off and crunched hard, her tears silent, crying and chewing—offered me the rest, which I took a far larger bite of, seeing I'd barely had any food at all, the last twenty-four hours or so. Not since the Cornishes and I'd blasted our way out of prison on the wings of old Abramelin the Mage's famous SATOR box...

It was better than you'd think, but not by much. And at the third chew in a row, old Harlan sat up straight-backed, as if run on strings. Turned his flap-jawed face my way, and said, in a voice still deep-buried: "That all looks good. Is it?"

Doll's puke-face was back, full force. I just shrugged. "Hard to tell, without you taste it. Want some?"

"Well...just a bite."

"Care for a sip of something, too, to wash it down?"

"Wouldn't say no. I'm powerful dry."

I nodded, and withdrew a half-bottle of rye whiskey I'd found in Tad's inner pocket. Harlan slugged it down, what was left of his throat working queasily, then handed it back, peering.

"Don't know you, do I?" he asked. "'Cause...you got some of the Queen's aspect to you, if I ain't mistaken."

"Don't know me, no, I wouldn't suppose. But I do know Her, and you—through that sister of yours, over there."

Another creaky turn, slick in its socket, sickness-greased. "Doll... that you, gal? Told you not to go messin' with my business, didn't I?"

Doll snorted. "You's the one went 'n got yourself killed, Harlan—left me an' the younger kids in a lurch so bad, had to turn 'em over to the State 'til I can produce you in court. Was stickin' your thumb in Orpah Cleves' eye worth all that?"

"She come at me crossways, when I wasn't lookin'. That ain't my fault."

"Her comin' at you any ways at all, that *is* your damn fault! Now I need you to go on to the nearest station and say your piece 'fore witnesses, then come back and lie yourself down again. Court or no, once you're on record, won't matter a piss in a windstorm if they never see you again—hell, it'll only prove you right, and Orpah that much more ready to kill to pay you back for whatever you said."

"Look at me, sissy. I ain't exactly fit to set under no hot lights."

Since Doll'd already done the heavy lifting, I thought I might as well throw in. "Might be I could lay a glamour would get you lookin' human-shaped once more, without even the stink to put a lie to it. How'd that be?"

They looked to each other, then back to me, and nodded just the once, in unison.

By the time Harlan set off to do what he'd pledged, he looked thin and mangy still, but more like a meth-head than the walking dead. Turned out those eyes of his were a slightly darker shade of blue than Doll's, his beard so fair it only showed at an angle. Doll and I huddled up in them swamp-side trees and dug deep, using the leaves and muck for cover, to dream the next half-day away. Letting my eyes drift shut, I chewed a few nightshade berries and slipped my body's bonds, hovering above the tree-line 'til I thought I glimpsed where Orpah might be laid in recovery—not her Momma's old trailer, but one awful similar. Saw her inner circle knitting hands all 'round her, greasing her wounds with a soothing slather of dogwood, club moss spores and Englishman's Foot rendered up in unbaptized baby-fat, while they roasted what was left of Harlan's familiar on the hot-plate; I guessed they probably meant to feed it to her later, maybe in a stew. For that'd get her back on her feet for sure, and smartish...but not quite fast enough.

I opened my eyes again to find Doll already upright, braced like a human pointer-dog, as Harlan shouldered his clumsy way back through the bushes, duty done and glamour long-dropped. Looking like nothing so much as a rag-doll stitched together from green meat whose joints were already giving way under pressure, and grateful-glad indeed to do so.

"Ma'am...sis," he managed. "That's an awful long way, ain't it? Here, and back."

Doll blinked, fiercely. "Ain't done both, just yet," was all she said.

"Well, take it from me. I do crave a rest."

"Lie down, then," I suggested.

"Can't. You know why."

We all did: He'd vowed himself to the Queen, to do Her worship and spread ill in Her name. Wouldn't get to quit 'til She Herself called halt, if She ever did. But then again...She had offered an alternative arrangement, too. As Miss Doll well knew.

I watched her a while, wondering if she'd share that knowledge, or what she'd do with it, after. For moral dilemmas do amuse me, when there's no other entertainment to be had.

"I'll take it on, then," she said, at last, so soft it was like she was talking straight into her own neck. And then...

...it was after, their pact sealed with a kiss, Harlan's barely skin-wrapped bones tumbled once more half-nude and sticky on the ground at Doll's boots. She had a trace of him still left on her mouth, black as axle-grease, and a look on her face like she didn't know whether to spit vitriol or bust out crying. A spasm shook her from the solar plexus out, a spectral upper-cut, but she didn't let it defeat her; just gasped, laid one palm on the place where I could only assume her long-deferred Mark was finally coming in, then straightened up once more, tall and proud. And licked her lips.

I clapped my hands, grinning. "Gal," I said, "here's proof the Queen misspoke, not that She'd ever admit it, 'cause you got grit truer than most I've seen. For just like Harlan stood up for you, you stood up for him, like I somehow knew you would—and now, your brother's debt is yours."

"That ain't what I wanted."

"No, but it's what you got. Listen, though: It's better this way, truly. Better you be what you are, 'cause the other don't work out—never, not really. No matter how much you might like it to." Saw her squint around a bit while I was talking, and knew her full

Sight must be coming in; this was only confirmed when her gaze wandered back my way, shock of what she saw making her gasp once more, and louder. Gently: "Yeah, that's right. So how do I look now, in my full ornament?"

"Like...somethin' I can't stand to see, hardly."

"Hmmm. Then you really do been holdin' out, pretty girl; what-all *you* got's far more'n just a smidge, and always was. Go on and enjoy it, while you can."

She gave a bitter, hitching little laugh of her own at that. "Think Orpah and hers'll stay content to let me roam, now they know I been workin' against 'em in *your* company?"

"Aw, well, now...I wouldn't worry yourself too much about *her*."

———

Nearest motel was in Step-Stair itself, though Doll left me long before that, trudging down-road with what-all I could find of my Momma hugged in both arms like a makeshift pouch-cum-bundle wrought from the skirt of Tad's hellacious-long jacket. Orpah and hers had rendered her skeleton like animals, cracked half the bones and cut the rest all to rounds for small magicks. But I'd found one gone hollow yet otherwise intact, maybe part of her femur, a one-note flute. I let 'em dry a while on the radiator while I had myself a nice, long hot shower, first in my clothes, then out of 'em. And then, once my jumpsuit, undershirt, bra, panties and socks were hung up on the show-rod to reassume their natural colours, I sat down naked and cross-legged to breath a few long, low breaths through that last piece of the woman I'd come from, waiting to see just how long it'd take before her voice came moaning out the other end.

...Whaaaat is't yooouuuu...waaaant fr'm meeee, Allfair...?

A bare whisper, marrow-caught: "You know, Momma."

A sigh came back, then a long silence. Followed, like night follows day, by this:

...Lisssstennn...

I put my ear to the bone's mouth and did, hard. And when I was done I said, "Thank you, ma'am," like any dutiful daughter, before crushing the fragile little tube of calcium and rot to dust with my bare hands, letting the last of it fall free onto the towel I sat on.

—

For this is what she'd told me, at least in part: Every coven does have its devil, just like Orpah said. But whoever it is ain't never the Adversary Himself, any more than every corner-shop drug dealer's the Man. Hell's a franchise that way, like any given Piggly-Wiggly. And back in Chatouye, France, where my kin come from, that devil was one of them who chose wrongside-wise during the Schism—a mighty creature, silver-tongued and armed to the back teeth, well-versed in every sort of chaos. When I'd last seen him, he'd looked like a man, dark-bearded and sad-eyed as any given Homeland Security wanted poster sketch, but back when my Momma first saw him, he might've looked somewhat different. Still, I didn't much care so I didn't ask, and she certainly didn't volunteer.

He knew *my* name, of course—that'd been the basic point of my meeting him at all. And now, thanks to Gley Chatwin's new-laid ghost, I finally knew his.

"Come to my call, first of my blood; come quiet, come sweet, in a form most pleasing to my eyes, meaning me no harm. O Raum Goetim, teacher of warcraft and morality, I invoke thee: *Venez, venez, diable des belledames Chatouyennes. Venez, o antrecessor. Venez, venez, prince et pere. Venez, dieu.*"

I shut my eyes and waited, expecting—hell, I don't know. A bad smell. A scratch at the door, like claws. A pounding of hooves along the roof and a clatter down where the motel should've had a chimney. But when I opened them, all I saw was Samaire Cornish sitting 'cross from me, with eyes the colour of cancer and pupils set slant as a goat's.

All at once, I recalled my rude state, and blushed. Felt my nipples come up so hard under the double ropes of my hair that they fair turned sideways, too.

"Gley's gal, is it?" this vision asked, soft enough, though it ran all through me like a hot shiver. "Haven't seen you in...hmmm. Never at all, I think, as an adult. Should I be insulted that you only seem to require my presence now, when you so obviously want something... or someone?"

"Hadn't thought you'd kept that firm a track on me, frankly."

"Seeing how many other seeds I've sown, over the years? But perhaps I'm sentimental that way, little Alleycat." "She" leaned closer, voice dropping further yet. "Still, I notice you don't answer."

"There *is* a gal I'm lookin' to find, yes. We got unfinished business, her and me."

"A woman such as you, I'm sure, could find more than your share of girls."

"No doubt, but none like this one. I think you might recall *her* Momma too, somewhat—Moriam Cornish?"

"Aaaah, yes. Sweet little Morah, reduced to salt and slime; her man fought monsters, so she made herself even more of one, to help him. But blood told in the end, as it always does. For hunted to truck with hunter is an invariably foolish choice."

"S'pose so," I agreed. "And yet..."

"And yet?"

Yet I was willing to test that theory nonetheless, loath though I might suddenly find myself to say so. But then again, it wasn't like I had to; "she" laughed out loud at the very thought, mocking Samaire's natural gravity. And I shivered again, want run all up and down and through me like a skewer, at the idea I might one day be able to make this illusion's sombre prototype chuckle the same way—if only a little bit, for a very little while.

Still wearing my sister's shape, my Daddy laid his hot hand on my forehead, invisible claws denting my skin, heavy with the thrown-star weight of frustrated millennia. And he told me what to do.

Family. Like I've said before, no matter where the various and disparate elements of yours may come from, once seen in action...it really is *something*.

—

Piece by piece, throughout the coming night, I pulverized the rest of Gley Chatwin's bones, making 'em into a sort of marrow-laced, grey-brown porridge. That handful on the towel I mixed my own blood with, fashioning it into a drab little wren-sized bird. The rest, meanwhile, I ate with a spoon rooked from the motel's restaurant, mouthful by gritty mouthful. And wished them into Orpah Cleves as I did—her stomach, her bowels, her bloodstream—for if she wanted my Momma's power so damnable much, I reckoned, she could just go on and choke on it, like them gals at Salem vomiting up their irons nails and rag-dollies and soaking hanks of hair.

Let her be filled so full it made a cage 'round her heart, a bone-meal box locked so tight that weary muscle couldn't even beat, let alone bust itself free; let her worshippers find her in the evening still and stiff, red lips gone blue, a discreet touch of vomit in her stormy hair.

For power has its price, after all.

Oh, I still think on Doll Tearsheet sometimes, unlike those fools the M-vale psych hoped I'd hold in my heart; think on her hard-bitten love for that brother of hers, the burden she'd fought so hard not to have to carry. I didn't begrudge her attempts to skew fate, either. Everyone'd dodge a bullet if they could, 'specially those can see it comin'.

But in the end, like Orpah—who I'd known far longer, and more intimately—she was just one more piece of collateral damage in my life's long rampage. Sweet Maybelle Pine, for example, who was my helpmeet and accomplice in lockdown, and who I do keep a small part of my memory left clear for, if only to recall how good she'd been at her marital duties. Or wonder, in turn, over how she could ever've been stunned enough to think she had to kill herself over me, when I'd gone so far out of my way to make sure she wouldn't have to.

Some people just don't like to be left behind, is all. While others—myself included—expect it. Because even when we're cheek-to-jowl with "normal" people, it's like there's no one else there at all.

Didn't have to be that way, though. Not anymore.

The bird, through whose tiny blinking eyes I aimed to glimpse the object of my desire, shook itself slowly awake, regarding me with that *Let me do thy will, Lady* fetch-stare. Then crept onto my palm so's I could throw it up into the air and watch it flap off north-wards with its tiny beak open, scenting the air for any trace of my something-sister's trail.

Mark me, Princess, I thought, hoping 'gainst hope that Samaire Cornish might somehow hear me, if only in her dreams. *I'm comin'. Straight as the little dust-bird flies, though maybe not quite that straight. Ain't no chain gonna hold me down, and nothin' in my way that'll be left standing, after—that sister of yours very much included.*

But first, I needed me a ride. So I paid my bill with the last of Tad's cash, strode out to the parking lot's gate, cocked my hip, stuck out my thumb...and grinned.

IMAGINARY
BEAUTIES

...hitherto we have been permitted to seek beauty only in the morally good—a fact which sufficiently accounts for our having found so little of it and having had to seek about for imaginary beauties without backbone!—As surely as the wicked enjoy a hundred kinds of happiness of which the virtuous have no inkling, so too they possess a hundred kinds of beauty; and many of them have not yet been discovered.
—R.J. Hollingdale's translation of
Friedrich Nietzsche's *Daybreak*

Rice Petty was leant up against the University of Toronto Medical Sciences Building cafeteria wall with Rammstein blasting in one ear, admiring the slick purple vinyl sheen of her own boots and wondering idly if she could get away with charging (yet another) new strap-on to her Daddy's Visa, when Horatia Wint slouched in: all head to toe in black, a weird Renaissance-style sugar-loaf wool cap with a gold brocade top jammed haphazardly down over her ears, dripping melted snow from the January blizzard outside. She stood there a moment shaking her head, waiting for her glasses to unfog; as they did, Rice saw her eyes were both slightly squinted against even this dim light, and probably far larger than that heinous degree of prescription made them look—a pale, peculiarly penetrating shade of green, like mouthwash, or maybe absinthe. Her nose was snub, her jaw square, her mouth decisive. She didn't look like she had any friends, or wanted any.

And: *Oh yeah, uh huh, save some of that for* me, *please. Hey baby, hey baby, hey.*

For Rice, it was violent pull at first (close-up) sight—like, lust, whatever. Certainly worth a walk-by, anyhow.

After relentlessly and heteronormatively fucking her way through high school, Rice had called dick break in university (with occasional time-outs to peg some random male bitch, here and there), and was enjoying the result; nice to have a different sort of reputation, if nothing else.

Meanwhile, though she'd also thus far coasted through her courses by playing the hypercognate card—previously registering Horatia's existence mainly through smart-dar, as potential competition rather than possible prey—Rice knew her own complicity in accepting that particular categorization had always been little more than a scam, a quick hit of public recognition without academic expectations. Sure, she had enough eidetic memory to ace any test she'd ever taken, but her study habits were for shit—and it was there, in the personal projects part of the equation, where the cracks were already starting to show.

Where Rice'd always excelled were the soft-skill areas of social intelligence: linking, cross-referencing, playing seat-of-the-pants mix-and-match games with names, faces, relationships, motivations. All the things that übergeeks like Horatia, the real deal in terms of sheer cerebral cannon-power, found either too boring or contemptible to master.

Notoriety clung to both of them in roughly equal amounts, an ill halo—automatic separation from the herd. It gave them something in common, a connection virtually begging to be built on. Add up the sum of *these* parts, and whatever alchemical combination you ended up with would probably blister paint, eat through walls, dissolve fools on contact: major damage in a Klein bottle, times two by infinity. And fuck knew, Rice had never felt up to resisting *that* sort of open challenge.

As Horatia scouted 'round for a seat, eventually deciding on the caf's single least passers-by-accessible table, Rice pondered her plan of attack. She knew she must be having a pretty good face day, judging by the cat-calls she'd gotten on her way down-campus, and that gave her an extra advantage.

As Horatia popped her MacBook Air open, revealing a screen mostly occupied with some chemical equation roughly the size of Pi to 1,000, Rice did a complex, basketball-inspired shimmy through the crowd and slid right in next to her, so close she was almost in Horatia's lap. "Hey," she said, grinning. "Antisocial much?"

Horatia scowled without looking around. "Do I know you?"

"Rice Petty, major Chem, minor Bio. And you—*you're* Horatia Wint, Girl Genius. Got the full ride on home-school, did 100 across the boards on your entrance exams, won that big…*thing* last year…"

"The Lasky Award for Excellence in Chemical Recombination Studies?"

"…Yeah, that's it, comes with $25,000 and a lab grant; think we've got, like…Prions for Perverts together, or whatever." Rice leaned a little further forward, deliberately invading Horatia's space to see what she'd do in response, if anything (answer: wrinkle her nose and stare at Rice like she'd grown another head, apparently). Then cocked her skull to one side while resting her chin on her steepled hands, and continued: "But anyhoo, enough shop talk…you like cunnilingus?"

"What?"

"Well, I'm just throwin' it out there, man. In my experience, though, most chicks do."

Horatia considered her again, a bit longer, and more closely. "Why are you even talking to me?" she asked at last.

Rice shrugged. "'Cause you're the only one here?"

"This place is full of people."

"Well, sure." Murmuring: "But, see…I've slept with most of them already."

—

131

Back at Gilmore Petty's West End screw-pad, to which Rice had had a copied key since she was around fifteen, Horatia watched with studied I'm-so-not-impressed 'tude as Rice cooked her up a quick batch of home-made MDMA. An hour later, she was explaining her thesis research to Rice at top speed and volume, gesticulating like she was on crack; a half-hour after *that*, Rice had her bent over the breakfast buffet, her tongue in Horatia's ear, three soaked fingers and an equally-wet thumb urging her girlie parts towards full, fist-ready dilation.

Why would she have even taken that first hit? On some level, Rice supposed, Horatia probably thought she was immune—that she could defeat simple chemistry through sheer Nietzschean will-to-power. The basic fact was, really smart people could sometimes do the dumbest shit imaginable; Rice herself was living proof of that truism. For most of her sexually-mature life, Rice had taken deliberate pride in cultivating a policy of enthusiastic polymorphous perversity—*live life to its most lurid extremes* was her motto, paraphrasing Rimbaud (or possibly Verlaine). In her time she'd seduced teachers, friends' parents and parents' friends, the occasional pet; she'd inserted any object inside her which would fit, plus many which really didn't (though she'd certainly had fun trying to make them). Hell, she'd spent the better part of Prom Night sucking off her best-friend-who-was-a-boy's same-sex date in the faculty lounge girls' washroom, while simultaneously taping the whole encounter for later YouTube distribution on camera-phone. If it was doable at all, she'd pretty much already done it.

But even in a short life of complex thrills, sex with Horatia had to qualify as a serious career high. Cold and efficient to near-Spockian degrees under almost every other circumstance, Horatia had no moral hangups, a vivid carnal imagination (Rice suspected she'd attended the School of Porn for some time now, functional virgin or not), double-jointed thumbs, and seldom remembered to wear underpants. Considering her entire *modus vivendi* revolved around a constant diet of hypertension and overwork, it probably shouldn't have been any sort of surprise that with the proper encouragement she could—and did—go off like a string of firecrackers.

They spent the next day in bed after a pleasantly exhausting night out of it, in various other locations (and positions). Rice lounged back and watched Horatia elaborate on the experiment that'd consumed her life up to this point, eventually breaking in to clarify—

"So you're working on, like…human flesh spackle."

Horatia, flushing: "I most certainly am *not*."

Rice really had to laugh, long and loud. "Aw, c'mon! You know you are, man—that's *exactly* what it is, and that's totally fine; very…chick-friendly. Very marketable."

"It's a damn *cellular matrix force-growth reagent* in a *collagen unguent base*, you whore."

"Comes in a jar? Goes on with a spreader?"

"…I hate you."

Ah, but *that* didn't last too long.

—

Just supposed to be a simple hook-up, a trick, like everything—or everyone—else Rice did. But she found herself taking Horatia's numbers anyhow, and actually using them; indisputably, there was something about finally having another high-three-digit IQ case on speed-dial. Besides which, Horatia had…qualities, and those qualities were already starting to grow on Rice like sympathetic mold. Rice soon got used to having her around in the background while she ran through her normal daily grind of low-level super-villainy—-so much so, after a lamentably short while, it almost seemed like she couldn't function optimally without Horatia. Which was…

(creepy)

…evolution, maybe. Like calling to like. And likin' it.

By the end of February, Rice had bought Horatia in on the bottom floor of an only half-built, all-but-discontinued condo out near the old abandoned sugar factory on Lakeshore, and put up for a bunch of shiny new lab equipment on top of it. A few weeks later, she let her dorm roommates kick her out at last, and moved in too. By April, when her Dad wanted to know just where the fuck her perfect GPA had gone and just what the fuck those $40,000 worth of unspecified expenses on his Visa bill were, she told him to go screw himself and he told her—fucking finally—that she was officially cut off. Annoying, but not unexpected.

After all, it wasn't like she didn't have a viable back-up plan.

—

But: "Listen," said Horatia, with surprising patience, "I am not going to let you boil the greatest potential discovery of the 21st century down for parts and sell it as a recreational drug, just because we have bills to pay. I'm just *not*, Clarice."

"Rice, please. 'Clarice' is Doctor Lecter's long-distance crush."

Horatia rolled her eyes. "Why would you want everybody to think your parents named you after a staple foodstuff?"

"Why would your parents really-for-truly name *you* anything that reduces down to 'ho'? 'Cause that kinda had to suck, back in school, right?"

"Moving on…"

It was April 22, Earth Day. Good time of the year for moral debates, but Horatia's position on this one would've rung a whole lot stronger had she not just been turned down for a follow-up grant to her now-exhausted Lasky Award funds—as Rice well knew, having overheard at least one half of the entire shrieking phone call which preceded this particular plot twist.

As far as Rice could make out, the Lasky Foundation's main objections had seemed to be A) but what are we supposed to *do* with something that keeps functionally dead rats alive indefinitely, yet unable to breed? ("Sell it to rich people who think they're too important to die at a ridiculously inflated price, you morons!" Horatia had screamed. "Then use half the initial profit to mass-produce it, give it out gratis to everybody else, and freeze Earth's population explosion!") Which then led directly into B) shut the fuck up, you freak.

"You do get how you just kinda shot your credibility wad there, right?" Rice had asked, helpfully, after Horatia threw the phone across the room. "I mean, fighting Death-the-archetype *mano a mano* for the salvation of the world is…pretty cool, but to the corporate mindset? Counter-productive, to say the least. They *want* mortality left in the equation, man. Makes it a whole lot easier to sell people shit they don't really need, when they're scared."

"I took the same Intro to Microeconomics requirement you did, thank you very much."

"Okay, sure. But were you actually paying attention? Or were you maybe just working on Reagent Draft One under the table, while making fun of the prof's heinous nose hair?"

To which Horatia snarled something unintelligible under her breath, so Rice began again, taking it nice and reasonable.

"Look," she said, "you already stacked the deck at the design stage so this stuff would induce euphoria, right? With no side effects?"

"That we've *seen*, yet."

Rice nodded. "And you *could* make a lot of it, pretty fast, if you needed to."

Horatia, shrugging: "Absolutely. But I don't need to."

And there it was again: Horatia's marvelous people-blindness—so endearingly hilarious when watching her trample over everybody else's feelings, so infuriating once you realized she really didn't even grasp that you *had* them too.

"Don't you?" Rice leant back in her chair as if the whole topic was boring her. "'Case you hadn't noticed, 'Rache, you're not the only one whose income just dried up—I mean, you do remember who paid for all this, right?" A dismissive wave at the lab. "Sure, you could take what you've got to any major Big Pharma group, but you know they'd keep you on rats for at least another ten years, and you could lose intellectual property rights at almost any stage of that curve." Sly: "This'd be just like skipping straight to human trials...if you can even call junkies human."

"Says the woman who thinks 'E' makes any first date better. And you'd find a paying customer base—where, exactly?"

"Where wouldn't I? Some of my best friends...oh, all right, more like all of 'em, actually. Everyone I've ever taken a class with, shared a club with, hooked up with..."

"...Except for me, that is."

Now it was Rice's turn to nod, her grin stretching wider, as she locked Horatia's hot gaze with her own, even hotter, stare. "All except for you, yes."

Horatia did hem, haw and fume a bit more after that, but by post-Afternoon Delight snack-time, it was a fully done deal. They attacked the sub-equation together that night, worked 'til 5:30 a.m., and spent the rest of the weekend on cooking/packaging. Friday evening after that, the hot new party favour known as "reA" was officially out on the street. Rice hit the circuit with fifty tiny baggies stashed in her purse's lining, wearing a winning combination of Victoria's Secret lingerie on top, red pleather fetish gear on bottom: salesperson mode, plausible and charming. Her twin trade secrets were a head-full of previous contacts and a complete willingness to do that all-important first little bump while her targets watched, ostensibly to prove she wasn't "wearing a wire," or some shit.

Test passed, the marks soon took a snort of their own, and sagged back, eyelids fluttering—*oh* man, *shit, that's* good! Followed at speed by the one-hit-you're-hooked routine of immediately double-dipping, rubbing it on their gums, all the while wondering out loud: *Uh, Rice…it wears off kinda fast…can you, like, shoot this stuff, or what?*

Well—

—let's find out, shall we?

—

Sometime later, Rice, too, would have occasion to wonder, the way she once had on Horatia's own behalf. *So why* did *I even take that first hit, anyway?* Fully knowing, in her heart—and elsewhere—the only possible correct answer:

…Oh yeah. 'Cause I thought I was immune, too. Or indestructible, at the very least…

And the funny thing, in hindsight? *That* was the part which turned out to be true.

—

Start-up fees alone kept their penetration of the Greater Toronto Area's synthetic drug market fairly shallow at first, though Horatia's demented insistence on tracking—and analyzing—their clients' habit-based bell-curves rendered functional invisibility not really an option. Still, Rice made sure they stayed close to the radar, if not actually under it. She had no doubt their main competitors knew of them, but it seemed unlikely they could gauge exactly how much of their profits reA sales might be cutting into, let alone who its creators were or where they lived.

By summer, however, the inevitable finally became evitable…

and Rice and Horatia woke, one way-too-early morning, to find their lab-loft suddenly full of thugs with guns. Their leader, Dieter Dorfmann, was a rooster-proud flyweight boxer of a guy with a shaved head, albino-blond eyebrows, inept jailhouse tats and a scary little lisp; Rice had bought crystal meth off and on from his various club dudes for about a year now, and always maintained there wasn't much wrong with him that a good swift dick up the ass wouldn't cure, plastic or otherwise. Still, it was funny how much less innately ridiculous he seemed when bolstered by five other well-armed guys of varying sobriety, all of them busily tossing the place for whatever they could find.

Rice and Horatia froze, stranded, halfway down the stairs from their sleeping platform—both barely dressed, with Horatia maintaining a white-knuckled clamp on Rice's wrist. The good part: nobody'd knocked over anything likely to explode, as yet. The bad part...everything else, pretty much: guys with guns, no guns of their own (not that Rice even knew how to shoot a gun, but she thought she could probably work it out fairly fast, given sufficient contextual pressure). No way to reach the door without being seen and/or stopped...

...so Rice went with her most basic instinct, instead—chill hard enough to cool down the whole room, thus keeping people calm enough for she and H to stay alive. In her best amused drawl, therefore, the knot in her gut thankfully inaudible—

"Yo, D, man...I *can* call you D, right?"

A rippling wave of pistol-cock clicks brought six separate barrels their way, at this; Horatia had already ducked behind Rice before Rice could even react, which might've looked bad from the outside, but provoked a weird rush of affection: *That's my girl.* Dorfmann turned, cutting her the only-slightly-curious wall-eye. "DD," he said.

Rice shrugged. "Yeah, well, whatever, D-squared—looks like you're looking for something, so maybe I can help. What's the issue?"

"Uhhh...*you* two rich bitches, shitting where *I* eat? Pushing your homebrew crap in my territory, without even kicking some back to me for the privilege?" Adding, as his chief button-men—equally large, brown and unimaginatively monickered brothaz Big Trey and Lil Trey—smirked behind him: "That's just *rude*, dude."

"Granted. How 'bout we rectify that right now, then?"

"Okay. You turn over what you got, you don't make any more, and you pay up for what you screwed us out of. Then you get to live… maybe."

Rice clicked her teeth together, "thought" a moment, then smiled wide. "Nah," she said. "Not really workin' for me, as an offer. Care to try again?"

"Listen, little miss gay-'til-grad—"

And now Rice could feel Horatia's nails really start digging in—but fuck it, her blood was up, and if she had to die today, she just didn't feel like doing it while sucking anybody's dick (metaphorically or otherwise). "Oh, fuck you, little mister Aryan Brotherhood-'til-parole," she snapped back, a contemptuous sweep of her hand taking in both Big and Lil's multiracial faces at once. "Your White Power click-pals know exactly who you got carrying the weight for you, out here? Or do you just skip conveniently over that part, come contact visits day?"

"Hey, insults. That'll make me *want* to cut you a break."

"Dieter, who the fuck do you even think you are, aside from the guy who couldn't cook up a new drug if somebody made you deepthroat an Uzi? Get out of my damn place!"

DD flushed (creepily deep, even given his colouration); he cracked his neck from side to side, then said, with remarkable restraint—

"Make me."

—and shot Rice, right in the chest.

Horatia's shriek was louder than the bullet's impact itself, and weirdly more painful. Rice lost her balance and fell backwards, like she'd been punched hard in the ribcage. Her ears rang. The light felt heavy. As she lay there, she saw Big Trey and Lil Trey moving slow-mo past her to grab Horatia in a double arm-lock, hauling her down right on top of Rice's body. DD was blabbing on, thick and dying-battery deep, about "teaching" somebody some fucking thing, while Lil Trey undid his pants; Big Trey had put his weight on Horatia's shoulders, holding her down on top of Rice's body. Horatia flailed, scratching at Lil Trey's eyes, and got a backhand in return that looked like it almost cracked her jawbone.

Oh, you don't *hit her. Ever.*

Without thinking, Rice simply reached up, grabbed Lil Trey

by his ears and broke his neck with one sharp twist, yanking his head clean off like snapping a pencil in two. Carotid and jugular popped, spouting blood like a busted tap. With a single wordless cry, Big Trey fell off the stairs, base of his skull connecting hard against the floor; Horatia scrambled backwards up the steps, mouth gaping, glasses smeared with crimson. A second later, Rice had vaulted to her feet, Jedi-style, and kicked Lil Trey's twitching body off the steps too before heading straight for DD at full-out stalk, ignoring the shots he kept pumping into her body until the gun ran dry, until she was close enough to lift him off the floor by his throat. As he dangled, gurgling, she leaned and hissed, right in his face:

"*Now.* Like I already said…you wanna try AGAIN?"

(Or *what?*)

—

Perhaps because he also spent much of his own time constantly caffeinated, DD seemed to get broken in to the whole *Herbert West, ReAnimatED* idea a whole lot easier than most other people—people not Rice or Horatia, specifically—might've. But he did have to work his way through it at least once, maybe just to hear it out loud:

"So…you're all dead but not, 'cause you been gettin' high on your own supply?" Rice, leaning on the kitchen island counter as Horatia fussed around her, nodded. "Which means…you must'a been makin' that shit out of shit that, like—makes you all not dead and shit."

A snort: "Oh, you're *smart*," Horatia observed, not even vaguely sounding like she meant it. Switching over to Rice: "You do know what you've obviously done to yourself, I take it…"

"'Obviously'? No, not really—and your bedside manner *sucks*, by the way." To which Horatia just scowled, taking yet another blood sample (though what she thought she was going to learn from this one she hadn't from the pint or so she'd already taken, Rice seriously didn't know); as she did, Rice turned back to DD, snapping—"And as for you…seems to me like you got crew problems that go waaay beyond the whole total-lack-of-discipline thing." She glanced significantly past him, first at Lil Trey's bisected body, then over at the still-open door, through which the rest of his gang (all but Big Trey, now lying semi-concussed on the couch) had already booked. "So if you still want to get in on this with us—"

DD blinked. "What?"

Horatia wheeled back up from the microscope, jaw dropping. "Excuse me, *what*? He *shot* you, Rice!"

"Yeah, thanks—might've missed that, you hadn't pointed it out to me." Rice ignored Horatia's near-purple flush and looked back to DD. "Like I was saying, the assholes who tore out of here, they're your guys. What are they gonna say happened, once they're back on the street?"

DD shrugged. "Nothing anyone'll buy; shit, I'm lookin' right at ya, and I don't even buy it." He scratched his head, oddly quizzical. "So, you like Wolverine now? Whatever happens, you just heal back?"

Horatia shook her head, impatience-quick. "Not how it works, not at this stage; the reagent builds a collagen-silicon neurocompatible tissue scaffold that sustains cells while they're living, redirects around them when they're dead or damaged...."

Rice yawned. "Tech, tech, techitty tech tech..."

"You're not even listening to me."

"Not as such, no. There a chase we can cut to?"

A slow, deep breath. "I'll need more tests to make sure, but I'm guessing your whole nervous system is probably more reagent than living tissue now. But since inert cells means no reparative process—"

"—I can't die, but I can't heal. Meaning I'm stuck full of holes for...ever, basically."

"I'd tell you to be careful with yourself from now on, but..." Horatia shrugged, helplessly, as Rice shrugged back: *given.*

Big Trey looked at them, then at Lil Trey's corpse, then back at DD; his face twisted, half-disgust, half-sorrow. "Listen, bossman—what these bitches got, this, this is really ill, man..."

Rice: "Says the on-command *rapist enabler.* Just step the fuck off, Sasquatch."

"Hey." Dorfmann raised his hand, abruptly hard. "My call, not yours, even if we partner up on this, and that's a way fucking big if. 'Cause I'm still not sure how much I trust you, Zombie Hooker from Mars—"

"Oh, you have *got* to be kidding me!" Rice exploded. "You shot me in the fucking *chest*, you dork, and I'm the one offering *you* free fucking money—does the Aryan Brotherhood only take retards these days, or what? You unbelievable fucking pussy!"

"Okay, okay; Jesus!" DD took a second to get composed, then braced himself against the other side of the kitchen island, lowering his voice like he thought 5-0 might be outside right now, listening in. "So…how soon before we can start to ship this shit?"

Far too many fricatives to that sentence for comfort, which Rice almost felt like telling him—but didn't, 'cause she'd already been shot more than enough times today. Besides which, at least he'd finally remembered that the primary active ingredient in dealing was making fucking *deals*.

—

Later, though—long after DD and Big Trey had gathered Lil Trey's remains up in a couple of sacrificed pillowcases, and departed—

"I'm beyond pissed, Clarice," Horatia began, almost conversationally. "Using the reagent recreationally is perhaps the single stupidest thing you've ever done, let alone using it *this* much—and now you're planning to play Scarface with some moronic methhead meatbag?" Considering that her voice didn't even rise while cursing, Rice actually found herself paying attention. "Not to mention how we don't know nearly enough about prospective side effects to begin mass-producing *anything*…"

"Those seem pretty cool, to me." In an infomercial announcer's voice: "'Side effects may include: if it so happens you end up getting shot in the chest, don't even worry…plus, as an extra-special bonus offer, free head-ripping ability!'"

Horatia shook her head. "You really don't get it, do you? For fuck's sake, Rice—is it really too much to ask that we occasionally approach the science part of all this like, oh, I don't know… scientists?"

Rice straightened up, grabbing for the old familiar sweet, hot flush of rage—though now, even with effort, all she suddenly found she could conjure was an offputtingly uncomfortable tinfoil-bite sting which rippled her nerves, from dry mouth to equally dry crotch. "Define terms, bitch," she said. "Did *we*, or did *we* not, just already spend three months manufacturing this exact same shit in large quantities, then selling it to people to get high on?"

They stared at each other for a long moment. Then:

"Oh, *fuck*," they both said, at pretty much the same time.

—

It wasn't until two weeks after the first major incident that TV newscasters co-opted the street-name, and started referring to people who unwittingly overdosed on reA, wandered into some public area and spontaneously combusted in a spray of potentially contaminative material as "Dusters." Rice and Horatia watched shaky black-and-white security camera footage of one poor bastard, as narrated by an equally shaky voiceover: he came weaving up to the counter of an all-night Tim Horton's, abruptly dissolving seconds later in an explosion which covered the horrified, easily infectable people around him in dried-out human matter.

Horatia stared. Muttered to herself: "Heart attack, aortic embolism, or...for him to go off like that, he must've died weeks ago, overdosed and just not noticed. So—one of the initial buyers, the first wave..."

"Yeah, I guess." Rice tried vaguely to summon some faces from that particular party run, but couldn't. "Eeeugh."

"We've released a plague of zombies, and all you can say is 'eeeugh'? Rice, this is *bad*."

"Look, that's not going to be me, if that's what you're worried about."

"What? *How? How* is that not going to be you?"

Rice grinned, and lowered her voice, conspiratorially. "Human flesh spackle. We got it; they don't."

"I *really* wish you'd stop calling it that." A pause. "Besides which...they aren't supposed to OD!"

Which Rice supposed was true—but to be fair, they probably weren't *supposed* to be taking drugs at all. In lieu of saying so, however, she started macking on Horatia instead, to change the subject—Horatia relaxed into the clinch initially, but soon drew back, nose wrinkling. Said: "Your tongue tastes...weird."

Rice took a swallow, considered the result. "Huh. It sort of *feels* weird, too..."

She turned away, snagging an empty coffee cup, and spit. It came out black. "Well," Rice said, at last. "Probably some new kinda side-effect, huh?"

Horatia, barely able to keep herself from spitting too: "Oh, you *think*? You see? You *see*?"

"Man, stop being all *Plan 9*, and let's just fix this shit."

"Again, *how*? You don't know—*I* don't know! *Anything*! Because both of us were too goddamn busy getting high or fucking with each other to ever run any motherfucking *tests*!"

"Okay. So here's what I don't get, H—if you think I'm such an ir-redeemable idiot, why don't you just up and *leave* my dumbshit ass?"

Horatia breathed out through her nose, just once, a short, con-trolled huff. Saying, eventually—

"I'm certainly *not* going to do that. Because—"

(you took my virginity)

(you're the only friend I have)

(you're the only person, friend or not, I actually know...let alone like)

"—this is *my* apartment, too," she finished, finally. And went right on back to whatever she'd been doing, before Rice getting herself corpse-ified in the service of keeping Horatia's narrow ass strictly reserved For Ladies Only had so rudely interrupted her.

—

(Un)naturally enough, of course, black spit soon proved to be only the tiniest tip of the New Model Zombie iceberg; Rice ca-reened blithely from symptom to symptom, dead heart not even skipping a beat between fresh new disasters—already starting to shrink a size or two overall, like the Grinch's leftovers. Her tape-tum began to scrape away, eyes throwing light like a cat's, while her skin grew iridescent with dust, proteins calcifying and rising everywhere she looked, fine and sharp as mica. A pheromonal miasma, decay-in-the-mist, exuded through her pores. She wore her shades all the time now, even at night, like the old song went—but it didn't look so cool anymore, not even in a retro way. Just...tired.

As things cooled off between Rice and Horatia, meanwhile

DD began hanging around a lot—far more so than their mutual three-way business "relationship" really warranted. One lazy summer afternoon, Rice walked out of yet another spackle-bath—stark naked, natch—to discover him sprawled out on their bed, shirtlessly inviting, like he'd picked up his entire idea of how a *Cool Guy Who Wants to Impress a Cool Girl* acts from watching home-made pornos.

"Oh, man," Rice said. "Necrophile much? Pervin' away on the Living Dead Girl; no, *that's* not creepy at *all*."

"You don't look dead. You look…slammin'."

"Oh, do I? Hadn't noticed." Rice sat down to gel her hair, and grinned at him in the vanity mirror. "Dieter, you do get that some people are just gay, right? All DC, no AC? And thus unlikely to be quite as interested in your eight inches as—say—you are, or would like them to be?"

"Sure, I get that—like her, right? But you…" He grinned at the thought, offputtingly wide. "I think I might'a found, like, clips of you doin' it old-school, all penis in vagina and what-not, right there on the Internet. True or false, missy?"

Rice shrugged. "Busted."

"So you *can* get down with the bone, if you wanna."

"Well, proven—but see, that's just not what's gonna happen, with you and me. 'Cause I don't even like you *that* much."

"This is still 'cause I shot you, right?"

"Somewhat, yeah. 'Course, I *might* be persuaded to rev up Ol' Faithful and do *you* up the ass 'til you screamed, if it turned out you were into that."

"Why would I be?"

"I don't know. Why *would* you?"

"You're—just—makin' this ten thousand times more complicated than it has to be."

"Ah, my cunning plan revealed. Think of it like…space exploration. Broaching the limitations of human endeavour; broadening people's minds, proving points, keeping accurate notes while you do it. Science."

DD frowned. "Are you really high right now?"

"Sure am. All the time, pretty much—I think it's one of those infamous side-effects. And guess what? This could be you. Take enough of this stuff, and you too could be pushing the walls of perception back 'til they fall apart. Take enough, and after a while you'll be all: 'Okay fine, I'm in! Soup it up, bitch!'"

Unexpectedly, as DD blushed bright at this last idea, Rice felt a sudden tweak of interest; she realized for the first time that A) she was a full head taller than him and B) he was sort of cute, in a maybe-trainable feral/rabid puppy kind of way.

"Listen," he said, "more'n enough with that crap, okay? I pimp, lady; I don't get pimped. I mean, I didn't even put out in jail, and I was there a good long while…"

Rice leaned over him, assaulting him with her just-washed scent—gave him a close look at where the paste-on jewel she'd put over the original entry-wound went, a little off-centre, right between her boobs. Working that *you know I could pull your head off right now, little boy* vibe *hard*, and murmuring—

"And just how well *did* that work out for you, anyhow? In the long run?"

—

Hours later, Horatia walked in on them, took one look—then walked back out, twice as fast. But she had to come back, eventually. All her stuff was there.

Rice sat in the dark, alone, 'til she heard the key in the lock, but didn't bother to turn around when the door opened. "Where've you been?"

"Does it matter?" Horatia sat down, heavily. Then said, after a long pause: "You…listen, I think you need to *stop*. Doing…things. Like that. You *need* to, Rice."

Rice let out a breath which—even to her—sounded more like a sigh, especially in context.

"…I don't think I can," she replied, at last.

"Why *not*?" No answer. "And more to the point—Jesus, Rice, what the hell? Pegging some straight thug in the middle of our goddamn living room? Why would he even go *along* with that?"

Rice's hands rose in a flourish of dismissive disbelief. "I don't know, man—I mean, that is a little weird, isn't it? Maybe he just likes having somebody tell him what to do." But now it was Horatia's turn to sigh, sharp and angry, and that finally made Rice look at her directly, laying on the charm. "Hey, c'mon, though—it didn't

145

mean anything, 'Rache, you know that. Not really. Not like—"

"—Like us? And I'm just supposed to, what, take that one on faith, because you tell me to? You lie for fun!"

"Not about that," Rice snapped back, without even thinking it over first. Which, once again, was…

(Surprising. Uncomfortable. Inconvenient.)

…*typical*. Especially coming from somebody who'd never, ever, in her entire life, known when to leave well enough alone.

"'Scuse me," Rice finally said, softly, as though lack of volume alone could really negate the reality of what she'd just let slip. Then walked out herself, shutting the door in Horatia's still-gaping face, and prowled downtown Toronto's increasingly empty streets until dawn.

—

Between the rising *did you say you loved me/Uh…maaaaybe* tension, Rice's increasingly permanent crazy-high and physical deterioration, and Horatia's insomniac cure-hunting mania, DD took on far more of the business end of reA sales than anyone had really planned for—and un-higher-educated as he was, he certainly knew how to move product. Too well, it turned out. But with Horatia too desperate for formula fixit funds to care, Rice too stoned, and DD just too plain greedy, their peripheral awareness of Toronto's response to the duster phenomenon—the reappearance of surgical masks as a fashion accessory; WHO health warnings triggering a free-fall economic collapse; ever-more-frequent and deadly street riots, whenever some poor calcified bastard went up in public and set off a crowd-wide bug-out—remained just that: peripheral, at best.

When she thought about it at all, Rice could only chalk the authorities' helpless flailing up to her own personal conviction: smart just made you stupid in different ways. As long as the WHO remained stubbornly certain it was a viral or bacteriological vector they were looking for—subconsciously influenced by five decades of movies, for all Rice knew—they'd never put two and two together with the cops on the reA drug, barring some lucky (or unlucky) break.

So (un)life went on, work vs. play vs. some arcane combination of the two—nothing Rice couldn't work around, just business as usual. Until the day it wasn't, any of it.

—

"Yo, cook-bitches!" DD shouted as he came through the loft's door, loaded for bear with a gun in either hand, and all tricked out like some pimpy Elvis from Hell, otherwise. "Grab your crap, we're on the run!"

Rice, thankfully fully-dressed this time, was checking her La-vaLife profile on Horatia's laptop, trying to figure out whether adding "vitality-challenged" to her profile would be more a draw than a drawback. "What you mean 'we,' White Power man?" she asked. "Better yet, where's your posse?"

DD found Horatia's camping-sized rucksack, and got busy shoving the wads of cash which lined his ridiculous suit inside it. "Uh—dead, I guess. Big Trey started givin' me shit about...shit, so we drew down, and I took his fuckin' head off. Then the fuckin' cops show up, but they got, like, Feds with 'em and everything. Plus these other people started breakin' in, all dressed in plastic bags and crap..."

"The CDC broke up your firefight?" Horatia had just emerged from the bathroom; as Rice stared: "Prime Minister called them in on Monday, to help with the WHO initiative. Don't you even vaguely try to keep up, these days?"

"That'd be a 'no.'" To DD: "So how the hell did *you* make it out?"

DD didn't miss a beat. "Threw a lighter into the main cook tanks and booked out the back. You need to do the same, and *fast*."

"Threw a—that was *you*?" Rice remembered, now—one more sound-bite, between videos on Loud; another (supposed) meth lab gone up in smoke, adding a boost to the simmering dog-day smog mix of August-end. "Yo, Dieter. Tell me you didn't just blow our entire backstock of reA into the fucking *atmosphere*."

At her tone, DD finally looked up, blank: *Yeah, why?* "You can make more, though, right?"

Rice and Horatia locked eyes, equally amazed—and for just a moment, a little of the old shared smugness came back, that communal telepathic prayer: *Oh Christ, save me from fucking morons.* And bitter as realizing just how stupid some people could be always was, it was oddly sweet, too. In context.

They packed fast, leaving most of Horatia's equipment behind, and ended up in a "safe house" that had started life as DD's first crack-house: no power, no phone, no cable. Its very walls themselves so saturated with chemicals even the air seemed to itch. There Rice lay in bed staring up at the ceiling, increasingly sleepless, while DD snored obliviously on one side of her and Horatia kick-moaned through a nightmare on the other. Her once-talented tongue gone cold, stiff and silent in her own mouth, like something already dead.

So two or three weeks passed, long enough for August to collapse into a cold and rainy September, as Horatia continued to work furiously towards some sort of cure with what little Rice and DD earned on their last few reA sales. With none of them talking about what they'd do when the stock finally ran out, or how Rice—deprived of her sustaining spackle-baths—was getting drier by the day, let alone what the ever-heavier presence of soldiers and CDC mobile clean-labs in the streets of Toronto might mean...

Around 3:00 a.m., Rice's aimless wandering took her up to Parliament, where a closed pawnshop's window display TV had been left on, tuned to CityPulse 24. Pausing to watch a "Rewind" segment from 1987 on how to shampoo your dog, she couldn't quite avoid reading the caption-snippets of news running beneath, words fading steadily in and out:

...fifth week of curfew, city councillors deny rumours that full quarantine of Toronto being considered...

...source in Prime Minister's office hints that War Measures Act may be reactivated...

...Center for Disease Control consultants report possible breakthrough in identifying primary 'Duster' vector...

Curfew; well, that explained the empty streets. Rice got off the main drag, double-quick, and used alleys to work her way back while thinking about hazmat-suited strangers ransacking the loft, disassembling Horatia's lab, shredding the mattress she and Horatia had slept on. She stopped across the street from "home" and its piss-stained concrete front steps, next to the pay phone, and felt a weird impulse—dug out change, dialed. By about the fifteenth ring, she'd almost convinced herself the man on the other end had long since done what she would have, in his shoes, and high-tailed it down to Gran-and-Grandad's condo in Florida—

Click. "Hello?"

No air in Rice's lungs. It was an act of will just to breathe, to force out the words—

"Hello?"

—but then she managed it, without even a crack in her voice to show for all her effort: "Hi, Dad."

A long, long pause. "Clarice?" And...shit, it didn't sound like Gilmore Petty at all. He had *never* sounded like that. "Clarice, is that *you?* They told me—" A wet, indescribable cough, almost a...

(sob?)

Yeah, *right.*

"They told me you were...dead," he said. And all she could think to say, in reply, was:

"...I guess...I sort of am," Rice told her father, before hanging up.

—

It was drizzling when she came in, sky beginning to go grey with morning; she found Horatia working by the wavering glow of a few tea-lights over a series of slides and eyedroppers. Alkaline catalysts, if Rice was reading the labels on the nearby bottles right, breaking up reA doses in different ways; measured by no more than hand and eye, with all Horatia's ridiculous, incredible precision. She looked up at Rice's entrance, and Rice wasn't sure exactly what that look meant.

"Well?"

"I figured it out. The molecular key to let reA hook right into a cell's master DNA for full-on regeneration—so we can actually repair damaged tissue, not just shellac it up until it disintegrates. So nobody else will ever go Dust."

"Regeneration." Rice wondered if this was how other people felt around her, that stumbling feeling, perpetually out of step, too slow to catch up. "Like, eternal life-type regeneration?" The grin took her over, like something alien. "That's—holy shit, 'Rache, that's great! You fucking did it!"

"Yeah." Horatia nodded, not looking too triumphant, for some-one who'd just broken the Grim Reaper's back and made it say "aun-tie." "'Did it' for the next batch of users. Not so much for anybody who already..." She covered her face with one hand. "I mean, um..."

"...Not for me," Rice finished, toneless.

Horatia stared miserably at her, too upset even to nod. And right then—

—was when DD stumbled out of the bedroom, holding his throat with both hands, as if choking on something. Eyes so wide with fear and fury Rice could actually see the madness brewing, he advanced on Horatia, who recoiled, slipping backwards off her stool. "Yah, fahk'ng, bihhhhtch," he wheezed, and Rice saw thick, dark drops of blood squeeze between his fingers, as blood flaked off his sodden shirt. "Cuht mah fahk'ng hroaght—"

Then let go of his neck and lunged at Horatia, mouth still working—but the gash across his larynx gaped wide, shrinking his voice to a bare wheeze. Living Dead Girl-fast, Rice snapped out an arm; they wrestled for a second before Rice pinned him, face to the floor, open throat whistling. Rice shot Horatia an exasperated look, and Horatia just shut her eyes, comprehension dawning.

"Riiight, 'course. You shot him up too, didn't you?"

"Well, duh. But he would have hooked himself up anyway, I hadn't—am I right, D-man?" She put her head down next to DD's: "I let you up, you gonna behave?" This induced a renewed bout of struggling, but Rice had far too good a grip to break, without risking further injury. "One more time, Dieter. *Behave.*"

Helpless, DD finally nodded, so Rice turned him loose; he stood up, shooting Horatia a hateful glare, and pinched his throat back together. To Rice: "Hwheeerre...th'fahk...hyouhh bihn?"

"Out; who're you, my—?" Rice stopped, remembering the phone call, and began again. "Doesn't matter. You missed the big news, dude; Horatia cracked the code. Now we got something that'll buy our records clean of anything, even the Dust-plague. Isn't a government on this planet won't set us up for life, once we start shopping immortality to the highest..."

But here, suddenly, she stopped. DD lifted his head too, a dog sniffing prey, as sick dismay whitened Horatia's face.

Screeches of rubber on wet asphalt; the clunking slams of car doors; the hammer of boots on the ground. The grey light filtering in through the filthy, half-shuttered windows began to wash with alternating red and blue.

And a megaphone-enhanced voice whipcracking through the

morning quiet, all the old standbys: "THIS IS THE ONTARIO PRO-
VINCIAL POLICE...BUILDING IS SURROUNDED...EXIT THROUGH
THE FRONT DOOR, HANDS ABOVE YOUR HEAD..."

Rice took a deep breath, mostly to steady herself. Said: "So,"
to neither of them in particular. "That's it, then." She looked at
Horatia, gone green in the weird light. "If DD and I go out the
front door together, we'll probably distract them enough you could
maybe slip out the back..."

"No. Forget it."

"Look, *one* of us needs to get out of here alive, okay? And given
you're the only one knows the Highlander formula..."

"No!" Horatia backed away, until she stood silhouetted against
the light from one window. "Rice, I am *not* leaving you, so don't
even try to make me—" She staggered and fell to her knees, glass
breaking behind her with a clean tinkling punch, as a spreading
blotch darkened her shapeless green sweater.

"'Rache!" Rice dove across the room to catch Horatia, while
DD hit the floor on the other side, peering upwards; felt something snap inside her as she did so, grating inside her ribcage as
she lowered Horatia across her lap. "Oh Christ, no, please, no..."

Horatia sighed. Then said, in a ridiculously clear voice: "Oh,
give me a break, Rice." She parted the hole in her sweater, probed
the wound beneath, then let her head fall back. "No, that's it.
Clean shot, police marksman. No repairing *that*."

Rice touched the matching hole in her own chest, from which
the paste-on jewel had long since been lost. Sparkling powder
drifted down, scattering across her fingers. Amazingly, she found
herself smiling.

"You fucking *liar*," she said, tenderly. "So what, more tests? Or
did you just absorb it, by osmosis?"

Horatia sat up, shaking her head. "Sample doses. Thought I was
still below the critical exposure threshold." A beat. "Guess not."

"Hmh. I think maybe I *do* love you, you know that?"

Horatia just rolled her eyes. Cool: "Well, I *know* I love *you*."

"Bitch."

A spasmodic hacking came from DD, and they both looked
over to see his chest rising and falling in what Rice realized, freak-
ily enough, was laughter. He covered his wound with one hand,
jabbed one thumb at himself with the other. "Sssooh hwhat's

151

that...maahke *me*?"

"You?" Rice grinned her old I'd-fuck-the-world-if-I-found-the-right-hole grin. "You're the boy with the toys, Dieter. Just how many guns you got stashed around this shithole, anyway?"

After a second, his own grin almost reluctantly answering hers: "Mhor'n...enough."

DD caterpillared across the floor into the bedroom, staying below the windows, and came back dragging a suitcase. Rice flipped it open. Boxes of clips and shells spilled across the floor, along with a half-dozen Browning automatics and a greasy-sheened shotgun.

Rice looked at Horatia, who took her hand and squeezed it hard. She picked up a pistol and slapped in a clip, just the way she'd seen in a thousand movies—and hey, she'd been right. It *wasn't* that hard to figure out, with the right incentive. Then again, she always had been the smartest person she knew...

(...well—second smartest.)

"Okay, then," she said.

HIS FACE, ALL RED

"You're up very late, my dear," the old man said, when Leah came over to hand him a menu and pour some complimentary water. It was 3:37 a.m. by the clock above the range, and the place was pretty much deserted—just her, him, and Amir and Gue back in the kitchen.

She shrugged, indicating the sign in the front window. "Twenty-four hours. Means somebody's always gotta be up all night, and that's me."

He turned to study it a moment, quizzically, like he hadn't even realized it was there, even though he must've passed right by it to get to the front door. Then replied, without much surprise, or interest, "Oh, well, yes."

The old man had one of those crazy accents, prissy and kind of hot at the same time, every vowel struck like a bell—sounded like Gandalf, basically, or maybe Jean-Luc Picard. Leah couldn't begin to reckon his actual age. Also, the nearer she got to him, the more she saw how his skin was kind of...flawless, creepily so. Eyes like blue glass, narrowed by smile-lines; perfect teeth, too, and wasn't that weird, for an English dude? When he smiled, he looked like everybody's favorite librarian. But he was wearing a decrepit, faded Lamb of God T-shirt that'd seen better decades and a pair of bright pink sweatpants, both much too big for his hawk-slim frame, with a cracked and battered set of Crocs Leah swore to God she could see his (slightly over-long) toenails through.

"What's with the clothes, sir?" she asked, trying to make it sound funny, charming even—but she had to guess it probably didn't sound like either of those things, because his good cheer faded on contact; he frowned slightly and looked down, studying the outfit like (again) someone had stuck it on him without his noticing.

"What *is* with them?" he repeated, genuinely baffled. Then: "Oh, these aren't mine; I found them in a trash-bin, I think. The one at the end of that alley beside your fine restaurant, with 'Twister Relief' written on its side."

"I don't think that stuff is meant for...somebody like you," Leah began, immediately feeling even sillier; now it was the old man's turn to shrug, however, giving her an excuse to change the subject. "What was wrong with what you were already wearing?"

"Oh, it simply wouldn't have done at all, my dear, not for a public venue. For one thing, my suit was almost completely covered in blood. And for another, I had been wearing it a good twenty years already, at least."

Leah only realized she was staring at those amazing teeth of his—so white, so straight, so *sharp*—when he snaked his tongue out, unexpectedly, and licked them, like an animal. Completely out of left field, and gross, too; perverted, somehow, or at least profane. For anybody that age to be getting such an apparent charge out of being hungry, breathing in deliberately, holding it like a mouthful of weed-smoke...tasting the air itself, sensually, as though it were a steak he longed to take a bite out of...

"'Covered in blood,'" she heard herself mimic as he stood up, seemed to almost eddy forward, near enough to touch. "'C—covered in—'"

"Yes, dear. Just like that."

"Whose...blood was it?"

"Oh, I don't believe I ever got their names; professionals, you see. No element of friendliness about *that* transaction, I can tell you. Not like you and I."

"...Can't move."

"No, of course not. That's what the hypnotism is for, you see."

Perfect teeth, so straight and white and shiny. She felt a tear streak down one cheek, thinking: *He's such an old man, and I'm not. I could—I should—*

But she didn't, of course, for far too long. And then there was a sudden, terrible pain, a tearing just above her collarbone, quickly followed by nothing at all.

—

When Leah came to again, everything hurt: her eyes, her guts, her skin. It was bright outside, enough to make her wince and flinch at the same time, cowering back, shoving herself as far underneath the table the old man'd been sitting at as geometry would allow for. Thank God, though, the two women standing in front of her seemed to have already figured out they should probably close the blinds before she woke, or lose their only witness to spontaneous inhuman combustion...

(*What?*)

...and oh, such an additional pain, so sharp and coring, to even think—let alone voice—that name. The one she was now forbidden access to, forever.

I don't know where this is coming from, any of it, Leah realized, suddenly sick. *Or how I know it...what I think I know, even...*

Eyes flicking first left, then right, as though bracing herself for further attack; hands fisting so hard she could hear her nails grate on the floor beneath, scratching the linoleum, like claws. But the vertigo that immediately welled up made her want to put her head between her knees and moan, like a poisoned dog, so she did, while the women—sisters, they were definitely sisters, she could smell it on them—simply stood there and watched, the taller one projecting an aura of quiet authority and genuine sympathy even as the smaller simply rocked back on her bootheels, her sniper's gaze never wavering from Leah's face and one hand sneaking behind her back, feeling for some kind of weapon.

Better put me down quick, bitch, you want to keep me there, the unfamiliar mind-voice (that doesn't sound like me) whispered in her head, gleeful-sly, all its worst instincts pricking up in anticipation of slaughter. *Better not let me get a good jump in, 'less you want to be wiping little sis's blood off the wall...*

Leah shook her head again, just once but sharply, to dismiss it. And made herself look back up, trying her level best to not only look harmless, but be so.

"That old man...is he still here?"

The taller one shook her head, blonde braids swinging. "Long gone, I'd say. Given the temp on your friends."

"Gue—Amir?"

"That's what their badges said, yes. And you're Leah, right?"

Leah nodded, sniffed, eyes blurred and stinging. But when she put up a hand to wipe away the tears, she drew it away smeared with red.

"Oh Jesus," she said, staring at the result, no matter how the word hurt to use. "Oh God, oh Christ. What *happened* to us all?"

The taller woman sighed, and took a moment, like she wanted to choose her next words carefully. In the meantime, Leah found her eyes drawn to the tattoos she could suddenly see crawling up along the woman's arms, weaving underneath the sleeves of her shirt to climb the sides of her long neck like vines. They were snaky, deep-carven things, some of them roughly keloided as though self-inflicted, a strange contrast with the woman—girl, really, Leah now understood—herself, who seemed gentle, almost sad. *I want to help,* her gray eyes seemed to say, though they both knew that was impossible.

(*Yes, yes we do*)

(How, *though? Why?*)

"His name is Maks Maartensbeck," the tall girl began, reluctantly. "*Professor* Maartensbeck. Highly respected in our field; did a lot of good, once. Saved a lot of lives. But he hasn't really been that man for a very long time now."

"Then...what is he?"

"Oh, Leah, come on: you've seen the movies. He came in here at night, put you to sleep with a look, drank from your neck, then ripped your friends apart. So if you just let yourself think about it for a minute, I kind of think you already know."

(Running her tongue along the inside of her lips, across her teeth, and feeling skin part, seamless. Knowing without even having to check how they would shine just as brightly as the old man's now; white-sharp like the new moon. Her empty stomach contracting, and the rush and pulse of blood—*not* her own—rising in her ears, more beautiful than any remembered song.)

The smaller woman was visibly tensed now, biceps gone hard beneath the sleeves of her many-pocketed East Coast gangsta parka; she had thighs like she pumped prison iron, so cut Leah could see definition even through her jeans. Such a tough little cookie, with her narrowed brown glare and her dirty blonde Boot Camp haircut, and Leah felt herself beginning to kind of long to see what exactly she was reaching behind her for, the roots of all Leah's brand new dental accoutrements set aching at once. With the bad voice whispering yet again, up and down the dry rivers of her veins: *Yeah, go on ahead and whip it out; get it over with, 'cause I'm tired of talking. Sun's up, my head hurts, and better yet, I'm—I'm just, just so, so—damn—*

(*hungry*)

But: *This is not me*, she told herself. *Not while I can still refuse to let it be.*

Then added, out loud, like she was arguing the point: "That stuff's not *real*, though, is it—not outside of...*True Blood*, and whatever? It just doesn't *happen*."

The taller woman cocked her head slightly, neither confirming nor denying—though one tattooed shoulder did hitch just a tick, automatically, a movement perhaps only kept from blossoming into a full shrug by some arcane version of politeness.

"Not usually," she agreed. "But sometimes. This time."

"But..."

Now it was the smaller woman's turn to shake her head, punctuating it with a snort. "Just skip the counselling, Sami," she told her sister. "You were right the first go-'round—she *gets* it, just doesn't like it, 'cause who would? Now get your whammy on, and let's do what's gotta be done."

"Dionne—"

"*Samaire*." To Leah: "You got a bad case of the deads, kid, and it stops here, before you start treating the next diner's staff like your private buffet. Nothing personal."

"Dee, *Jesus*."

"What about him? Oh, that's right: not here. As usual." The thing behind her back was a machete, carving fluid through the air, already nicking Leah's throat; Leah felt the creature inside her leap, vision red-flushing, and knew her teeth must be out, lips torn at their corners. But Dionne didn't flinch, barely turning to yell, over her shoulder: "*Do* it, goddamnit, 'less you wanna be doing *me* next!"

(*Yes yes and fast do it fast*)

Something caught Leah then, square in the back of the skull, like a hook; it lifted her up and soothed her slack at the same time, a novocaine epidural. She was sewn tight, paralyzed, unable to fire a single nerve—the voice, the hunger, all drained away, replaced by a smooth, warm feeling of peace. Behind Dionne, she saw Samaire's long fingers flicker, drawing symbols on the air. Her many tattoos were glowing now, right through her clothes, each too-black line somehow rimmed in vitriolic green and sulphur yellow-touched at the same time, like light reflected off a shaken snake-scale.

I didn't ask for this. Yet even as she willed her lips to shape the words, failing miserably to bring them to completion, she already knew Samaire could hear them anyhow. And thought she heard, in reply—echoing, as it were, from another part of her too-full head entirely—

No. No one ever does.

Seeing the cores of the tall girl's eyes twist sidelong, little black swastikas at the center of two pearl-gray pools. And letting her own drift shut, letting go of everything at once; barely feeling the pain as Dionne's blade slashed through her spine, severing her new-made vampire head with one quick, expert blow.

—

Take the night shift and lose your life, maybe your freaking soul; wake up with a killer hangover and a cannibal thirst, catapulted into a world where the best you could hope for was somebody like Dionne and Samaire Cornish to put you down before you did the same to anybody else. That was their cross to bear in a nutshell, Dee knew: the family curse, spelled out coast to coast in monster-blood and mayhem, still-live warrants for prison break and felony murder notwithstanding. But at least they could trust the Maartensbeck's to use all that career vampire-killer money of theirs to cover their tracks for them this time, supposedly, so long as they returned the favor...

She stepped back just in time to let poor Leah's skull fall one way and her body the other, neatly avoiding the tainted geyser of blood spraying out every which-way, cellular-level desperate to find something else to infect before its time ran out. But Sami was already twitching the diner's blinds up again, letting in enough sunlight to crisp that evil shit to ash so fine it wouldn't register on any CSI test. Of course, they could've just taken the former waitress down that way in the first place, but it was messy, to say the least, and beheading was a clean, relatively painless death. So saving the daylight exposure option for body disposal suited both Dee and Sami fine.

No time for much more than starting to think: *Good work, little sis, however,* before Dee found herself stopping short once more, machete automatically whipping back up, as an all-too-recognizable voice drawled, from the diner's conveniently propped-open doorway—

"Hmmm, *messy.* Not s'much as the old boy I just did somethin' similar to, 'course, but that's probably 'cause practice makes perfect. Y'all truly do know your stuff when it comes to supernatural creature disposal, you two."

Oh, you have gotta be fucking kidding me.

Both of them turned together, then, to see well-known holler witch turned cellblock pimp Allfair "A-Cat" Chatwin standing there with both hands buried wrist-deep in her hoodie's front pocket, large as life—which really didn't work out to be too damn large at all comparatively, though grantedly bigger than Dee—and twice as skanky. Her bush of malt-brown hair was jammed down under a backwards-turned trucker cap so gross she might've rolled an actual trucker for it, and Dee was amazed (yet not, somehow, surprised) to note the crazy bitch was still wearing her prison jumpsuit, albeit with the shucked top hung down like shirt-tails, so it probably read to the uninitiated as nothing more than a particularly heinous set of bright orange parachute pants.

Had a big book tucked under up one arm, too. Bible-heavy, though Dee didn't have to see Sami's nose twitch to know it probably had a very different sort of stink to it.

Sami would claim they owed Chatwin something for helping in the escape from Mennenvale Women's Correctional, Dee believed, if pressed. For herself, Dee was pretty sure all they *owed* her was a quick put-down, an unmarked grave and the promise not to piss on it after, but she'd long since had to reconcile with the fact that whenever Sami's highly flexible conscience was involved, things didn't always go her way.

"We should talk, that's what I'm thinkin'," Chatwin suggested, black eyes glinting with ill charm and a touch of sly humor both, like she could read Dee's mind right from where she stood. And hell, maybe she could—Dee'd seen Sami do something similar enough times to not bother counting anymore, using the half-demon blood she and Chatwin shared, supposedly from the same source. That was if you could trust Chatwin on that one, which Dee very much didn't, having watched her calmly lie about the sky being blue in her time (metaphorically speaking) for the express purpose of messing with both their minds, not to mention seeing how far she could slip inside Sami's pants while doing it.

Moriam Cornish's sin made flesh, Dee's dead Daddy would've called it, they hadn't already shot his veins full of poison for killing her over lying down with the Fallen. Of course, she'd only done it to help him fight a crusade she apparently felt worth sacrifice, but that sure hadn't saved her, once he found out. It was the key event of both their childhoods, Sami's birth out of their Mama's useless death—the thing that'd sent Jeptha Cornish to jail and both his kids into different degrees of foster care, kept them separated 'til they were both adults and well past the age of consent when they'd made their own pact together: a vow to take up the reins and keep fighting their parents' Anabaptist crusade, with that solemn troth plighted on Moriam's grave and sealed since in a hundred different variety of strange things' blood.

Dee'd already started up where Jeptha left off, wielding rote-learned knowledge and home-made weapons she would turn to her sister's service, playing knight to her reluctant sorceress—just as Sami had committed on her own to Moriam's path, though without the shamefaced layer of secrets and lies that had eventually dragged her down. Had already taken the first few steps along it back when Dee turned up at her university dorm room's door, in fact, so long since. When she'd opened it gingerly, scratching at the first few raw, hand-scribed lines of Crossing the River—the Witches' Language, Jeptha'd called it, a foul tongue good for nothing but spell-work

160

and bindings on things too awful to force the thousand names of G-slash-d to touch—she'd just inscribed along her left wrist, and squinted down at Dee from under floppy blonde bangs, asking: *Can I help you?*

Samaire Morgan? I'm Dionne. Cornish.

Morgan's not my real name.

I know. Can I come in?

Standing there in her fatigues with a stolen sawed-off full of salt-cartridges in her backpack, and looking shyly 'round at the detritus of a life she'd never once thought was possible to achieve on her own—track-meet photos, scholarship documents, the tricked-out laptop with all its bells and whistles. The *friends*, grinning from half a dozen frames—one in particular, familiar from various news stories and police reports.

Heard about Jesca Lind, she'd offered.

Did you. Wouldn't've thought that'd've made the papers, over in Iraq.

Well, I got it from your Mom, actually, when I was tracking you down—Mrs. Morgan. She said you guys went to prom together, picked out the same university, all that. As Sami nodded, slowly: *Yeah, that's a damn shame, losing somebody you love so young.* A beat. *She really possessed, when she died?*

She was something, all right—and she didn't just die. Why do you ask?

You know who I am, Sami?

I'm—starting to get an idea; Mom showed me coverage of the trial, when she thought I could handle it. You're Jeptha Cornish's daughter.

Your sister.

That's what it said on the birth certificate. So, Dionne...you here to kill me, or what?

They looked each other over a moment, taking stock; Sami was bigger but lankier, and Dee was fairly certain she hadn't had a quarter of as much training, not physically. Then again, if she took after Moriam the way Jeptha'd thought she would, she wouldn't need it.

I'm your sister, Sami, she repeated. *How you think you got out of that trailer in the first place? I picked you up and I ran 'til I couldn't run anymore. Never looked back, no matter how hard he yelled at me to. So hell no and fuck you, 'cause I ain't him.*

That familiar/unfamiliar gaze—Mom's eyes, Dad's unholy calm. That set mouth, lips gone just a shade off-white, asking: *But you know, right? What I am.*

Sure. You're blood.

Only half. Half-human, too—by family standards.

To which Dee'd simply shrugged, throwing four hundred solid years' worth of witch-hunting genes to the winds, at least where it concerned one witch in particular—and not giving all too much of a damn as she did it. Because: How many relatives did she have left, anyways, in this frightful world? How many did she need?

Good enough for me, she'd said.

And Sami had nodded, eventually, once she saw she meant it. Then slipped her sweater off to show the rest of what she'd been doing to herself, all up and down and every which-way, penning the forces she had no choice but to know herself capable of wielding carefully back inside her own skin. Tracing marker with razor, then rubbing the wounds with a gunk made from equal parts ink, salt and Polysporin, 'til the result began to heal itself out of sheer contrariness. Lines of power digging themselves down deep from epidermis to dermis, burrowing inwards like worms of living light, sinking 'til they could sink no more.

Help me, then, she'd told Dee, a hundred times calmer than she'd had any good reason to be, given the circumstances. *You see my problem, right? 'Cause long as my arms are, I just can't seem to reach my back.*

And she'd handed Dee a blade, and Dee had taken it. Said: *I got you.*

And...

...that was it, slang become fact. It was *done.*

In the here and now, Dee hiked her eyebrows at Chatwin, trying her best to project every ounce of contempt she had across five feet of space, without moving more than those thirty tiny muscles. "Team up again, uh huh," she replied. "'Cause that worked out so well, last time."

"Still outta jail, ain't you?" Continuing, when neither of them answered: "Naw, just listen—not exactly like I want to, ladies, given the acrimonious way we parted, 'cept for the fact that it sure does appear we're workin' the same case for the same people, from suspiciously different ends. An' if yours told *you* the same pile of bull mine told *me,* might be we should throw in together regardless of past conflicts, just to keep ourselves all upright for the duration."

"Pass," Dee started to snap back—then sighed instead, as Sami waved her silent.

"I want to hear," the big idiot said, stubborn as ever.

"The shit for, Sami? She dumped your ass in the woods, left me stuck inside a *wall*."

"Didn't expect that to happen, just t'say," Chatwin pointed out. "Neither a one."

"Not like you tried all too hard to stop it, when it did."

A shrug. "Well, in for a penny."

Sami rolled her eyes. "Look," she told Dee, "you were already sure the Maartensbecks couldn't be trusted in the clinch, considering who we're chasing. And it strikes me A-Cat probably knows a dirty deal when she hears one—better than us, given we're not exactly social."

Dee had to smile at that, since it was nothing but true; hell, even Chatwin knew it. As they both watched, she sketched a little bow, shrugged again, tossed her head like a hillbilly beauty queen. And drawled back, without any more or less malice inherent in the words than usual—

"Well, ain't *you* sweet, still. Princess."

—

When most people talked about the Maartensbecks, they concentrated on their twinned academic prowess and charity-work, not to mention their storied geneaology—elliptical mentions of them stretched all the way back to the ninth century, when Holland separated from Frisia to become a county in the Holy Roman Empire, and a man named Auutet from Maarten's Beck ended up qualifying as a student of the Corpus Iuris Civilis at the newly-founded University of Bologna. For those in "the life," however, the name carried a very different sort of weight.

"They're Dutch, and all they hunt is vampires," Moriam Cornish had told her eldest daughter one night, during a Hammer Horror movie marathon. "Sure, they don't use a 'Van' when they sign anymore, but you do the math."

Though not rich in a conventional sense, their consistent ability—and willingness, even when it cost them bad enough to denude whole generations—to tackle the Rolls-Royce of monsters head-on had produced a wide-flung funding network of grateful, financially liquid patrons. And with the foundation of the Maartensbeck Archive in 1968, they'd begun to amass a vault full of magical artifacts other people wouldn't touch with a literal ten-foot pole: grimoires, cursed objects, holy weapons, all of which the family's surviving members either caretook or banked accordingly, loaning them out at a fair rate of interest to anyone who could afford their late fees, and was in search of a way to kill the unkillable.

Occasionally, someone would be dumb enough to think they could go full supervillain with whatever it was they'd borrowed, then find out better once the Maartensbecks came to retrieve it; Dee had seen photos, and the results weren't pretty. These crafty stealth badasses might have multiple degrees and class out the wazoo, but they sure weren't fussy about coming down hard on whoever they considered evil, a category whose boundaries sometimes appeared to shift at whoever was currently heading the Maartensbecks' boardroom table's will.

For the Cornishes, who'd received their initial email while recuperating after the M-vale break in a motel Sami swore up and down didn't even have WiFi, contact had been made in the well-preserved person of matriarch Ruhel Maartensbeck, legendary Professor Maks's only granddaughter. She was a silver fox of a woman with Helen Mirren style and Vanessa Redgrave pipes, turning up to their highly public first meeting—at yet another all-night roadside greasy spoon, somewhere on the Jersey Turnpike—dressed all head to toe in retired teacher drag so good Dee would've pegged her for a civilian, at least from across the room. Then she drew close enough to sit down, revealing sensibly low-heeled lace-up shoes with enough tread for a high-speed chase, a no-grip Vidal Sassoon crop, and the discreet lines of a high-calibre pistol packing modified rounds under one arm. The overall effect was of a stretched-out Dame Judi Dench, voice almost accentless and tartly crisp, as she slid her long legs under the plastic table and opened by saying—

"Congratulations on your recent return to circulation, my dears. Believe me, I'm not usually one to interrupt a celebration, but...well, the truth is, my family finds we have a problem that requires an outsider's touch, albeit one educated in very—specific ways. I know you'll understand what I mean, given your background." A pause.

"Beside which, we've heard *such* good things of you both, it seemed a pity to look anywhere else."

Dee had to bite down on the urge to laugh, hard. But a quick glance Sami's way told another tale; she had a look on her face that read as partly stunned, part wistful. This was civilized talk, Mrs. Morgan-grade, of the sort that hadn't come her way in years—not since that last phone call, when Dee'd tried not to let herself over-hear as Sami told her former "mother" how she not only wasn't gonna make it for Christmas, but wouldn't be able to tell her where to get in touch with her anymore. 'Cause yes, what those cops had told her was true, to a point: they had just killed a bunch of people in a Beantown bar, deliberately and with premeditation, just like the charges said. But only their bodies, because the things *inside* those bodies weren't the people they were claiming to be at all, what with the whole tempting transients down to the basement, then killing and cooking them routine they'd gotten into recently...let alone the additional part about feeding the remains to their customers as a Tuesday Night Special afterwards.

Thing was, when stuff'd already gone that far, that was pretty much the point where prayer and a 911 call stopped being any sort of use at all, and white magic against black took over; magic plus a bullet, or a load of cold iron buckshot mixed with salt. 'Cause just as Jeptha'd always said, *Exorcist* movie franchise aside, sometimes the Power of Christ alone wasn't up to compelling shit.

And: *Oh God, Samaire*, she could remember Mrs. Morgan crying, tinnily, on the other end. *I told you it was a bad idea to take up with her. Told you that nice as she seemed, she was probably just as psychologi-cally disturbed as that man, her father...oh baby, and you were doing so well, too, even after Jesca! My smart, smart girl. Where's it all going to end now?*

Good enough question, back then; even better question seven years on, parade of victories balanced against the occasional defeat or not. Though it wasn't like Dee really had the first or faintest idea of an answer, either way.

Ruhel Maartensbeck had come equipped with two fat files that night. One was full of background stuff on *them*, which Dee found creepy, enough so to mainly skip over, but she'd seen Sami studying it off and on since, apparently fascinated by how the Maartensbecks had managed to trace the exact moment where the long-defunct

European Cornîches had broken off into their only slightly less so Americanized brand, after a younger brother of witch-finder Guilliame Cornîche converted to Hugenot Protestanism, fleeing France for Québec in the wake of the St. Bartholomew's Day Massacre. The other file, meanwhile, was about Miss M's "little problem" itself, a crisis forty years in the making—one that'd started all the way back in 1971, with Professor Maks's tragically quick and surprisingly unheralded passing, from Stage Four prostate cancer...

...except, well, that turned out to be a bit of a face-saving fib, on the Maartensbecks' part: i.e., for "prostate cancer," read "undeath."

"'Vampire-hunter turned vampire, no news at eleven,'" Dee'd commented, munching a fry. "Understandable, right? I mean, that's really gotta rankle."

"Somewhat, yes."

Sami, nodding: "Be hard to cover up, though. Unless—oh, tell me you didn't."

"Didn't what?" Dee'd demanded, watching Ruhel Maartensbeck nod, sadly. But then the penny dropped, with an almost audible *clink*—'cause while she might not've been able to get much schooling beyond what her Spec-4 called for (high school equivalency, plus some Engineering Corps courses and a whole two years of Explosive Ordnance Disposal training), no one could accuse Dionne Cornish of being *completely* unable to follow things through using plain old logic.

"You stuck him in the vault," she said, out loud. "'Course you did. 'Cause given that place is like a toxic dump, 'cept for magic crap, there must be some real full-bore sons of bitches trying to slip in *there*—and a live-in vampire? Best security system money can't buy. Don't even have to feed him, just let him keep what he kills, long as he doesn't actually *turn* any of 'em..."

"Well done, Miss Cornish the Elder." Ruhel sighed. "Yes, that was the plan—his idea, actually, a contingency protocol decided on long before it happened, which he made me swear to honor, if and when. Imprison him in there and wait for the vampire who killed him to come free him, as a trap. But it never showed up, and after a certain amount of time, I simply ceased periodically dropping by to check on...that thing."

"Not like it was really your grandpa, anymore."

"No, of course not. *You* understand: everything I know I learned from him, and it knows everything he did, so it knows not to even bother claiming to be him. Vampires aren't people; not the people you hope they are, anyhow."

Sami, took into care far too young to remember Jeptha and Moriam's bedtime stories, raised one eyebrow. "So what *is* it, then?"

"A demon wearing my grandfather's skin which says horrifying things to me in a beautiful voice, such as 'Oh, you're pregnant—it's a boy, how lovely. Babies taste so good, or so I've heard.' Not to mention one entirely capable of biding its time, fashioning an escape plan and just waiting, as such things can, until I'm too old to do anything about it."

Said without rancour, so far as Dee could tell. This swank old lady had killed a thousand similar monsters in her time, probably—more than she and Sami'd ever seen—but when it came to emotional weaknesses, everybody had their something; if she wanted to contract hers out, Dee could certainly relate. No different from any other job, long as the money was good.

"We're still wanted," Sami reminded her. "Sticking around in the States wasn't part of the plan."

"Oh, no doubt. But you'll need new identities, won't you, to cross the border into Canada? Unless you're planning on using magic, that is—and that does leave a trail."

"Not one the FBI can follow, far as I know."

"Ah, yes. But what of Miss Chatwin, your former partner in escape?" Here Ruhel had tapped the second file, lightly. "Turns out, there's a fair deal of historical linkage between her family and yours, above and beyond the sad fact of both your mothers having decided to initiate, ahem, intimate contact with the same member of the Goetic Coterie—"

Dee: "Careful."

"I'm always careful, Miss Cornish; so should you be. Especially since I know you *both* know that Allfair Chatwin remains fixated on her half-sister, for...various reasons, all of them toxic. A dangerous woman."

Dee shrugged, reluctant to state the obvious. But it was Sami who answered, anyways.

"Look," she said, "I don't think we have any problem with hunting your grandfather down, per se. But what is it you want us to do with him, exactly, once we find him?"

—

"So she gave you a phone too, huh?" Chatwin shook her head, grinning. "Can't say they ain't a canny lot, them Maartensbecks. Particularly like her usin' me as a threat, too, to light a fire under your asses."

Dee snorted. "'Threat,' Jesus. Annoyance, maybe..."

"Now, now, Lady Di. No need t'be insultin'."

But: "Just *shush* it, both of you," Sami broke in. Then asked, of Chatwin: "So who'd you talk to? Ruhel again?"

"Naw, they sent me a pretty little brown gal in undercover cop slacks and a Kevlar neck piece, tough as nails. Said her name was Anapurna Maartensbeck, so I'm thinkin' she's probably this generation's granddaughter, but she didn't say nothin' 'bout her great-great-great...whatever. Just how there'd been a break-in at the vault, some big black books took, an' now they needed somebody t'get 'em back, an interested third party knew enough of what magic smells like t'sniff 'em out."

"They sent you after books." Dee shook her head. "The fuck."

"Funny, that's what I thought; them books weren't the only things stunk, by a long shot. Most 'specially so 'cause when I did track 'em down, they turned out t'be mainly no great shakes—I mean, sure, I guess if you never seen a grimoire in your life, you might get all het up. But really: Agrippa, Paracelsus? The *Petit Albert*? They're the Time-Life series of black magic—ten a penny, find a copy any damn place. Hardly worth the lockin' up, 'sides from *this*..."

Bitch meant what she had under her arm, of course—that squat, thick tome, more folio than book at closer examination, ill-bound in sticky-pale leather. She flourished it forth at Sami with a little half-bow, running her thumb along the embossed title, which Sami read out loud: "*Of The True Heirarchy of Hell, or Pseudomonarchia Daemonium*, blah blah blah. Greatest Magickal Hits bullshit, like you said."

"Uh huh. Now flip it open."

Sami did, gingerly. And Dee watched Chatwin grin even wider, so much so it was like the top of her skull was in danger of falling off, as her—*their*, shit on it all—half-sister's eyes widened, when she saw what was written inside.

"*Clavicule des Pas-Morts*," she said, amazed. "This is...this was burnt. Wasn't it?"

"Oh, more'n once, from what I heard. Then again, those might've just been rumours put 'round by whoever had it at the time, to throw everybody else lookin' for it off the scent. 'Cause once you got a copy of this bad boy, you probably want to keep it just as long as possible, don't ya think?"

Dee looked at Sami, the resident expert. "Okay," she said, "I'll bite. Why?"

"Because whoever has the *Key of the Not-Dead* can cure vampirism," Sami replied, eyes still firmly riveted to the thing in question. To Chatwin: "How'd you find it?"

Chatwin shrugged. "Easy enough. Miss Anapurna give me a box of forensic samples, said they took 'em at the crime scene—I whipped up a trackin' spell, but didn't get more'n one trail and that gone cold hours back, 'cause it looked like the old boy who made it was already dead. Odd thing was, though…"

"He was still moving?"

"Mmm. Just like old Professor Maks, I'd bet—or like that gal he left behind here would've been, you hadn't performed an emergency head-ectomy."

"So you figure out he's a vampire, kill him, grab the book—and? Maartensbecks are the ones who lied to you, why aren't you takin' it up with them? How'd you even know where to find us?"

"Aw, now you're drainin' all the fun out of it." Chatwin waited for Dee to rise to the bait, then sighed when she didn't. "Well—as it ensues, Princess here was always gonna be my next stop already, but let's lay that by, for the nonce. Given Mister Book-Snatcher didn't look like he'd been undead too long, I decided t'use his blood and see how near the one'd turned him was, just in case it decided to come lookin'; that's what brought me this-a-way, though I guess I'm runnin' a bit late in terms of catchin' up with the head monster-maker himself. Imagine my surprise, though, when I snuck up t'peek through the diner window and saw the two of *you* standin' there, all large as life, 'bout to cut yourself some fresh new vampire's throat!"

"Like Christmas," Sami agreed. "Or Hallowe'en."

"Six of one, darlin'. And now…here we are."

A pause. Sami looked away, tapping two fingers against her lips and cogitating so furiously Dee could almost smell the gray cells burning. Chatwin took advantage of her distraction to run a frankly admiring look up and down Sami's frame that made Dee long to knock her into the middle of next week, thinking: *Eyes front, bitch. I got a cold iron knuckle-duster in one pocket and a shaker full of salt in the other, both with your name written all over 'em.*

But: "Okay," Sami said out loud, interrupting Dee's reverie. "Professor Maks is a vampire, been one since 1971, and Ruhel still seems pretty cut up about it—so if they have the *Clavicule*, why don't they use it? 'Cause…"

"'Cause—they didn't know they had it," Dee answered, slowly. "Not until it was already banked. Only thing that makes sense."

"Yeah. They take the cover at face value, then find out they were wrong. But by that time, it's already inside the vault, with not-Professor Maks guarding it."

A-Cat frowned. "Just a second of enlightenment here, ladies, for all those who ain't in the biz…wouldn't havin' a vampire squattin' over your stuff put a kybosh on the Maartensbecks' whole magic item-loanin' sideline?"

"Oh, I'm pretty sure they could negotiate with him to get him to send things out, considering how dependent on them he'd be," Sami replied. "Give him extra blood, maybe even donate their own…but they certainly wouldn't tell him about the *Clavicule*, because he'd know what they wanted it for."

"Granted," Dee agreed. "So—say they *did* want to get it back out—"

"Arrange a break-in. It's pretty much the only way."

Dee frowned. "They must've known he'd get out, though."

A raucous snort, from over Chatwin's way. "Known? Lady Di, I'll stake my box they was *bettin'* on it."

They both turned to look at Chatwin, who nodded, almost to herself. Then added, for clarification: "Yeah, just before I told that old boy to put the book down and step back, I recall he was goin' on about how he didn't understand why 'the money people' hadn't shown up yet. In fact, I think he kinda thought I *was* one of those people."

Dee: "Why'd you want him to step back?"

"Oh, that was so's none of him'd get on the book when I opened the door t'let the sun in, basically. 'Cause one way or another, I knew I was gonna need it, later on."

That smile again. Sami looked anywhere but, while Dee met it straight on, glaring extra-hard: *You're gonna get yours, Chatwin, and sooner than you think. That's if I got anything to say about it.*

Would she, though? This was starting to be the baseline problem, whenever Sami and Chatwin got in close proximity. There was no denying the witch could be useful, in her way, but Christ.

She's evil, Sami, Dee tried to signal her sister. *And you, no matter what happened, 'fore you had me help you cut those binding tattoos into your skin—you're not. Don't matter how much blood you share; you and me must share the same amount, right? And human trumps demon, or should...*

But it wasn't like Sami could hear her, anyways. At least—

(—she didn't *think* so.)

Chatwin was leaning forward now, hand raised tentatively, like she actually thought she was going to try and lay it on Sami's shoulder in mock-sympathy, or some such shit. If she did, Dee thought, it was more than likely she—Dee—would respond to that unbearable provocation by leaning forward herself, and sticking her vamp-killin' blade so far through the part of Chatwin's wrist that didn't connect with Sami's flesh she might succeed in severing both bones at one *chunk.*

Luckily for everyone concerned, however, it didn't prove necessary, after all.

"We need to get to Professor Maks first," Sami said. "Then hold him, 'til his relatives show up. After which we can discuss all the people they've let him kill so far just to get a chance at turning him back, not to mention whether or not we were supposed to be three of them."

Dee sighed. "There go the spankin' new IDs."

Chatwin laughed at that, heartily. "Oh, Lady Di," she said, "that's precious. You should'a heard what they promised me, to get me t'deal myself in."

No, I shouldn't, Dee thought.

—

Dee left the magic shit to Sami and Chatwin, just like last time, when they'd ended up using a spell called the SATOR box and a scrap of dead girl's soul stuffed in an aspirin bottle to bust themselves out of M-vale. Just sat there and listened to them hash out how to use blood from two of old Prof Maartensbeck's spawn and

171

that goddamn book a whole bunch of people who'd never heard of him had all paid so much for to locate where he was right now, then drag them towards it, like iron filings to some tainted magnet. She was trying to remember everything Jeptha and Moriam had ever told her about vampires, which wasn't much, aside from *don't get within grabbing range* and *only thing really works for sure is the head comin' off*, so...

(And here she had a clearish image of Jeptha shrugging, somewhat baffled by his own contradiction. Shooting Moriam a smile as he did and seeing it returned, softly, yet with interest.)

Thinking: They did love each other, once. Just like Sami and me. That's the fucking pity of it.

Then remembering a little further on, the last time she'd seen him, after the date'd finally been set and all his appeals wrung out. Sitting there across from a man she barely recognized anymore, listening to him rant about how if she ever found out where her little sister was he was counting on her to *finish the damn job, this time, sentiment aside. You hear me, Dionne?* To which she'd just shook her head and answered *no, on no account, no fucking way—you hear me, Dad? Just goddamn no.*

They'd sat there a minute, glaring at each other with the same fierce eyes. *Because she's my sister, and I love her, no matter what. You do remember how that goes, right? Family is family, that's what you always said...up 'til the night you decided it wasn't, anymore.*

Think I didn't love your Mama, Dee? he'd answered, finally. *I did. Still do. But—*

—sometimes, that didn't mean as much as it should, in context. Sometimes it *couldn't*. Not when civilians were involved. And she knew that, too.

Britishisms aside, the Maartensbecks had to "understand" it just as well, if anybody did.

(*Civilians like Jesca Lind?* that voice at the back of Dee's mind asked her, though its tone also Jeptha's, as it often was. Not that that likeness was ever enough to keep her from ignoring it.)

I made my choice, Dee thought, giving her machete a last quick, sharpening scrape. And tuned back into the conversation still going on to her right, even while stowing the whetstone away in one of her jacket pockets.

"Now, you got to keep a tight hold, this time, Princess," Chatwin was warning Sami. "Don't wanna go spinnin' off all unexpected-like, not given the forces we're playin' with, here..."

"You just make sure we all arrive together—me, you *and* Dee," Sami replied. "Because if I come out of fugue and find her gone again, first thing I'm gonna do is put a thrice-blessed iron cross-nail right through your Third Eye."

"Witch's lobotomy? Perish the thought."

Dee stood up, tucking the machete out of sight. "All that mean we're good to go, or what?" she demanded, eyes firmly on Sami, who sighed. Replying, as she did—

"Good as we'll ever be, I guess."

Things contracted, then: there was some old-fashioned Appalachian hair-knotting and a bit of haemoglobin fingerpaint action, followed by a three-way handfasting and widdershins footwork on three, two, *one*. Seconds later, with a pitch-black spacetime *rip* through a wormhole where only Sami's lit-up tats showed the way, they stumbled like one clumsy, six-legged animal into the parking lot in front of one of those weird new airport motels with the courtyard inside the building, six stories of glass-fronted apartments looking only inward, where a sunken fountain-pool combo and some scattered built-in couches lurked.

Those apartments were all vacant now, though not exactly empty, their redly hand-printed vistas giving only the impression of drawn blinds, or maybe a fall of particularly virulent-coloured cherry blossoms. While down in the pit sat Professor Maks Maartensbeck, leant back in the now deep-dyed fountain's bowl with his equally-scarlet eyes half-shut and his long legs delicately crossed at the ankles, frankly luxuriating, dyed head to toe in unlucky moteliers' blood.

He'd swapped his Twister Relief dumpster outfit for what looked like the remains of a security guard's uniform along the way. Still slightly too big for him, but a far better overall impression.

And: "Well, ladies," he called up to them as they stood rooted in the doorway, ridiculously polite voice anti-naturally resonant, some distant silver key dragged over ice. "Two witches, both demon-blooded, both by the same sire—and one full human, by the same dam; hmmm, let me see. The fabled Dionne and Samaire Cornish, I presume, here to chastise me for my many sins...but who, pray tell, are *you?*"

Chatwin shrugged, then sidled in crosswise and sauntering, though Dee could tell even *her* hackles were up, under that don't-care prison swag show. Calling down: "Allfair Chatwin's my name, sir, thanks for askin'. But you can feel free t'call me A-Cat, you find yourself so inclined."

"Ah, yes. Descended from the fabled *demoiselles de Chatouye*, I'd wager, whose village was burnt by none other than these two's equal-distant genetic author, Witchfinder Corniche. *Voulteuses* of great power, all, as I'm sure you must be yourself, to find me so quickly... especially once one takes into account your—other connexions."

"Too kind, Professor. Just a humble holler-worker out of Black Bush, that's all."

"Oh, hardly."

They're fast, too, Moriam'd said, that long-ago night, *so don't forget it*—and holy shit was that ever true, what with all that fresh type whatever jacking up Maartensbeck's system. Because all it took was a blur of movement, a single tiny eyelid-flick, and there he was, right up in all three of their faces at once and smiling horribly, a highly-educated human shark with blood-breath sporting a manicure that—now you saw it close on—read halfway between Fu Manchu and full-on ten-fingered raptor.

"You see, modesty truly does ill-become creatures such as we, my dear," he told Chatwin, who stood there frozen for once, while Sami and Dee both shifted a half-step back into automatic attack-stance. "Why quibble terminology? Be proud, whatever you choose to call yourself."

Chatwin breathed out, visibly smoothing her face back into its usual smarm-charm lines. "No argument from me on that one," she replied, lightly. "In fact, you'll find monster pride's pretty much my middle name, under most circumstances...unlike *some* I could mention."

He smiled, gore-mask crinkling. "Well, then. Since you've mentioned her—" Switching over, to Sami: "What a very decorative object you've made of yourself, Miss Cornish, to be sure. Can those be binding sigils? In Crossing the River, no less?" She nodded. "One would think they'd make it rather more difficult to summon your power, even when faced with imminent threat. And yet one can only assume you thought that a desirable outcome, when you carved yourself all over with them."

Dry: "Uh huh."

"Why?"

"Less people get hurt this way."

Dee saw one stained yet elegant eyebrow tic up in disbelief. "Ah yes," the professor replied, with fine contempt. "*Morality.*"

"Kinda heard you had a thing for that, back in the day," Dee couldn't quite keep herself from snapping, though she knew it'd turn him her way—but hell, she was ass-tired of things like this supercilious old fuck always talking around her, just 'cause her Daddy wasn't the one with horns. So when Maartensbeck's blood-charged gaze met hers, she just smiled: not as sharp as him, but sharp enough. Only to be more surprised than she'd expected to be when, a moment later, he did the same.

"Little soldier," he called her, with what rang like a gross parody of affection (though for all she knew, he actually might've meant it). "How you remind me of Ruhel, at your age..." Then threw back over his shoulder without turning, diction still crisp, yet tone gone melting: "...or you, of course, Anapurna—is that the correct pronunciation? What a joy! I still remember what your father's heartbeat sounded like, in Ruhel's womb. You also have his smell."

Dee looked up, and found herself locking eyelines with what must be Chatwin's recruiter: little, yes—small as Dee herself—and definitely a shade darker than the Maartensbeck norm, curly beech-brown hair drawn back in a tightly-practical French braid, though her Bollywood movie-star eyes were as blue as his once must've been, or her grandmother's still were. Had a modified flare-gun held in a two-hand grip (white phosphorus? That would've been Dee's call) trained between the professor's shoulderblades, with the famous Kevlar gorget peeping from her silk blouse's collar. Much like Ruhel, she had her game face down pat, given that was undoubtedly who she'd learned it from. But—

It's different, when it's one of your own. Always.

"Great...*great*-grandfather," Anapurna Maartensbeck said, finally.

"Oh, that does seem a touch over-formal. Do call me Maks."

"I've—always wanted to meet you."

"And I you." Cornish sisters and Chatwin apparently equally forgotten in the face of this long-desired reunion, the professor turned his back on them and took a pace forward, chuckling when he saw

Anapurna's finger tighten on the trigger. "But where is my pretty girl, my dear-beloved granddaughter? Where is my Ruhel?"

"Here, grandfather. On your nine o'clock."

"Excellent. You never disappoint."

So here they all were, weapons either out or on the verge of being so, with the walking corpse of Professor Maks playing monkey in the middle. To her right, Dee had Anapurna, gun-barrel still levelled; to her left was Ruhel, having materialized out from behind what used to be the motel's front desk, toting what looked like either the world's biggest Taser or a high-tech portable flamethrower scaled down far enough you could hide it under your coat, like a shotgun.

Must be nice to get paid corporate rates, Dee thought.

"I'm sorry to have lied to you, at least by omission," Ruhel Maartensbeck told them, voice only slightly shaky, "but I needed that book, as well as my grandfather's location, and I needed whoever brought it to me not to know why. So while I must admit that Miss Chatwin turning out to be able to recognize it took me somewhat by surprise—"

Chatwin shook her head, trucker-hat bobbing. "Tch. Why does everybody assume just 'cause I never got my GED, I must'a stopped readin' for pleasure altogether?"

Dee could sympathize, not that she was going to say so. "Well, it's here now, one way or the other," she told Ruhel, instead. "It, him, and...about twenty dead bodies I can see plus six more floors of ones I can't, plus whoever else he might'a happened to kill, on the way over..."

"Plus the team you sent in to get it," Sami added, "up to and including the only guy he didn't gut right then and there, the guy A-Cat got your book from. Plus Leah, the waitress, who didn't even know what was happening to her, 'til Dee cut her damn head off. Her, those two guys in the kitchen, a couple more people who came in before Maks here was finished, just looking to get a midnight snack..."

The professor threw back his head and hooted, delightedly, while Ruhel's mouth trembled. "Please," she said. "I know what we've done must seem—excessive, to an outsider—"

Dee rounded on her. "'*Scuse* me? We're *hunters*, lady, just like you—that's how you fished us in, in the first place. So no, I don't

176

give a shit how nice he used to be, or whether or not you can maybe make him that way again: you let your granddad *eat* people, *real* people. The kind we're supposed to save from things like him."

"Be polite," Anapurna warned, her voice chill.

"Or *what*? How old are you, man? You don't even know him!"

"True enough. But I know *her*—when my mum and dad died, she's who took me in. So—"

"—She tells you he's worth however much collateral damage it takes, then that's what goes, huh?" Dee didn't quite spit, but it took effort. "Yeah, well—know what my parents told me? How you people were heroes."

At this, the professor laughed so hard he had to bend over just a bit, bracing himself, before finally trailing off. "Oh," he said, "that was delightful. Do you know what a hero is, my dear? As much a killer as anything he kills, but with far better public relations."

"That what the guy who made you this way told you?"

"Amongst other things." The professor sighed. "Ah, and now you've made me sad. I did think, you know—he and I having been nemeses for so long—that if I only caused a long enough trail of damage once I finally got on the other side of those five-foot-thick walls, he might hear about it, and come join me." A hapless shrug. "But...as you see."

"*Men,*" Chatwin commiserated, deadpan.

"All that effort, and all for nothing," the professor continued, as Sami and Dee shot each other a quick glance behind his back while Anapurna's eyes slid over to her grandmother, who was starting to look queasy. "I'd discorporated him five times already, throughout my career, which I now suspect he took as a variety of flirtation. But then I was old, and one night I dreamt he appeared in my bedroom, telling me he'd slipped some of his blood into my food. *You will change either way, Maks, but if you meet me directly, if you let me do as I please, I can keep you from harming Ruhel, at the very least.* I agreed, naturally enough—"

"—Because that was the sort of man you were," Ruhel broke in here, desperately. "Because you were good."

"No, child: because I was a fool. Because I didn't know, then, how little I'd care about hurting you at all, once the deed was done." If he heard her little gasp, horror-filled and breath-caught, he gave no sign. "So I went out past the point where my home's protective

wards ceased to work, and I bared my neck to him. Even thoroughly
infected, I had time to make my peace and write out instructions
before falling into a trance; when I woke, Ruhel had already pris-
oned me inside the vault. Of course, I understood why he wouldn't
try to free me himself—I'd designed it, after all. A dreadful place,
and booby-trapped, to boot. But still I warmed myself over those
intervening years with the idea that if and when, he'd surely be
bound to come and meet with me, at last—just drop by for a little
look-see, no social obligations assumed. No...pressure."

"So you could kill him," Anapurna suggested.

"Oh no. So I could *thank* him."

Ruhel gasped again, the sound deeper this time, more of a half-
sob; Anapurna jerked a bit, as if face-slapped. Then said, with a op-
timism she didn't seem to feel: "But we have the book, yes? The
Clavicule. So we can put it all back, the way it should be. The way
you should be."

"And how's that, exactly?"

"*Human.* That was...the whole point, of all of this."

With mild disbelief: "Oh, dear. My poor, sweet girl, *really*—why
on earth would you think I would ever want *that?*"

And there it lay, at last, between all seven of them: the gauntlet.
Dropped like it was proverbially hot, a mic, or a fuckin' bomb.

"Well, there you go," Dee heard herself observe, ostensibly to
Anapurna, who she almost thought she saw give a tiny little nod in
return—before Ruhel jumped in on top, crying out: "But you can't
possibly mean it, grandfather—you, who taught me to always keep
fighting, no matter what! This isn't your fault, for pity's sake. You
have a condition, but it's curable, and with the book's help, you'll be
exactly the person you were again, before all this...oh God, why are
you still laughing?"

Because he doesn't give a shit, Dee wanted to blurt at her, to grab
and shake her, bodily—anything to keep her from abasing herself in
front of this goddamned ghoul, this *sacrilege,* just because it wore a
rough approximation of the person she'd once loved best in all the
world's face.

But—

"Well, one never does know 'til one's in it, so to speak," Professor
Maks explained, grotesquely reasonable. "But the fact is, I may have
told you a bit of a fib, my darling, without meaning to—because so

far as I can tell, I am exactly the same person I was before, right now. I know what I've done. It's just, as I've already said, that I simply can't seem to bring myself to *care*."

And: *Oh, we got trouble now,* Dee's brain told her, stupidly. As though it'd somehow convinced itself they hadn't had any, before.

Out of the corner of one eye, Dee saw Chatwin reach to slip her hand in Sami's, brazen as ever—and Sami, with no other alternative, close her fingers on it, hard. Saw those sketchy sigil-letters start to light up all up and down her arms, hair haloed and lifting; saw the trucker hat pop straight off of Chatwin's asshole head, as her own mane did much the same. And felt the power they were both suddenly funneling into her start to light her own medulla oblongata up like a bulb, switching her over to full berserker mode without her even asking. The machete's blade glowed horizon-flash green as she struck out, burying it hilt-deep through the prof's long-dead bicep; he whipped 'round snake-quick, all fangs, but Dee managed to dodge and slip anyhow, steering him straight into a twinned blast of arcane witch-juice from Sami and Chatwin's upraised, fisted fingers that sent him reeling, almost flipping back into the fountain.

At almost the same instant, Anapurna pulled the trigger, firing into his side. White light bloomed, taking half her great-great-grandfather's ribcage with it; he gave a shriek, spinning sidelong, then shrieked yet again when Ruhel discharged her own weapon, half-harpooning him with species of grappling-hook that chunked in deep and sizzled as she juiced him hard: once, twice, three times, 'til his hair stood straight on end, smoking, and his eyes rolled up white in their sockets. But did he fall?

(No.)

Sharp teeth set and grinding, Maks Maartensbeck clambered grimly to his feet once more, shook himself like a wet dog, throwing off sparks. And began, by slow, tug-of-war degrees, to pull the cable between them ever tighter, reeling her steadily in.

Though Ruhel fought him all the way, it was a foregone conclusion; Anapurna scrabbled in her vest for another cartridge, tore her palms reloading, but his claws were already closing on her grandmother's throat—so she threw a glance Dee's way instead, too angry to beg, and Dee found herself punching Sami's arm, gesturing at the book Chatwin still clung to. "*Read it!*" she yelled.

Sami's brows shot up, startled by the very notion…just as Chatwin, predictably unpredictable, flipped the folio open one-handed, and started to do exactly that.

"*O judge of nations!*" she yelled out. "*Ye who threw down Bethsaida, Chorazin, Sodom! Ye who raised Lazarus up, whose voice spoke out of the head of the tempest! Ye who made the bush of the Hebrews burn!*"

"*Lift up this carrion flesh, and make it clean!*" Sami chimed in, scanning the page over Chatwin's shoulder. "*Ye who made wine of Your own blood and bread of Your own meat, heal even this mortal wound! Ye who harrowed Hell, put fear into this black and fearless heart!*"

At the first few words, a shudder straightened the professor's spine, whip-cracking him erect. His mouth squared in pain, "You—" he began. "You, I—stop it. Damn you! Stuh, stuh—stop—"

Not likely, motherfucker. One more time, Dee glanced at Anapurna, who nodded, and whistled at Ruhel: a three-note phrase, very definite, clearly some signal. Still vainly fighting against the pull, Ruhel reached inside her jacket for a glass ampoule of some red liquid, which she broke open with her thumb and deftly tossed, splattering its contents across her grandfather's deformed face. The bulk of it landed straight between those snapping jaws, sizzling as it went down; Maks Maartensbeck coughed smoke, then retched outright, bringing up a rush of hot, black, stinking mess. His hands slipped off the Taser's cable, letting Ruhel leap away even as Anapurna jumped forward, landing a vicious kick to the small of his back that sent him crashing further down, face against the floor.

"*Adjuramus te, draco maledicte!*" Sami told him, every word a blow, under whose impact Dee watched him writhe. "*Exorciso te! Humiliare, sub potente manu Dei!*" To which Chatwin added, without any apparent shred of irony: "*For my God is frightening in His holy places, since all places are those He has made, and thus it is His name before which all terrible things must tremble.*"

The professor looked up, punished face-skin starting to darken and tremble, almost to melt and run—and was it just the light in here, or did his squinted eyes suddenly look less red, more blue? "Whah *wash* thah?" he demanded of Ruhel, then spat yet more black, before continuing: "Ih fehlt...*blashphemous.*"

"Communion wine, blessed by the pope. The literal Blood of Christ."

"Buh ohny a priesht—"

A sad smile. "You told me yourself, grandfather: we have an

indulgence, because of what we do. Who we *are*."

Yeah. 'Cause Sami and her, they were just itinerants like Mom and Dad, riding 'round from town to town in a series of stolen cars, dodging Feds and killing things out the back. But the Maartensbecks were Templars, for real, Vatican giftbags included...and for all Dee'd found herself thinking *must be nice*, earlier on, maybe it wasn't so much. Not the way Ruhel made it sound.

"Sympathetic magic," Sami murmured, to which Chatwin snorted.

"Or some-such," she replied. "Ain't religion grand?"

They looked up to find Anapurna glaring at them both, eyes wild enough to make Dee automatically reach for her drop-piece, the little .22 she kept holstered up one sleeve. Hissing, as she juiced the Professor twice more, in quick succession: "*Did she tell you to stop?*"

"*Do not keep in mind, O Lord, our offenses or those of our parents, nor take vengeance on our sins,*" Sami replied, not skipping a beat, while Maks Maartensbeck—him, increasingly, rather than the terrible force that had driven his frail form hither and yon these forty-plus years, gulping down anything stupid enough to come near—shuddered at her feet. "*Lift this sufferer like Lazarus, out of the grave. Bring him forth, whole once more.*"

"*Restore him,*" Chatwin agreed. "*Change his gall for blood, corruption for health. Set him free.*"

"*This we pray: liberate him from the mouth of the Abyss, ex inferis, in nomine patris, et filis—*"

"*—Et Spiritus Sanctii,*" they all chimed in on this last part, seemingly without premeditation: Ruhel, Dee, Ana. Dee glanced down herself as she said it, eyes drawn back to the sheer spectacle of the professor's—Jesus, who knew, at this point: salvation, ruination. One out of the other, out the back and right back in, straight on through 'til morning...

Saw his lips move, whitening, firming. Saw his wounds begin to bleed, first clear, then red. And heard him gasp as the pain came rushing in, at last—a torrent of it, others' as well as his own, deferred almost half a hundred years. The pain, so long forgotten, of being merely human.

"Ruhel..." he managed, just barely, but she heard it; fell to her knees in the mess at the sound, all uncaring of her lovely suit, and hugged him so hard he screamed. Exclaiming, as she did: "It *worked*, oh God, you're cured. I *knew* it would. Oh, grandfather..."

Anapurna, boot still on his back and her gun leveled between his shoulderblades, seemed unconvinced, but Ruhel laughed and wept like a child; Dee wanted to look somewhere else, but was sort of starved for options. The professor, meanwhile, took it just as long as he could before gingerly shifting back, Taser's cable dragging painfully between them. And—

"No, Ruhel," he managed, lips twisting wry over a mouthful of newly-blunted teeth. "It...simply won't do, you know."

"Grandfather?"

"Oh my girl, you *know* it won't. Look around you. *Someone* has to pay for...all this."

She shook her head, shamed, dumb. Put a hand up to stop him speaking only to have him print a kiss onto her palm, so light and sweet it made her groan out loud, then fold to sag against him, sobbing against his frail, torn chest. He patted her awkwardly with the arm that wasn't left hanging, Dee's blade still stuck through it, and addressed the others over her shoulder, head turning in a short half-circle to them in turn—Sami and Chatwin, Dee, Anapurna. "Ladies," he began, visibly exhausted, "there is...so much I must leave unsaid, and for that...I apologize, most of all for how quickly I must discard this gift you've bled to grant me. The last thing I wish is to seem ungrateful. But...blood sows guilt, as we Maartensbecks well know. And I..."

Gaze left steady on Anapurna alone now, her stepping back, regarding him for the first time as anything but a threat. Those fine blue eyes, both sets of them, shining with unshed tears.

"I understand," she said.

"I have...been damned, all this time, utterly. But what they did saved me..." Nodding down, as Ruhel continued to cry: "*She* saved me, as she always said she would. I was the one who...tainted it. Do you understand *that*?"

"I think so, sir."

But she didn't move, and neither did he—gaze holding steady while hers slipped sidelong, supplicant, almost. Pleading. For what?

Dee wondered, but only momentarily.

"You want to die, again," she said, out loud. "For real, this time. But you can't pull the trigger—damn yourself all over, if you do. That right?" The professor didn't answer, but didn't object. Dee nodded at Anapurna. "So you want her to kill you, instead."

"'Want' would be a...strong word."

"For her too, given she fights monsters and you're not one anymore. Plus, you're family."

(*I know a little about that.*)

Anapurna stiffened, gun jerking back up, as though challenged. "Never said I wouldn't," she snapped, to which Dee shrugged, making a placatory movement: *Peace, lady. Managed to get this far without shooting each other—let's go for the gold, huh?*

"Just think maybe it'd go better if it wasn't either of you," she said, mainly to Maks. "'Cause when you're bent on doing good, doing bad—no matter why—don't ever seem to help."

He didn't bother to nod, but Anapurna did it for him, so...good enough, Dee guessed. Pressed tight to her granddad's clavicle, Ruhel covered her eyes with both hands and wept on, bitterly. And Dee reached into her sleeve, for real this time—not knowing if Sami was watching, but sure as hell not wanting to check, either. Hoping Chatwin was, though, and attentively, as she cocked back and dug the barrel into his fragile, rehumanized temple.

Been dead a long time, she reminded herself. But: "I'm sorry," she heard herself tell him, nevertheless. To which he merely smiled, answering, with amazing self-control—

"I'm not."

(*So thank you, dear girl. Thank you.*)

Over his shoulder, she saw Anapurna not quite close her own eyes because somebody had to stay on point, and thought: *Damn, if you didn't get the exact same training I did. We could've been friends, maybe, if not for this.*

But that's just me, right? Always the bad cop.

"Okay, then," Dionne Cornish said, to no one in particular, as she pulled the trigger.

—

In the motel battle's immediate aftermath, nobody but the surviving Maartensbecks was greatly surprised to discover that Allfair Chatwin had used the Professor's death as distraction and run off while the getting was good, taking the easy-to-sell-for-travelling-cash *Clavicule des Pas-Morts* with her. Since Ruhel—icy veneer firmly back in place—was already on the phone arranging cover-up plus retrieval for her grandfather's corpse, however, now finally set to occupy the tomb bearing his name at last, Anapurna was the one who offered the Cornishes a ride to the Canadian border, along with those fabled clean new IDs.

"Chatwin'll be our next project, if I have any say in it," she promised Dee, too.

"Good luck with that," Sami replied, crossing her arms, not quite allowing herself to shiver.

Later yet, as the miles were eaten up beneath them and Dee stared at the back of Anapurna's head, rubbing fingers still a little bruised from the recoil, Sami leant over to assure her she'd done the right thing—"The *only* thing, Dee, under the circumstances. He knew it. You do too."

"Do I?" Dee shook her head. "Don't feel that way. More like... well. Kinda—"

"—Like it sets a bad example?"

A pause. "There is that," Dee eventually agreed, so quiet she could barely tell herself what she thought about it.

CANADA: ONE HUNDRED FEET, the next sign said. Above, the moon hung high; Anapurna Maartensbeck tapped the wheel as she drove, beating out some tune Dee couldn't identify. "So who's this guy your—the prof kept on talkin' about?" Dee asked her, falling back on business, for lack of better conversational topics.

"Juleyan Laird Roke," Anapurna replied, not turning. "Wizard first, then graduated to vampire at the moment of his execution, during the Civil War—ours, not yours—through some spasm of ill will and sciomancy. Helped that he was a quarter fae on his mother's side, with ten generations of hereditary magic-workers on the other...a rancid bastard, too, from all accounts. Doesn't surprise me a bit that he left poor old Maks to rot, once he'd had his way."

"Uh huh. So tell me, Miss M—is some holler witch you barely know *really* at the top of your list, with *this* guy still on the loose?"

"Perhaps not."

"Good luck again, then. Twice over."

"And let's hope the chase ends better for me than it did for my great-grandfather? Why, Miss C, I'm touched." An expert swerve took them into the express lane, where Anapurna slowed to an idle. "Enough so to wish you the same, in fact, on your journey. Since, after all..."

But here she broke off, maybe thinking better of finishing the thought, considering how Sami was sitting right there all extra-large as life, listening. Or how she already knew Dee had a gun.

Because: *Some hunt monsters,* Dee thought, *and some become monsters, in their turn. But some are just made that way, with no say at all in the matter—collateral damage, already born fucked, just waiting for the worst possible moment to fall down.*

Family as destiny, its own little ecology, forever struggling forwards, forever thrown back. But...it didn't have to be a foregone conclusion, was what Dee believed, at the end of the day. What she had to make herself believe, to keep on going.

What's the difference? she wondered, knowing there wasn't much of one—that there couldn't be, for any of it to work. And reached out, in the darkness, to take her sister's hand.

THE
SPEED OF
PAIN

ive o'clock a.m., and all's definitely *not well.*

That's the thought to which Nimue Ewalt wakes, more or less, as she pulls herself headlong from the shreds of her latest Valerian-influenced nightmare. She reaches for her nightstand sketch-pad before the connect-the-dots "narrative" behind that cold hand in her sternum can dissolve into complete uselessness, shivers plucking up and down her arms as she scrabbles for a pen in the half-open drawer, while Veruca Luz snores asthmatically on the futon couch across the room...

...and shit, what *was* it, now? A hazy wash of images overlaid like bad Flash on an overburdened browser, shucking files Trashbound right and left and spiralling headlong downwards towards the final Big Freeze...

Out on a deserted beach at night, maybe Cherry, maybe not; the Island's polluted shore spread out behind her in a blur of garbage, rocks cold against her naked back, black lake-water lapping at her toes. No stars above. And this sensation of being watched by something hidden, maybe from above, maybe below. Of laying herself open—physically, psychically—to wait for an unseen enemy, already settling down upon her like a cloud: entering by the mouth, leaving by the sex. Splitting her from stem to stern entire, in a sudden spray of heat and blood and waste.

Then being buried in the beach's wet sand, spade-full by hideously slow spade-full—broken, paralyzed, yet somehow still alive, a turtle's egg stewed fast in its own leathery shell. A chrysalis, waiting to hatch.

But with that, Nim abruptly finds herself shaking all over, so hard she can't hold the pen straight enough for legible notes anymore. So she lets it go instead, pulls the covers close around her, while Veruca sleeps on. Keeps her unspectacled eyes front, focus lost against the far wall's blurry stucco veneer, and waits for morning.

—

There's an early frost in Toronto this August; no big deal, a few black tomatoes here and there, but try telling that to somebody who's used to running on California time-slash-weather. So Veruca wraps herself up like Arnold Vosloo every time they set foot outdoors, complaining endlessly about how the cold could affect her septal piercing, how if it goes below a certain temperature it could set off one of her migraines. How since of course she left her medicine at home, or maybe lost it in transit someplace, that leaves her prospectively SOL when the hypothermic muscle tension comes a-callin'…

So: "Just take the fucking thing *out*, then," Nim snaps back at her, finally—not exactly wanting to be too much of a bitch on wheels, but not willing to seem too sympathetic, either; this *is* Veruca we're talking about, after all. And with Veruca, there's always *one more thing*.

She feels bad about it almost immediately afterward, though, especially when Veruca looks down and sniffs, bolt swinging. Saying, quietly:

"Dude, you don't have to be like that. I mean…I'll be fine, totally, I'm sure. For tonight, I mean. I'm just, y'know…"

(Just what? But for the love of God, please please please don't say)

"...just...sayin'."

And here endeth the lesson, Nim finds herself thinking, for neither the first time nor (probably) the last: *File under Truism 'cause it's true, and never again let yourself think that because you like somebody online, you'll like 'em in person. Or, say—*

(at ALL)

Because virtual friendships should stay just that: virtual. Or risk spawning prospective justified manslaughter charges, on BOTH sides of the equation.

Nim takes another sidelong glance at Veruca, bundled well beyond the tenth power, with the very roots of her bleached-blonde skater grrrl-cum-faux chola cornrows visible where her hoodie meets her hairline; eyes with a semi-epicanthic droop peek out from under boxy black-rimmed glasses, half-squinted against any light brighter than that of a screen set on PowerSave. Doesn't help that Veruca seems to revel in the same chin-to-chest geekslump Nim's spent hours trying to yoga away, either, or that her voice constantly ricochets back and forth between whine (when upset) and monotone (when anything else), like she's never even taken the time to consider how she might sound to other humans.

It all makes being near her familiar and dreadful in teeth-grittingly equal measure, cringe-worthy the same way flipping through your Mom's hidden stash of high-school snapshots is—Veruca's everything Nim used to be, back before Nim wised up, *grew* up. Back before she knew, or cared about knowing, any better.

The funny thing being...in e-correspondence or chat-rooms, on ICQ or her blog, Veruca's one seriously impressive cyber-chick: She can actually spell, for one thing, which helps sort the wheat from the chaff straight off; got a strong grasp on punctuation and sentence structure, can debate without degenerating into FlameWar territory, always backs up even her oddest points with quotes or links, or both. A delight to "hang" with, no matter the URL occupied, and somebody Nim's always considered one of the closest non-RL friends on her friendslist.

But in person, Christ Almighty, in *person*—

—in person, Veruca is shy, awkward, adenoidal to the point of incoherence, scarily opinionated, possibly hypochondriac. Inside

Nim's apartment, she's barely communicative; outside, she exhibits all the fine interpersonal skills of Kaspar Hauser.

She's also so obsessed with each and every facet of (say it with me now, in unison) The Late Timothy Darbersmere's life and work as to literally talk of very little else, no matter the context or circumstances…a fact, Nim is forced to admit, that she A) certainly can't say she hadn't already known, given the two of them first hooked up when Google directed her to Veruca's Darbersmere fanlisting (*A Man of Wealth and Taste*, for those who like their Stones references so old as to be practically crunchy) and B) once considered far more a plus than a minus, way back when. I.e., in those halcyon days before she'd actually met her, or been forced to squire her around in public, where they might occasionally collide with those few people whose good opinion Nim truly cares about keeping.

Still. After tonight, after the Speed of Pain opens its doors and Veruca walks through them—eyes darting 'round like she's on crack, continually peeled for any brief glimpse of The Late Tim's mysterious heir/nephew Tom, the Speed's new co-owner—Nim's probably (hopefully) never going to have to see, talk to or think about her again. She'll have served her purpose, gross as that sounds. And if, a second past the Speed's midnight, she tells Veruca to lose her number—along with her addy, her ICQ handle, and any other bloody thing Veruca can remember about her—well, to be frank, Veruca will have only herself to blame.

But that prospective relief, either cutting contact with Veruca for good or finding an environment where she's once more bearable, is still hours off. If pain really has a speed, then right now Nim would have to call it pure glacier: heavy, cold, creeping. Going out only seemed like a good idea in comparison to remaining trapped in Nim's tiny no-bedroom; she's since been forced to settle for the Second Cup three blocks away instead of the Starbucks two doors down, because Veruca (surprise, surprise) considers the funky green mermaid logo Ground Zero for the Evil Empire of Globalization, and refuses on principle to contribute Dime One to it.

So here Nim is, making do with the second-class blends Second Cup specializes in, while Veruca's green tea cools untouched on the table in front of her—unable to compete for even a second, in terms of interest, with Veruca's latest Darbersmere monologue.

"You see the same threads running through every story," Veruca rambles. "Like, if you look at the first couple of stories Tom came out with, it's pretty obvious he's picked up where Tim left off: Human relationships are based on deception, people adapt to crisis by cannibalizing their own minds for parts, run rampant 'til sooner or later, God cuts 'em down. His word choices, his phraseology, all lifted straight from Tim's." She leans forward. "Know what happens if you take the profanity out of Tom's story 'Starfucker,' though? I did that—transcribed the whole thing, dropped all the swears and translated all the automatic street cred shit back into, like, 'proper English.' And guess how it comes out?"

"Two thousand words shorter?" Nim's dry response fails to adequately cover the profoundly nonplussed, almost frightened, bemusement she feels.

"Sounding exactly like Tim."

"And you know 'exactly' how he sounds because…?"

"He spoke to me." For a minute Nim thinks Veruca's being metaphorical, but no. "On his last tour, for *The Bodiless and Embodied.* I might've been the last person to see him alive."

Oh, riiight.

Because now Nim remembers this story…she's only heard it half a million times before, after all. How Veruca sold her first motherboard to get down to St. Louis in 1999, so she could get her '79 first-printing copy of *Jaguar Cactus Fruit (a Novel in Slices)* signed in person, and tell the Late what "a babe" he was as he did it. To which stalkerish infringement of personal space he apparently smiled, and said—Veruca's treasured imitation sliding quickly into *Withnail & I* territory here, every vowel a languorous string of same, sing-songing happily like she doesn't even get how pedophile-creepy its actual content is—

—*You should have seen me when I was twelve, my dear.*

Tim isn't exactly available anymore, though: Took a header off the interstate two days after and went up in a classic Bruckheimer-movie fireball, along with his driver (some Chinese-British guy hired for the tour) and all his prospective works. Aside from whatever was in his rhetorical bottom drawer, all of which Tom now has V.C. Andrews-style legal access to…

That's the rumour, anyhow.

"People say he'd just sent 'The Emperor's…' off to the printer," Veruca continues, rapt and hushed. "Like, he might've finished it

191

that same night. People say—"

"People say Pop Rocks and Coke melt your insides, 'Ruca. 'The Emperor's...' is a myth."

"I've read excerpts."

"You've read fanfiction. Shit *you* could've written—hell, I could've written. Any Darbersmere groupie with a keyboard and a modem."

Veruca's lower lip pooches out. "You're wrong, Nim. It's not just hosted text somewhere, okay? I've seen *scans,* I've seen—" She stops, resets herself. "Besides, it's classic Tim," she goes on, weakly. "His life, pulled out further—like that thing he wrote about that accident he had, or how his first wife left him stranded in Kiev with no papers, or how he got diagnosed with cancer and thought he had six months to live..."

None of which is anything like provable, Nim wants to counter. None of which stands up to even the slightest real scrutiny. None of which we have anybody's testimony for but his, *in the final analysis—that stuff, right? I.e.,* fiction?

"Great, sure, okay. So maybe *Tom* wrote it," Nim says, finally. And leaves it at that.

In her crappier moods, Nim now sometimes doubts she ever really liked Tim Darbersmere's writing at all; never in the same way Veruca does, anyhow. She spends a moment musing over the relative merits of "coolness" for coolness' sake, as Veruca drones on...how when you're fifteen or so, something can seem really great simply because it's really alien, but that's a reaction you eventually (hopefully, if you're lucky, or normal) grow out of. It sloughs off relative to your own RL experience: The more you rack up, the less you feel the need to surf through somebody else's consciousness, especially when all you get out of it is feeling cool by osmosis.

That sick glamour, that *Fin du Monde* decadence, that faker-than-thou exoticism. It's the sort of classic Art School push-pull you get from certain Cronenberg movies—like "ewww, gross!" mixed with "show me more, show me more!"...and definitely the exact kind of creepy high you'd have to be riding in order to make reading about pledging your true perfect love in some kid's still-living flesh a plus, rather than a minus.

(Because yes, Nim's read the spoilers; she knows damn well what "The Emperor's..." is *supposed* to be about, thank you very much, just like everybody else who claims to have seen the thing itself does. Or everybody else who'd willingly sell their soul to do so.)

Still: *This is yet another thing that she's never going to get,* Nim finds herself thinking. *Because to Veruca, her own tiny opinions about irrelevant crap like this are as close to 'RL experience' as she's ever going to come.*

Thus this whole trip, potential chance to hit up Tom, Darbersmere 2.0, the exact same way Veruca did his uncle: autograph, anecdote, squee! And when Nim first volunteered (*let's not forget that: you* did *volunteer*) to host her, the over-the-top delirium of gratitude Veruca responded with had been as endearing as it was gratifying—all now, in 20/20 hindsight, nothing but a bright red warning sign.

Why do you even need to meet him, anyhow? she keeps on asking Veruca, even now; idle curiosity turned psychic self-defense, news at eleven. Tom, *not Tim, right? Dude...he's just a guy.*

To which Veruca always replies, simply: *No. He's not.* The sheer weight of faith behind her words so scary-blind, it drains Nim of any sort of satisfactory response.

Strictly speaking, she can't deny Thomas Caudwell Darbersmere carries his own cloud of intrigue: Sole executor of the Darbersmere Estate and Trust, he runs the family Import/Export business, even though he's less a straight-up nephew than a sort of half-cousin once removed—illegitimate son of the dead drug-addict daughter of Tim's dad, Eustace Darbersmere's first wife, with her second husband. There's speculation that since Tom didn't pop up until after Tim kacked it, maybe he forged his name on the will somehow in order to get hold of the business and/or the books...after all, he does apparently make part of his current dough from a publishing deal allowing him to "complete" any of Tim's unfinished manuscripts, extant or conveniently hitherto-undiscovered.

Does bear a scary resemblance to Young Tim, though, from what Nim can make out by comparing recent 'Net-snaps of Tom-and-his-wife (Alicia, social-climbing American former nobody turned instant somebody, the Speed's real ringmaster) with those awful 1970s photos Veruca dug up. For an otherwise sleek Christian Bale clone, the dude had some seriously funky polyester fetish, and unfortunately, bad fashion sense seems to have *not* skipped Tom's generation.

But like most digital snapshots taken by overexcited amateur paparazzi, the majority of Tom's pics tend to be caught in mid-motion, too smeary to make much out, his face flashbulb-haloed, back-lit, blurred equally often by laughter or the smoke from Alicia's ever-present cigarette. It's possible that in person Tom may look disquietingly unlike his revered uncle, and be nothing like him in personality, either.

"Y'know, V," Nim says now, all casual, "I was thinking, just for tonight, we—"

(meaning you)

"—should maybe go easy on the Tim stuff."

Veruca blinks, mid-sip; puts her cup down. "How do you mean, 'go easy'?"

"Well...the club, the launch, this whole night, I mean—" She hesitates. "Given who's running the show, it might be kind of, I don't know—rude."

Nim lets a heartbeat tick by, bracing herself. But Veruca, surprisingly enough, nods.

"Listen," she starts, so quietly Nim has to strain to hear, "I get that. I just need to...figure something out, and I think if I could only see Tom, hear his voice, it might all come clear for me. Plus—I might have something for him."

"Like what?"

"...Something," she replies, mysterious to the Nth degree. And it makes Nim want to—

(laugh, cry, puke, punch her in the mouth, hard)

Sitting there with half a muffin in hand, rehearsing comebacks she'll never quite have the balls to make, Nim huffs out, angry at her own cowardice, then tries to cover the sound with a cough. Then looks up, reflexively, to find Veruca staring right at her.

"You okay?" Veruca asks, the very pitch of it enough to make Nim snap:

"Do I seem *not* okay?"

Veruca flushes. "Uh...well..."

(get to it, get to it, get to it)

"...you seem really pissed off, actually. Is something wrong? Are you...not gonna take me there, tonight, or something?"

Yeah: 'Cause that's the deal-breaker, right there. Isn't it?

"Of course I'll still take you," Nim snarls, eventually. "Jesus fucking Christ! Couldn't get there on your own, that's for sure. Besides which, I already goddamn said I would, didn't I?"

"Yeah, you did." A beat, then: "Why?"

(Why indeed?)

"Because I didn't know you, back then," Nim says. And gets up to pay their tab, back stiff, turned flat one-eighty to Veruca. Like she's shutting a door in her face.

—

From Scarwid and Ffolkes' *Overview of Millennial Fantasists* (Coldwater Flat Press, 2000)—

FFOLKES: I'll begin with a few of your late uncle's more noteworthy reviews, if I may...

TOM DARBERSMERE: Oh yes, please.

FFOLKES: "The bloody meat of Tim Darbersmere's stories is always the exact opposite of the soothing, reasonable tone in which he communicates it." "Never has such beautiful and clever prose been suborned to the service of such decadent and puerile ideas." "Solipsistic to the point of sociopathy. Darbersmere is the sole protagonist of every story he's ever written...the hero, the villain, and (most certainly) the love interest." As you begin your own writing career, does the potential after-effect of these remarks disturb you?

DARBERSMERE: Not at all. I aspire, one day, to a similar critical impact.

FFOLKES: And "Ellis Iseland," what about her? Why has she become central to your fiction, too—carried over from your late uncle's work, for continuity's sake? Or does she represent some more personal archetype, perhaps?

DARBERSMERE: Ellis who? Oh, you mean the chainsmoking war profiteer *femme fatale* from that last story Uncle Tim's supposed to have written, the one no one's ever reliably found a copy of?

FFOLKES: "The Emperor's Old Bones," yes.

DARBERSMERE: Wherein we find out the secret key to eternal

life and renewed youth is making a meal of filleted ghetto child? Well, that's a bit like quizzing me on a viral Internet meme, one of those things that seep into the creative community's groundwater without anyone noticing how, and wondering why you don't get more of a distinct response.

FFOLKES: But she turns up here too, doesn't she, in Tim's own "Echidna Comes Rising"—he calls her Lisha Illen, granted, but each version is described using much the same language. Or here, from your novella "Copshawholme Fair": Elfis Isham. Essa Highman in *A Dull Wind Blows from the North*, Ester Smallwaterhame in *Safe in Their Alabaster Hives*...

DARBERSMERE: Does she? I suppose she must. How extraordinary! You know, I never read my own stuff once I'm finished with it, no more than I re-read his. I really must start.

FFOLKES: Everyone's got a type, I suppose.

DARBERSMERE: Oh, certainly. Every woman I write is my wife, to one degree or another.

—

The package is waiting for them when they get back to Nim's. As Veruca trudges past, still sunk in the same kicked-puppy misery haze that made their silent walk back so excruciating, Nim unlocks her mailbox and frowns at the result: a flat rectangle wrapped in subtly-striped brown paper with a registered-mail barcode in one corner, poking up out of the rest of Friday's bills. The return is a name she doesn't recognize, in Australia; scrawled across the front in letters two inches tall, meanwhile, is—

ATTN VERUCA LUZ C/O NIMUE EWALT

"Veruca!" Nim's a little startled by, but not really sorry for, her own shout's volume; Veruca skitters back down, eyes wide, as she holds up the parcel. "What the hell? You gave my mailing address out to some guy, without even asking me? You—"

But Veruca throws herself headlong to rip it from Nim's hand, tearing at the paper, all the while emitting such a fast high-pitched squeak it takes Nim a second to decipher it: "Ooh, owemjee owem-jee owemjee owemjee owem*jeeee!*"

Owemjee, equalling OMG as in Oh My God, in 'Net-compact-ed typespeak for terminally lazy hunt-and-peckers. As in—

Let's get this straight…you can't be bothered to fill in four extra let-ters, like you were actually saying something out loud? Like a GENUINE *FUCKING ADULT?*

"What is it?" Nim makes herself ask, at last. And Veruca turns it towards her with a *The Prestige*-y flick of the wrist, showman-like, conspiratorial: Ricepaper cardstock cover, deep Chinese red, embossed carp design. Pretty classy, actually, for some cheap little one-story printing…

"Read the title," she says. So Nim does.

(Oh.)

For a moment, she's back on that blackwater beach, under that starless sky. It sort of hurts to breathe. The letters swim in front of her, drunken and dripping, pixilated in some almost tidal way—twenty characters if you count the apostrophe, letters slightly raised, DomCasual BT script at 22-point font. The Late's name under-neath, silver-stamped; his real signature or a very good imitation, probably traced from a treasured memento, by somebody like Ver-uca.

Because: There it is, the thing itself, its lacquered cover slick like skin under her increasingly sweaty fingers. And she can't take her eyes off it.

While Veruca watches, her own green gaze reflective, serene. Al-most sad.

"You see why I had to come, now?" she asks, gently. To which Nim can only nod, once. And then—

—

Flash-cut to later, as Nim logs on to CreepTracker.org while Veruca cat-naps, getting herself good and charged for the full-fron-tal assault on Darbersmere Central. CreepTracker's Nim's favorite chat-hangout of choice, not to mention run by another "friend" she's yet to meet in the non-virtual flesh (and man, is she starting to think that may never seem like a good idea again, no matter how calm and reasonable Ross Puget may seem when he's just text on a screen, plus a blurred icon that's all crested prematurely-grey hair and wide, crooked smile...)

Word on the 'Net, and it's not like he denies this, is Ross used to co-run a three-way hazmat cleaning service—Glouwer-Cirrocco-Puget, currently defunct due to one of the founding members being kind of dead, the other kind of nuts—that was either a total scam or less about asbestos removal than scouring sites of "psychic fragments." <not ghosts, there are no ghosts. just, stuff.> With a space/pause between <just,> and <stuff> that's somehow more convincing than the most detailed explanation could *ever* be—in person, or otherwise.

Nim's fingers fly over the keyboard, 60-words-a-minute speedy, more sure than she's felt since she first touched "The Emperor's..." fabled frontispiece. Asking—

GirlInTree: <the speed of pain, whats the deal? hear anything?>
KirlianPhotog: <how so?>
GirlInTree: <like psychic fragments etc.>
KirlianPhotog: <aaah. comprehension dawns, hold on>
<clicky-clicky>

Her server sings its "you have mail!" song, and she keys the link Ross just sent her: more like link salad, actually—different sites, different names, different angles. But the key-words stay the same: BODY FOUND...C.O.D. NOT APPARENT...NO CHARGES...WITNESS TESTIMONY LATER DISCOUNTED...INTOXICATED...UNDER INFLUENCE OF DRUGS...EXTREME COLD...BRIGHT WHITE LIGHT...

KirlianPhotog: <got it?>
GirlInTree: <yup:)>

Seven people over three years in two separate clubs—one in New York, one in San Francisco. OWNER ALICIA DARBERSMERE HAD NO COMMENT...

KirlianPhotog: <thats tom ds wife right?>
GirlInTree: <the very same>
<taking veruca to the speeds opening tonite, just wanted>
<uknow>

A pause: *Know what, exactly?* Then—
KirlianPhotog: <ok, sounds dicey 2 me>
GirlInTree: <cmon>
KirlianPhotog: <u asked man>

And then there's another chime—another email. Man, Ross

codes almost faster than Nim can read…

(but not quite)

GirlInTree: <radiant boy?>

KirlianPhotog: <horribly murdered kid turned harbinger of death; the bright white lights a big giveaway. also, in the emperors>

GirlInTree: <that whole cannibal dinner thing?>

KirlianPhotog: <i got eaten alive just so 2 freaks could be young again, id be pretty pissed>

GirlInTree: <good point>

"Saying" it ultra-cool, a throw-away snark-snap, old-school *Buffy*-style. But feeling the hairs on the back of her neck go up nonetheless, oblivious to cliché, as her stomach clenches and flips: The disgusting gastronomic concept from which Tim's notorious "memoir" takes its title playing itself out behind her eye-sockets, utterly unwanted, bad enough when done to a damn fish. Let alone a child…

Except, he didn't. No one did. It's a frigging story, Nimue.

GirlInTree: <so>

<whats the 411? according 2 the monster manual>

KirlianPhotog: <on what, the radiant boy? like>

GirlInTree: <2 stay safe>

<if u have 2 get near it>

A *long* pause, this time. Long enough for Nim to remember the last time they "spoke," when she spilled on Ross about Veruca's RL nutsiness. Only to get a similarly wry line in return: <u do know ur probly no RL treat urself, right?>

And thinking: *Yeah, granted.* Which may well be why she and Ross keep it strictly between the lines—why they've never thought to hook up for real, even though they live in the same city. Like they're afraid to meet each other in the flesh, for fear of being disappointed that their "soulmate" might come attached to tics they can't stand: Veruca, all over again. Thinking…

Shit, am I that *easy? That* hard?

But all things must come to an end, even this. And so the pause breaks at last, with Ross's final post—

<*if u have 2 get near it*>

KirlianPhotog: <dont>

<just>

<just dont>

—

Hours later, meanwhile…

…they're already through the door, inside the Speed of Pain, where the bass is loud enough to blow your hair back, bottom-heavy enough to sound like an abyssal snake coiling and uncoiling in some parallel dimension. Up on stage, two women gyrate in a black-lit go-go cage, each using a hand-held buzzsaw to strike sparks off the crotch of the other's metal bikini. Posters are plastered everywhere, blurring together in the changing light; there's a livid yellow flyer on the floor at Nim's feet, one of many, piled in clumps so high they brush the ankles. It reads:

TONIGHT, GRAND OPENING, AFTER MIDNIGHT. NO COVER. DEE-JAY CEMETERY OX 'TIL DAWN. FEATURED BANDS—FUDGETONGUE, DUST-GOWNED, PLUS RANCIDULCET (THE SOFT SOUND OF ROT).

Nim looks around, throat already raw with stray pot smoke and heat, vaguely recalling what it used to be like, back when this was still something else. But now it looks somehow darker and bigger, offputtingly so—a huge overhanging ceiling strung with lightbulb stars, a dance-floor inset intermittently with stained glass and lit from beneath, to weirdly patterned effect. Everything swims, hyp-nagogic, dream-sick.

And it's at this point, naturally enough—when she's already off-centre, and the noise conspires to render her all but unintelligible—that Nim sees Veruca's face assume an awful look of slack hunger as somebody she can only assume is Tom Darbersmere appears in the middle distance, near one end of the room-long bar: that man-shaped thing with the laughing white null for a face, arm wound around the shoulders of a woman (Alicia?) whose long brown hair hangs heavy, interrupted only by a rising dragon's tongue of smoke.

Veruca surges against the crowd, chapbook already in hand, but Nim grabs her by the arm before she can quite start to move.

"You know there's no way any of that actually happened, right?" she bellows over the roar.

"What part?"

"Like, *any* of it? Holy crap, Veruca, get a fucking grip. I mean, this is some sick sort of shit right here—"

Veruca purses her lips, a disappointed *moue*, like: *Oh, Nim.* And says, only:

"I have to go."

"Veruca, *look* at them!" Nim has to scream now, feeling her face distort with the effort. "Does he look seventy? Does she look, what, a fucking *hundred*?"

"Not anymore."

"They couldn't get away with it. Not today. They *couldn't*. Veruca!"

But she's gone. Vanished into the crowd, a salmon slipping effortlessly beneath the rapids, heading upstream.

And it's stupid, but Nim keeps on glitching on that…story. "The Emperor's Old Bones," which she finally read in full on her way up here, under streetcar-light. That scene in the kitchen, that last phone conversation between "Tim" and the head chef at the Precious Dragon Shrine…

Sure, the author makes it sound "plausible" enough, in the moment—that's his damn job. Even if you accept "The Emperor's…" as Tim Darbersmere's work to begin with, though, all the Wiki'ing in the world won't let you skip over the fact that he did this exact same sort of shit before, a couple of times: the case-study for a disease that didn't exist, that 1960s piece where he convinced everybody who was anybody he'd lost his arms to gangrene, after a car accident outside Cannes… And yes, glamour and exoticism turns tarnished if it's revealed that the gruesomeness is factual, not just squeamish, gleeful metaphor—but it doesn't matter, does it? After all—

—things like that *aren't true*. Thankfully. Because if you thought, if you even suspected, even dreamed they were, then it'd be time to—

(bury yourself in the sand, face-down)

And besides which: How could it go unnoticed, even if? How could such a price be paid over and over again in a world of SINS, DNA and GoogleEarth, of YouTube and datamining, a world drowning in celebrity poon-shots and political blowjobs, where nothing stays secret for long?

Yet: That's exactly why, Nim suddenly realizes, silent and unmoving amid the rave, completely unconscious of the odd looks she's getting from the crowd. *Veruca thinks she's stumbled across the greatest story never told, so she wants in.* Not to take part, never that—but just to know, to be certain, to be on the inside, for once. If only the once.

So either Veruca's just batshit and about to get thrown out for spouting craziness all over the host, or…

But Nim shies away from the *or*, on principle; she doesn't believe it, doesn't need to. Forcing herself into movement, shouldering her way through the crowd, sliding between bodies where she can't force them apart, ignoring the passing gropes and the leered invitations; nothing matters now except heading Veruca off, before she can render both their chances at a genuine life even more remote.

Then—*thud*, stumble, recognition: anticlimax. Veruca stands (more accurately, sways) at the edge of a small circle ringing the good-looking man and his smoke-wreathed wife. Her face is pallid, her eyes wide and bright, and she clutches the chapbook to her heaving chest like a shield.

A second later, Tom Darbersmere can't help but see her; his eyes widen, ever so slightly. Almost as though he—

(*recognizes* her)

He leans towards her, lips moving. Something that might be: *My dear.* And Veruca, Veruca...

Recoils, falls back. Goes whiter than white. Then backs away 'til she hits somebody, blunders further, turns tail—

—and flees.

—

Nim follows after, into the maelstrom. Past couples dry-humping up against the door-frames, through room after room of excoriatingly loud music of every possible type, a thousand-song playlist set on infinite shuffle. In one of them, people toss wreaths of lit sparklers back and forth, like they're putting on some carny magic show. In another, a man hangs from the ceiling by Sundance hooks, a softball stuck with nails held tight in either hand; his friends stand underneath, videotaping the ordeal, as blood drips onto their camera's lens. Each successive room is hotter, louder, stranger—

Nim wipes sweat away and checks her watch, only to find she's lost more than an hour. Thinks: '*Cause time works differently, in here.*

Then catches a flash of blonde up ahead, ducking through yet another doorway, and heaves forward again, trying to bridge the gap between them. Ending up somehow caught inside what seems like ten or so feet of bead curtains strung one behind the other, instead—she swims through them, their warm plastic leaving a sticky trail behind everywhere it touches, and spills through to the other side: a cool, dim room so insulated she actually can't hear the music playing in the rest of the club anymore (though she can still feel the sheer erratic pulse of it coming up, floor acting as a remarkably efficient conductor, even through the three-inch soles of her shoes). The sudden contrast makes her heart slam up against her ribs, beating fast. She pauses, long enough to take it all in—

Dim and spare and hung with red, everywhere Nim looks. And it really must be later on, because the only people in there are Tom, Alicia (lighting a fresh cigarette with a flourish, then flipping her antique silver lighter shut) and a squat woman Nim doesn't recognize at all: thick glasses behind which her eyes swim like tiny fishes; a corduroy jumpsuit with purple irises printed all over it; beige hair, beige skin, beige voice.

She carries something small and squishy-looking in a baby-harness slung tight over her massive bosom—*not* a miscarriage that's been dug up and somehow laminated, as Nim horribly assumed at first sight, but a plush creature of some weird derivation, with a gaze as hooded and squinty as her own. It jiggles back and forth with her breath as she stares down at the table, a tealight candle slopping dangerously between her palms.

Tom, to Alicia: "Not *this* again."

And: "I need to know," Alicia replies, her voice nothing like Nim might have expected—flat, Midwestern, abnormally "normal." "Especially now. Think you'd feel the same, tai pan."

"Would you?"

"Yeah. You saying you don't?"

A spark passes between them, chased with a sigh. "It is *your* club," Tom points out, finally.

Alicia grins. "Well, okay, then." To the woman: "Is it here, right now?"

The woman gives a long sigh, lips twitching feebly, as though she doesn't want to answer. At the same time, beneath the frame of Nim's gaze, something stirs; she strains to focus on it for a second, before realizing—

(oh GOD)

—it's that *thing*, that mockery, the woman's snug-cocooned un-child, kicking out slightly in all directions, like it's testing uterine waters. While the bulgy eyes blink and the mouth pulses in and out, stop-motion slow, like it's clearing its throat…and from the woman's own mouth, a slurred voice issues, hissing:

"...Alwaysss herrre."

(Like it's puppeting her. Not the other way 'round.)

Oh MAN, I need to get out of here.

Nim backs up, praying Tom and Alicia won't notice; thankfully, they don't seem to. Not Alicia, anyhow—who leans forward, brows knit, and keeps on quizzing.

"Is it dangerous?"

"Nottt ttto youuu."

"How do we get rid of it?"

"Youuu can'ttt."

"Why not?"

A pause. "Becaussse..." the thing says, at last. "Itsss yoursss. Bothhh offf youuu. Yourrre..."

"...Part of it," Tom fills in, softly.

Alicia snorts. "Like fun, *tai pan*."

(That phrase: Chinese? Nim knows she's heard it before, just can't think when, or how—then feels the down on the back of her neck go up again, ruff-stiff, as she suddenly recalls exactly where.)

More snore-y breathing. The "doll" speaks on, ignoring them both. Says:

"Ittt...hhhe. Knowsss youuu aaate himmm. Hisss liiife. Hisss... paiiin."

"Well," Tom says, softly, "he would, wouldn't he? Can't really miss it while it's happening, not even if it's done expertly."

Alicia shoots him a look. "Enough of that crap," she says, warningly, which gets her nothing but a single arched brow in return. As Tom points out—

"Really, 'Lish: You're the one who *asked*."

And all through this, Nim is backing away, her face and body held equally rigid. She feels the plastic bead curtain hit her spine, stroke up her back, then collapse together in front of her; Tom, Alicia and the puppeted puppeteer blur and distort between the strands, as they fall into place. Step by step, Nim forces herself through, drowning in plastic. The music's getting louder again, still reverberant with distance and distortion, and underneath it there's a strange cross-current of sound; phantom cellos, sawing up from below.

Recognition's a jolt of ice and adrenaline to the spine: That second layer, the Apocalyptica version of "Until It Sleeps" is her ringtone. Nimue fumbles in her purse and digs the phone out, the muffled tinniness of its repeated music refusing to fade, like it's wrapped in invisible cotton. She puts it to her ear.

"Veruca?"

Static, broken by arrhythmic crackles that might be words. Nim feels her balance going out. She can't tell if she's pushing or falling. Her feet have gone numb. The plastic beads trail slowly alongside, kelp fronds in a nightmare sea that cling, and clutch, and—

Give way.

Nim stumbles back out into the Speed, the noise disorienting for half an instant. Then her mind seizes on Veruca's voice—now obscured by nothing but the ordinary background roar—echoing in her ear. *"Nim, where are you? Nim, please, talk to me—"*

"On the floor!" Nim shouts. She casts about, futilely seeking blonde cornrows or lens-distorted green eyes. "Where the hell are *you*? What happened? Why—"

"I couldn't do it. God, I was so wrong—sorry—" A hiss and a coughing huff follow, sounds Nim finds almost welcome in their previously-infuriating familiarity: Veruca's taking a stress-triggered blast off her inhaler. *"But I was right, too, you saw—had to see—tell me you saw—"*

"V, where the fuck are you?" Nim yells back, jamming a finger past her naked tragus. "Your voice sounds weird."

"It's HIM, Nimue. Looks exactly the same, just...young."

"Who looks the same?"

Another huff. Then, even fainter—like Veruca's talking through a mouthful of cotton—

"...im..."

Nim scans around again, frantically. Eventually, something— some light-sliver glimpsed from the corner of one tearing eye—sug- gests where Veruca might have gone. "Dude," she says, "listen to me, okay? Are you in the john?"

A fizzle-click "s"-slur is her only reply; might pass for "yes," on a bad day. Nim takes it as her cue to head for the pertinent sign at speed, a flickering Georgia O'Keefe rubyfruit done in flickering neon. As Veruca keeps on chattering, between white noise waves:

"...said, it's him. Them. They DID it...like the story says, not made up, it's all true. All of it."

"I'm comin', man. I'm almost there."

Puts her hand on the door, poised to push. And hears Veruca's voice from inside, twinned: once via phone, once through the wood itself, but shit-scared either way. Suddenly dropping to a dull, tiny whisper, cold inside and out, as she breathes—

"—Nim, stop, keep out. Somebody's here."

The phone gives a half-silent *pop!*, drained battery abruptly dead. Yet Nim hears another voice fading in, nevertheless—well, not hears it, exactly. More like remembering what it must have sounded like when somebody else heard it, a long, long time ago. A juvenile voice, pitched high, with that wandering edge that usually means drink, or drugs, or particularly high fever, saying...several things at once, it seems like, each sentence butting up against the one before, overlapping slightly. Like so:

I'm COLD...Where you goin', man? You said I could watch TV... Can't move my legs...Why won't you look at me? I'm right here, man...Just LOOK at me. Please...

Nim can't stop herself from applying her full weight against the handle, leaning steadily inwards. The door flaps out and back, spitting her into a washroom so ultra-cold and bright it's practically Kubrickian—and as Nim looks up into the mirror, for one split second, she thinks she sees somebody standing behind her, a shadow quivering against the crack between jamb and post on the nearest stall's door. So she turns, finds it gone; turns back, and finds the room is suddenly properly dim. All except—

—that other stall, the one within easy arm's reach with its own door swinging half-open, a single black Nike trainer-encased foot...

(Veruca's)

...wedged between hinge and jamb, not letting it rebound, let alone come to a full entropic stop.

And: *God*, Nim thinks again, though it's not like she believes in one. Not officially.

Because Veruca's inside, of course. Propped up on the toilet, pants securely fastened, *that book* wide open in her lap. But Nim can't think of much to do about it except take "The Emperor's..." from her, gingerly, holding it up by the corner like it's sticky; let the spine flop open to expose its ill-glued core, its cracked and fraying threads. Or press 911 on speed-dial, hoping she was wrong about her phone, while simultaneously averting her eyes—resolutely determined not to look down, not to try and read over her dead friend's shoulder.

Kneeling there, touching the book with as little of one fingernail as she can manage, like she's afraid it'll rub off on her somehow, its rough cover slick and dirty as dead scale under her hand. And then there's this sound from behind her, from the corner—somebody who doesn't really need to breathe doing it anyway, deliberately clearing their no-throat, so she won't crap herself with fear.

Child-light footsteps approaching, wetly, from behind her. A skinless little hand, slimy on her shoulder. An unwavering, pitiless light like a fifty-bulb night-shooting rack igniting with no percep-tible warning, back-haloing the floor, the stall, Veruca's sprawling corpse...

...while the voice, that voice, repeats every one of the phrases Nim heard through the bathroom door over again in an endless, profane loop: no ending and no beginning, just—pollution, ripples spreading outwards. Curdling everything in its path.

Just LOOK at me, man. I'm right here. So...LOOK.

(No. Not gonna.)

Can't move. So COLD.

(I'm sorry for that, kid. I really, really am.)

Yeah? Then turn around, right now. And look.

(You can't make me.)

Oh no?

(Is that what you think, little geeky girl?)

You'd be amazed what I can do, I only take a mind to.

Heart bruising itself against her sternum from the inside, a muscle-and-valve jackhammer. As the voice keeps on, never raising, never falling. Never slowing. Never stopping.

He said...he was gonna take...care...of me...

Nim sits there on the bathroom floor with her eyes closed and two fingers jammed deep into the book, still automatically holding Veruca's place for her, as hot red tears run down her face to drip on the bright white floor below. Sits there until it stops talking, until she's *almost* certain it's gone away for good. Then keeps on sitting there anyhow, hips and knees burning, cold creeping up through her pant-legs; her eyes still downcast, still shut lid-tight, afraid to open them again, in case.

Until, at last, somebody else comes in to pee. And the screaming finally starts.

—

Though the cops get there surprisingly fast, by the time they arrive, the Speed's already cleaned itself up (and out) with alarming efficiency. No more blood-sports in the corners, no more pot-stink or bad behavior. Even the soundtrack manages to reel itself back a notch or ten, so nobody has to shout to make themselves heard while they give their deposition.

They let Nim go at 3:30 a.m., waving her briskly past the same ambulance they loaded Veruca's bag-clad body into. And there, beyond the yellow tape, she finds Tom Darbersmere waiting for her.

"Your friend…" he begins. "…The girl with the glasses, same one who came up to me, 'round midnight?"

"Her name's Veruca," Nim finds herself telling him, mouth suddenly too numb to quite form every syllable. A fact he doesn't really seem to notice, observing only:

"Veruca: Was it really. How absolutely marvellous."

A statement, not a question, odd to the point of insult. It stings enough to make her look up, into his eyes—

—where she *does* see sympathy, of a kind. But only like a shallow sheen: all surface, china-cerulean, pale and dry and faded. And *not* young, when you come to look at them this closely—in no fucking way young, not at all. Not even a little, tiny bit.

"My dear," Tom Darbersmere says, pressing her hot hand between his two smooth, cool, dry ones, "I am so very sorry for your loss."

Sorrowful and civil, utterly archaic. And so much like Veruca's treasured imitation of his late uncle, it brings sick to Nim's mouth. Something burning in her nose, behind her teeth, choking her. Something deep down in her gut and lower still, sinking to where it makes her groin ache and her muscles flex, burning, burning, burning to cut and run.

("He's exactly the damn *same*…"

Who, Veruca?

"…*im*…")

Him: Tom. Or, rather—

—*Tim*.

(The not-so-Late.)

With Alicia—*Ellis*, Iseland—standing right behind him, at a middle distance, puffing away. Her smoke-coloured eyes boring into Nim, slow-motion bullets. As though she thinks if she just does it long enough, she'll be able to read Nim's address off her DNA.

And: "Thanks," Nim husks, at last, dropping his hand like it's radioactive. Before running off into the night, away from the Speed of Pain, never (hopefully) to return.

Later, she's over half the way home, sitting on the Vomit Comet with tears running down both cheeks—unsought, unstemmed—before she feels the edge of it touch her thigh as she shifts, and realizes she still has the only known copy of that nonexistent fucking book of his right there in her purse.

Thinking: *Something needs to come of this. This needs to COME to something. Bite your ass. Bite BOTH your asses, you lying, dream-killing, kid-eating, unspeakable fucking, FUCKING…*

Thinking: *Because Veruca's dead, and that thing, it's dead too. But you're alive, still.*

You always will be.

Thinking, thinking, thinking: Nothing relevant, not really, aside from the dreadful half-sob that racks her now from head to toe, epileptic. Because it's late, and she's tired, more tired than she's ever been in her life. Because her only friend in the world is gone, and—stupid fixations, obsessive eccentricities, annoying vocal inflections aside—the world she has to live in now, alone, is oh so much the poorer for it.

Nim hugs "The Emperor's Old Bones" to her chest with both arms, tight like she gave birth to it, and shuts her eyes once more, knowing she'll have to keep moving now, but not knowing for exactly how long. Certain she won't sleep 'til dawn, at least. Or, maybe—

—ever again.

Formerly a film critic, journalist, screenwriter and teacher, Gemma Files has been an award-winning horror author since 1999. She has published two collections of short work (*Kissing Carrion* and *The Worm in Every Heart*), two chap-books of speculative poetry, a Weird Western trilogy (the *Hexslinger* series—*A Book of Tongues*, *A Rope of Thorns* and *A Tree of Bones*), a story-cycle (*We Will All Go Down Together: Stories of the Five-Family Coven*) and a stand-alone novel (*Experimental Film*, which won the 2016 Shirley Jackson Award for Best Novel and the 2016 Sunburst award for Best Adult Novel). All her works are available through ChiZine Productions. Her novella, *Coffle*, was just published by Dim Shores, with art by Stephen Wilson. She has two upcoming story collections from Trepidatio Publishing (*Spectral Evidence* and *Drawn Up From Deep Places*), and one from Cemetery Dance.

CPSIA information can be obtained
at www.ICGtesting.com
Printed in the USA
LVHW050618040619
620063LV00003B/505